Praise for

kayla perrin's

Getting Even

"This story of exquisitely plotted revenge will have
every woman who has ever been 'done wrong'
quietly cheering...This is sexy erotica."
—*Library Journal*

"Well plotted and with an appealing chick-lit sensibility...
that's not to say it lacks heat—it definitely doesn't."
—*Romantic Times BOOKreviews*

"*Getting Even* is one wild ride!...Perrin is an author who
belongs on your must read list. Don't miss *Getting Even!*'
—*RomanceReaderAtHeart*

"Fans of contemporary girl loves boy, boy mistreats girl,
girl avenges mistreatment tales will want to read
this hot, spicy novel."
—*Harriet Klausner*

"[A] writer that everyone should read."
—*Eric Jerome Dickey*

kayla perrin

Getting
Some

Spice

Spice

GETTING SOME

ISBN-13: 978-0-373-60514-9
ISBN-10:   0-373-60514-5

www.Spice-Books.com

Printed in U.S.A.

This book is dedicated to the girlfriends
I know I'd have a blast with in Vegas:

Diane Kurtz, Melinda McGowan, Brenda Mott,
Leslie Gray and Heidi Familia

Maybe there's a trip in our future?

Part One

Revenge is sweet…but now what?

One

Samera

Sometimes, life's a bitch.

And when I say a bitch, I mean that literally. Like life is some crazy woman hovering over the universe, dealing with a bad case of PMS. She *could* let you be happy, but she's got killer cramps at the moment, and if she's got to suffer, you're damn well going to suffer, too.

So instead of giving you easy choices—like a clear path that's right, versus one that's obviously wrong—life is gonna mess with you. Present you with *two* paths you can see yourself taking, but you *must* choose one of them. And no matter which one you choose, you're going to feel bad.

Hell, I know what I'm talking about. I just chose Path B, which is the path my heart told me I was supposed to take. I should feel a sense of resolve right now, a sense of peace. I should have a smile on my fucking face because I'm taking fond memories with me from my vacation, but instead I feel like shit.

I just left a guy who likes me—no, adores me—probably completely heartbroken in Costa Rica.

"Miguel." I say his name out loud, and his image pops into my mind. His beautiful, bronzed body and smoky eyes. That gorgeous smile of his, which is both sexy and sweet at the same time. My face flushes as I remember other things about him—like how eager he was to please me in the bedroom, to give me one mind-numbing orgasm after another.

Is it possible I've made a mistake? I wonder as I stare out the small plane window, craning my neck for one final glimpse of the beautiful country where I spent the last two weeks of my life. *Have I made the wrong choice?*

Choosing to leave Miguel and get on a plane heading back to the States was the hardest thing I ever had to do. One minute Miguel and I were moving full steam ahead to what I thought would be a serious commitment. The next, my fucking louse of an ex showed up claiming he still loved me—and I bought his lies, effectively changing my destiny with Miguel forever.

Reed, my ex, actually tracked me down in Costa Rica, like he was Brad Pitt showing up at the end of the movie to claim his girl. He complicated the shit out of my relationship with Miguel. But even though I got wise to his game—realizing that Reed hadn't changed, he just didn't want to lose me—I had to accept one very certain fact: clearly, I didn't love Miguel the way a man deserves to be loved. If I did, Reed couldn't have walked back into my life so easily. And I care too much for Miguel to let him settle for half of my heart.

Knowing that, however, doesn't make my decision any less painful. I really like Miguel, and I'll always have a soft spot in my heart for him. But I'm just not ready to make the big Love Commitment with him—or anyone for that matter—so it was far better that I leave him now than that I stay and break his heart in a couple months.

I had to be fair to Miguel. If I didn't ultimately want what he wanted, I had to let him go.

Still, I wonder if I'll ever meet another man like Miguel. When I told him I had to leave him, he was so friggin' understanding. I'm used to guys punching holes in walls and cussing a blue streak when I break up with them. But Miguel—despite being sad—simply told me that I had to do what my heart told me I should.

Right now my heart is aching. I'm not sure what that means.

Moaning softly, I bury my face in my hands. Suddenly I wish I were back in my hotel room at the gorgeous oceanfront Marriott resort, Miguel's body on top of mine, his cock deep within me, and my legs wrapped around his waist. I want him whispering words of passion to me in Spanish as he did for much of my two weeks in his country, making me scream his name as I come.

That's what I should be doing. Instead, I'm sitting in coach class on a Delta Airlines flight, staring out the window like a lovesick fool, with the worst case of melancholy gripping my heart.

I glance to my left. The guy beside me, probably early sixties, wriggles his eyebrows when he sees me look his way. I roll my eyes and look past him, behind me. And that's when I notice a dark-haired man who reminds me of Miguel. He's with an attractive blonde, and the two appear to be totally in to each other. I watch them for a moment as the man whispers something into the woman's ear. Her face flames and she laughs, and that's all it takes for my brain to open the door holding back all my memories of Miguel and the time we shared.

Once again, I turn to the window, but I don't see the view. In the theater of my mind, I'm seeing me and my Spanish lover. The first time he stripped off my clothes, then ate my pussy until I screamed. How incredible his cock felt when he entered me as I was coming.

It had been the first time, and yet we had connected on a level I can't say I've experienced before.

My mind fast-forwards past the first time to the most memorable—at the Tabacon Resort. Miguel took me to the most beautiful place in the world, the most romantic. I picture us in the resort's stunning hot springs, secretly screwing as people strolled by on the paths, our bodies submerged in warm, bubbling water.

As long as I live, that sexual memory will remain forever etched in my mind. Hands down, it was my most romantic experience. From the magnificent beauty of the natural hot springs and lush foliage at the base of the Arenal volcano to a hot man whispering Spanish words of love in my ear, I know that experience can never be duplicated.

My nipples start to ache as I think about the moment Miguel covered my breasts with his hands—then his mouth—once I slipped my bikini top off. The guy knows how to suck a nipple, with this sort of gentle reverence that turned me on more than I thought it could.

I steal another glance at the couple a few rows behind me. Now they're kissing, so much in love that they don't mind showing it to the world.

What would Miguel do if he were here with me on this plane?

I would be the first one to make a move, I'm sure. Not that he wouldn't want to, but I'm more brazen when it comes to sex. I would tease Miguel with my fingertips, stroking his inner thigh from his knee on upward, not stopping until I reached the bulge of his cock.

I imagine Miguel's reaction—the look of pleasant shock spreading over his face. "Princessa, what are you doing?"

I glance around, make sure that there are no flight attendants nearby. "What do you think I'm doing?" I ask as I begin to undo the snap on Miguel's jeans.

A combination of a chuckle and sigh bubbles up in his throat. He places his hand on mine, as though to stop me, but I know better.

He wants this, too.

"That old couple across the aisle is asleep," I tell him. "The people in front of us can't see us, nor can the people behind." I maneuver Miguel's cock out of his pants, but make sure it's covered with the small blue blanket supplied by the airline. Then I whisper in his ear, "Tell me you don't want to feel my lips on your cock right now."

"Princessa, you are crazy."

"Yeah, and you love it."

I unsnap my seat belt, quickly look around to make sure no one is heading our way, then reposition my body so that it looks like I'm resting my head on my lover's lap. And then I flick the tip of my tongue over Miguel's hard penis.

He shudders, but doesn't stop me. The way he pushes up his hips tells me he doesn't want me to stop. His cock is as erect as a flagstaff in my hand.

"My, my, you really want this," I whisper as I lift my head to his. "Your semen is already coming out of your cock."

Miguel moans softly and strokes my hair.

"All I have to do is lie like this, hold the blanket like this…" I readjust my body so that my face is in his lap again.

"And everyone who walks by will think I'm taking a rest on your lap. Meanwhile, I'll be giving you the best head you've ever had at 20,000 feet in the air."

Miguel murmurs something in Spanish, and now tangles his fingers in my hair. That's his subtle way of telling me he is giving me total control, that I can do to his body whatever I please.

So I do. I can't bob my head up and down his cock without arousing suspicion, but there are other ways to give great head. I run my tongue around the top of his shaft over and over again, before taking the tip into my mouth and sucking on it. I brush my lips against his hard length, then flick my tongue over the same area of flesh, before gently tugging on his skin with my teeth.

Miguel breathes heavily, as though he's fighting a moan, and the more he does, the more I want to forget discreet and go at his cock with total abandon. I get a little bolder, taking his penis deep in my mouth to the back of my throat and holding it there. I tighten my lips around him and suck steadily, as though trying to draw out his sperm into my hungry mouth.

After a moment, Miguel's hand stills on my head. "I cannot take any more of this," he whispers.

I raise my head. Kiss him softly on the lips. "Want to go to the bathroom and fuck?"

"You are serious?"

Now I run my fingers through Miguel's dark hair. "You know I don't joke when it comes to sex."

We neck openly now, and I am so turned on I want to lie back, spread my legs, and let Miguel fuck me.

"Excuse me, Miss?"

The words penetrate my brain, jarring me out of my

fantasy. I open my eyes to see the man sitting in my row staring at me with concern.

"You okay?" he asks. "You kind of sound like you're moaning."

My cheeks flame with embarrassment. "Something I ate, I guess," I lie. Then I turn back to the window and stare outside.

I can't believe how caught up in my fantasy I got. But then again, I can.

Maybe I'm being too friggin' dramatic about the whole situation with Miguel. I mean, it couldn't work with him. End of story. Period. Forget that the attraction between us was totally hot. Sex isn't everything—and I can't believe I'm even thinking this—but it isn't.

Maybe Miguel has already found himself a new woman. Perhaps another tourist, whose heart will beat a little faster when he flashes that gorgeous smile of his…

The very thought makes my throat constrict.

You can't have your cake and eat it, too.

Best-case scenario, when I get my life together, say in five years, I'll call Miguel and he'll still be single, still have the hots for me. We'll get together like no time has passed at all, start tearing at each others' clothes before our lips even touch…

Why are you doing this to yourself? Anger flares inside me, and I yank down the window's blind. I can no longer stand staring out at the idyllic view, because it's messing with my brain.

Seriously, what is wrong with me? When did I become such a sentimental fool? Now is not the time to think about Miguel and what might have been. I have to concentrate on myself. Start thinking about what I want to do with the rest of my life. Trust me, that's a huge hurdle I have to overcome. Until now, I've worked as a stripper. I didn't go to college, and I passed high school with less-than-flying colors. It's time I start to think about my future, because I don't want to be taking my clothes off for a living when I'm fifty years old.

Quite frankly, I should be thanking Reed for being such an asshole. He's the manager at the club where I worked, and I dated him for months—until I found out that he was screwing another dancer behind my back. But if he hadn't fucked someone else, I'd still be in Atlanta now, still working at his club, still thinking I couldn't strive for anything more than that. So he did me a favor by setting me free, and making me concentrate for once on *me*.

Don't get me wrong. I'm not ashamed of being a stripper. But I'm fully aware that a girl can't make a lifetime career in that field of entertainment.

I try to avoid the gaze of the guy next to me as I glance around for a flight attendant. The Fasten Seatbelt sign is still lit, and no one has announced that we've reached our cruising altitude. But, fuck, I want a drink already. That and a cigarette. Liquor will have to suffice until we touch down in Atlanta and I can find a smoking lounge at the airport.

I don't want to feel this way, so conflicted. But worse than feeling conflicted over leaving Miguel, I don't want to admit that if I hadn't gotten my hopes up about Reed when he showed up posing like a Knight in Shining Armor, I'd probably have thrown caution to the wind and stayed with my Latin lover in Costa Rica.

Yeah, I need a drink. Scotch preferably, but I'll take anything.

Anything that helps numb me from thinking about the fact that I probably left the best thing to ever come into my life back in Jaco, Costa Rica.

* * *

Hours later I'm standing outside of baggage claim at the Atlanta Hartsfield airport, waiting for my hot-pink suitcase when I hear, "Hey, sis."

I turn around to see my sister, Annelise, her smile so bright it just might blind me. She's wearing her hair down as opposed to in a ponytail, and her long blond locks are tossed over one shoulder. It's clear to me just by looking at her that not only is she getting laid, she's getting laid good.

She certainly deserves to be happy after the crap her husband put her through, but the reality that she's getting some has me missing Miguel even more.

"It is so good to see you again." Annelise wraps me in a warm hug. "How are you?"

"All right."

"Uh-oh." Annelise's smile falters as she breaks our hug and stares at me. "You don't sound all right."

"I'm fine."

"Then why do you look so glum? You should be invigorated," she adds with a wink. "All that time you spent with that hot stud."

"Yeah, well." I don't say anything else. I'm not sure what to say. I *know* it wouldn't have worked with Miguel, but I still feel like crap.

"Oh my God." My sister's eyes light up. "You fell in love with him, didn't you?"

I don't answer as I watch my luggage go by me. I push past two fortysomething women standing together, excusing myself as I do, to grab the suitcase before it gets too far.

The moment I turn around, I notice that my sister's eyes are narrowed. There's genuine concern on her face.

"Did he hurt you?" she asks when I return to her side.

"He was seeing someone else? Oh, no. Don't tell me he was married!"

"He wasn't married. He didn't hurt me." I extract the suitcase's handle. "Can we go now?"

"You don't want to talk about it." Annelise states the obvious.

"Which way?" I ask.

"This way." Annelise starts for the doors off to the left, but slows so I can catch up to her. "Hey, I know what it's like to not want to talk about something. When it hurts too much to even think about it. But just know that whenever you *do* want to talk, I'm here." She rubs my back. "Okay?"

I can't believe myself. Just the act of Annelise giving me support has me almost ready to burst into tears. I hold them in check—barely.

Which is why I know I'm nowhere near ready to tell her about Reed, how he showed up in Costa Rica and told me he still loved me, and how I stupidly fell for the line like a moron. If I get into the story here, I think I'll have a meltdown.

So I change the subject, asking, "How's Dominic?"

"Amazing," Annelise responds right away, her face lighting up like a neon sign.

"In other words, the sex is good." I manage an actual smile.

"Good?" Annelise pauses before she heads out the automatic doors and whispers, "Sam, the sex is…out of this world!"

"Wow."

"Total romance cliché, I know. But, Sam, it's the absolute truth. I had no clue sex could be this amazing."

"So I take it you're not missing Charles," I joke as we start out the door toward the parking lot.

"Charles. Ugh." Annelise makes a face of pure disgust. "I hope he rots in jail for embezzling money from the Wishes Come True Foundation. Never in a million years would I think the man I married could be such a heartless son of a bitch. To steal money that goes toward helping terminally ill children…"

"What's happening with that?" I ask. I've only been away for two weeks, but it seems like much longer. A lifetime, in many ways.

"I heard Charles was begging for a plea bargain. Claimed the embezzlement wasn't his idea."

I snort at that.

"Exactly. He can keep dreaming, because with the evidence they have against him, he'll be lucky if the sentence is lenient."

"The evidence *you* found in Costa Rica," I say proudly. It was Annelise's bright idea to search her husband's tropical condo when she learned it existed. Honestly, I never thought my sister had it in her to become a modern Agatha Christie. With Charles, she accepted substandard treatment. She became a wimp under him, if you ask me. Always wondering what she could do to please him, how she could spice up their love life to keep him happy when he suddenly didn't want sex from her. It was no surprise to me that he'd been screwing someone else for quite some time.

"And it was so much fun," Annelise admits.

"Wasn't it, though? And when Charles showed up at the condo…"

"I know! I thought it was over, right then and there." Annelise pauses as she chuckles. "I can't believe that was my life, not some HBO movie."

"Did you talk to a lawyer yet, see if you can get any money from the house?" I ask. "After how you helped break the case, the last thing you deserve is to get screwed over in this."

Annelise nods as we approach her Volvo. "I have. Claudia set me up with one of her uncles, and he's really great. He seems optimistic, but I don't want to hold my breath."

"Claudia's the spoiled rich one, right?"

Annelise frowns as she meets my gaze. "Spoiled?"

"Yeah. She doesn't work, her parents pay for everything."

"So?"

"So I'd say that's pretty spoiled."

"Well she's not," Annelise says in defense of her friend. "Claudia does a lot of charitable work, as many rich people do. That was what she was going to do when she married Adam—devote her life to charitable causes. But then he screwed her over and the wedding was off."

Annelise opens the trunk for me, and I hoist my suitcase into it. Suddenly I smile. The two of us here like this, doing things that sisters normally do on a day-to-day basis—it's nice.

Even having a bit of a disagreement, as sisters often do, is welcome. Because it means we're communicating.

I should point out that my sister and I haven't been exactly close. She's older than I am, and for most of our adult lives she's looked down on the choices I've made. Like the decision to be an exotic dancer. But in the last couple months, our relationship has gone through a marked change. We're talking. Communicating again without judging each other.

In short, we've become friends.

We probably have a long way to go, but I'm hopeful about the future. At least when it comes to my sister, that's one relationship that's working out.

Two

Annelise

The moment my eyes open, I do what has become part of my morning routine over the past couple of weeks. I glance to my right, see my lover's naked body and smile.

My how times can change.

If you'd told me six months ago that today I'd be getting sex regularly and that my best friends and sister would be the ones now going without, I would have laughed in your face. No, I would have cried. That's how pathetically miserable my sex life was with my husband.

I had a husband who, after we'd been together for ten years, stopped touching me. Completely. Didn't want to make out, much less have sex. He started treating me like I was his grandmother in terms of the sexual contact between us, and I, like a fool, began blaming myself for his lack of sexual interest in me.

They say hindsight's twenty-twenty, and it's so easy for me

now to see exactly how much of a lying ass Charles was. To think I bought his I'm-so-stressed-I'm-impotent line. At the heart of the matter, really, was my religious convictions and deeply held belief in till death do us part. Being raised by a religious fanatic mother, I've lived much of my life being concerned that if I do the wrong thing, I'll burn in hell for eternity.

To my credit I can say I remained committed to Charles until I learned he was cheating on me *and* cheating the kids of the Wishes Come True Foundation, where he was a member of the board. I took my vows seriously when I married him, even though he didn't deserve my love. And I feel no guilt about moving on with someone else while I wait for my divorce, enjoying sex for the first time in nearly a year and a half.

Life is good now.

No, I think, glancing at Dominic again. *It's great.*

In many ways it seems like much more than two weeks have gone by since I dove headfirst into a relationship with him. Call me a romantic fool, but everything feels right between the two of us. We gel in every way.

Dominic is renting the top floor of a town house in Buckhead, which is where I've been living since my relationship with Charles ended. It's a nice place, but small, and we're already talking about finding a place of our own and officially moving in together. Things are moving fast, but it doesn't feel that way. It's not like I wouldn't have stayed in my matrimonial home a while longer, especially since Charles was arrested and carted off to jail so I wouldn't have had to share the home with him. But I had to leave the house, as it was seized by the authorities. They're investigating it as a possible proceed of crime. Scary, I know. Because if they deem it *is* a proceed of

Charles's criminal behavior, I will likely lose everything I should have gained from the house. Considering Charles and I bought the house five years ago, I know it isn't. At least, I think it isn't. But I'll be the first to admit that I didn't really know Charles at all, which means I can't be certain about what my future holds financially.

And this is where the situation gets worse. My lawyer has told me that, proceed of crime or not, my house might have to be sold in order to repay the victim—the Wishes Come True Foundation. My lawyer and I are awaiting word on this very matter, but the bottom line is that despite being entitled to half of my house, I might get nada. Zilch. Not one red cent. Sometimes I feel so much anger that I want five minutes alone with Charles in a room—me, Charles and the meat cleaver I'll use to disfigure him.

Then I think about the fact that were it not for Charles being the con artist he is, I wouldn't have met Dominic, the auditor investigating the embezzlement. And meeting Dominic has been the best thing for me.

If not for Dominic, I'd be homeless right now. Not that I couldn't stay with Claudia or Lishelle, but what can I say? I can't resist the lure of a hard cock every night and every morning. Until Dominic decides to kick me out—which I hope he doesn't!—I'm going to be staying with him.

Tilting my head to the right, I peer at Dominic's face. I love all those angles and grooves. The man is too darned sexy. His eyes are still closed, and the steady sound of his breathing tells me he's still asleep. My eyes venture lower, to his naked body uncovered by our sheets. Like every morning, Dominic's penis is erect.

I reach for it. Touch the tip ever so lightly. When Dominic

doesn't stir, I take his cock into my palm and stroke it. Now he moans softly, but still doesn't wake up.

All I have to do is touch him and I'm turned on. I want more of him.

Unable to resist myself, I ease my body down the bed and position my head over his cock. A quick glance upward tells me Dominic is still asleep.

He won't be for long.

I hold his cock steady and slip it into my mouth. Dominic's body jerks slightly, an involuntary reaction. I move my tongue slowly around and around the tip of his shaft before I draw it deeper into my mouth.

Hearing a deep moan now, I look toward Dominic's face. His eyes are still closed, and I don't know if he's in dreamland or realizes that this wet dream is reality.

I run my tongue up and down the length of his shaft, then lower, to his testicles.

"Baby…" Dominic's voice is groggy.

As I look up at him, I grin. "Morning."

"I thought I was dreaming. Shit, what a nice way to wake up."

I don't answer, instead using my mouth to skillfully torture him. I suck on the tip of his penis like it's a big, juicy lollipop, and soon, Dominic is groaning loudly.

He reaches for my shoulders and urges me forward. "Climb on top of me."

I do so, straddling my legs over Dominic's hips.

"I meant my face," he tells me. "Climb on my face."

Just the thought of it elicits a moan from my throat. I'm not sure anything gets me off more than sitting on his face and looking down at him as he's got my clit in his mouth.

As I move my hips upward, to Dominic's face, he grips my

ass with one hand while the other goes to my pussy. He runs a finger along my folds, then grins at me.

"So wet, baby. Before I even touched you."

His mouth is close to my vagina as he speaks, and his hot breath makes me quiver.

"I could probably come before you even lick my pussy. Just looking down at you like this, knowing how close you are…"

"Really? So you don't want me to do this?" Dominic's hot tongue flicks over my nub.

"Mmmm…"

"Or this?" Now he covers me with his mouth and suckles—hard and strong.

My hips buck and my right leg shakes. "It's too much…it's too intense…"

He pulls his mouth away but massages my nub. "You're so wet," he murmurs before laving me with his tongue. "I love how you taste… Can't get enough… Say this pussy is mine…"

The delicious friction of his tongue has me panting. "My pussy…is yours. Only yours."

Dominic slips a finger inside me before suckling my clit again, and this is when I start to unravel. I look into his eyes, and our gazes lock as he sucks on my pussy gently this time, making these soft, slurping sounds.

Sweet heaven, I come. Come hard. Arching my back, I cry out from the pleasure of my orgasm. My hips writhe against his mouth, as if desperate to be free of the exquisite torture, but he holds me in place. Still he tortures me with his teeth and tongue, still pleasures me with his fingers, making the orgasm as sweet as any I've ever experienced.

My body drained, all I can do is whimper. Dominic whips me over onto my back, finds my center with his cock, and enters me with one blinding thrust. My whimper turns into a loud moan. Already I'm at the edge of another orgasm.

Dominic rams me hard, giving me no mercy. And I don't want mercy. I want exactly this—passionate and crazed fucking.

Knowing I'm about to lose control, I grip the bedsheets and lock my feet around his waist as I go over the edge. This time, Dominic swallows my moans with a kiss. My entire body shudders as my orgasm passes through me like a giant wave.

And then Dominic rolls over onto his back, taking me with him. His cock, still burrowed inside of me, reaches me at an even deeper place. He holds my hips firmly and guides me back and forth, back and forth, over his crotch. My clit, already sensitive, responds to the friction of skin against skin.

"Dominic, baby…I'm gonna…" He takes one of my nipples into his mouth and hungrily sucks it. I'm lost in an ocean of overpowering sensations. "Oh, baby. I'm gonna come…*again!*"

I barely get the words out before my body explodes. This orgasm is the absolute sweetest, the most intense. I throw my whole body backward, squeeze Dominic's legs for support, and ride this wave of pleasure while I ride his strong, hard cock. His hands cover my breasts and I hear his deep groans. I know he's close.

"Look at me," he rasps.

With effort, I throw my body forward and gaze down at the man I love.

"Yes, that's it. Fuck, you're hot. So beautiful."

Dominic's hips buck slightly, and he grips me harder. I can see in his eyes the moment his orgasm takes control of him.

Now I kiss him, swallow his moans of passion as his seed spills inside me.

"I love you," he murmurs.

His words express everything I feel.

I stroke his face and say, "I know, sweetheart. And I love you, too."

After we make love, Dominic and I take a quick shower together. He has to head off to his office, and I…well, I don't know what I'll do. Ever since the news broke about Charles, my business has dropped to practically nil. Even some people who'd already booked photography sessions with me canceled. I was ready to refund all of their initial deposits, but Dominic told me that wasn't a smart business practice, and if people were going to fire me because of my husband's actions, they were far too judgmental and didn't deserve their money back. I followed Dominic's advice, even if I have mixed emotions about it. It's not in my nature to be so hard-nosed when it comes to business—which is likely why I haven't been more successful.

At least Dominic's brother, Sebastian, has hired me for his September wedding, and he and his fiancée have booked a great package. But I need more business than that.

Maybe I'm crazy, but I'm not nearly as stressed about the demise of my business as I should be. And if there's one thing I've learned, it's that crying about something will get you nowhere. I've decided to take a moment in my life to pause and reflect before moving on. Oh, I have every intention of making my business the success I've always wanted it to be. But I need money to do that—to advertise, especially—and right now I can barely afford to pay the property's rent.

It could be because of my religious upbringing, but I'm going to have faith that everything will work out.

As Dominic dresses, I slip into a silk robe. I lie on the bed and watch him. I like to watch him. And not just because he's got the body of a god, but because I take immense pleasure in watching him do the simple things he does every morning when he gets ready for work.

It gives me a sense of security, I suppose. And the sense of intimacy I so craved with my ex.

"Whoo, you are looking hot!" I exclaim. He's dressed in a neatly pressed white shirt, open at the collar, and a pair of black slacks. He looks as amazing with his clothes on as he does with them off.

He smiles softly at me, meets me at the bed, then lowers his head to mine and gives me a quick kiss on the lips. When he pulls away, I moan.

"You know I have to get going," he says.

"I know. That doesn't mean I *want* you to."

Normally Dominic and I would engage in a bit more sexual flirtation, but today, he eases himself off the bed, gives my hand a kiss, then heads out of the bedroom.

Hmm. Odd.

I scramble off the bed and follow Dominic to the front door. I give him a big, openmouthed kiss that promises there's plenty more where that came from. But Dominic doesn't respond the way I expected, with the usual growl from his throat, the one that tells me he hates having to leave me when what he wants most to do is get me flat on my back.

Now I really have to wonder what's going on.

"Dom?" I step back to fully look at him. "Honey, is something wrong?"

He shakes his head.

"Are you sure? You don't seem…yourself."

"I'm just wondering about the future."

Panic stirs inside me. "Meaning?"

"If you'll still love me as much in a couple months as you do right now."

Now I laugh. Is he actually insecure about my feelings for him? I move toward him, take one of his hands in mine, and slip it beneath my robe. Then I force his fingers to touch my naked pussy. "Ask me again if you think I won't love you as much in a couple months."

"Seriously, Annelise. Things will be coming to a head soon. With me testifying against Charles."

"Oh. That." I wave a hand, as if to dismiss his concern. "I couldn't care less what you do to Charles in the court-room. The son of a bitch deserves it."

"You say that now, but when you see me on the stand—"

"I wasn't planning to be in the courtroom, if that makes you feel any better."

"I guess a little."

Every time I'm around Dominic, I want to touch him. Literally, I can't get enough of him. I'm like a teenager in heat.

I run my hands through his black hair. "I know something else that would make you feel way better." I wink at him. "But I'd have to get down on my knees, right here in the doorway. The neighbors might talk. But, hey, I'm game."

Dominic shakes his head as he looks at me, a smile playing on his lips. "You're a total nymphomaniac."

Am I? I certainly am not the same woman I was when I was married to Charles. But almost a year and a half of no sex will make any woman a sex-crazed maniac.

Of course, a guy like Dominic does wonders for a woman's libido, as well.

Dominic gives me a soft kiss on my forehead. "I'll see you later."

"I'll be here."

* * *

For about a minute after Dominic leaves, I wonder if he's being truthful. Or if he's keeping something from me that I need to know. Then I brush those thoughts aside.

"Don't bring your baggage from your marriage to this relationship," I tell myself, thinking of the advice the Oprahs and Dr. Phils of the world would dole out. The truth is, Charles did a number on my self-esteem when he didn't touch me for nearly a year and a half. But just because Charles was a liar doesn't mean Dominic is. I have to take what Dominic tells me at face value, not start questioning anything unless there's a real reason to.

I busy myself with household duties like dusting, laundry and cleaning the toilets. And as I do, a smile creeps onto my face. No, I'm not trying to set the feminist movement back forty years. I'm just saying that it feels right, being in Dominic's home, doing housework like we've been together forever.

And maybe, just maybe, that's what's at the heart of my insecurity with Dominic. I don't know him well enough to know all his quirks and nuances. The two weeks we've officially been a couple is hardly enough time to discover all that.

And not enough time for me to be totally secure about where our relationship will head, no matter how much I know I'm totally into him.

"You know he's into you," I assure myself as I head to a large, leafy plant with a duster. There haven't been any middle-of-the-night calls, any hushed whispers as Dominic talks to a mysterious person on the phone. And perhaps more important, I haven't had any hang-ups when I've answered the phone.

The telephone rings and I jump, then chuckle at the coincidence of having thought about telephone calls before it actually rang, I hurry across the living room to answer it.

"Hello?"

"Annelise?"

"Yes," I answer, somewhat guarded.

"Annelise, it's Nick Foster."

"Oh, hello." I settle into a leather armchair, wondering what my divorce lawyer has to tell me.

"Do you have any time to come and see me today? Say in a couple hours?"

"Sure," I answer. "You have news?"

"I think it's best if we talk in person."

I can't imagine what my lawyer wants to tell me, but already I've got a bad feeling. The fact that he wants to see me in person probably means that he's got bad news for me.

I wince. Damn, this isn't what I was hoping for. I need money. For my business and my day-to-day life. Yes, my friends have helped me out, and because I've been staying with Dominic I haven't really needed much. But still. I want to be able to make it on my own. No more relying on a man.

The next two hours pass in slow motion, with me dreading going to my lawyer's office but knowing I don't have a choice. Even when I arrive at his office, I have to encourage myself to get out of the car.

"Bad news or not, you have to get this over with," I mutter.

I finally open the door and exit the car.

"Annelise." Nick Foster, a tall and attractive black man, stands when his secretary ushers me into his office. He pumps my hand from across his desk. "How are you?"

"Truthfully? I'm a little bit stressed about what you're going to tell me."

"Stressed? Don't be stressed."

"I am…unless you tell me otherwise. That I don't need to be."

Nick cracks a smile as he sits in his chair. He opens a folder on his desk and says, "You don't need to be."

Now my heart leaps with hope. "Are you saying—"

"I've got great news for you, Annelise. Your portion of the house—it's all yours."

My hand is shaking as I raise it to my mouth. "Oh my God. This isn't a joke? This—it's for real?"

"It's for real. The matrimonial home will be sold, and you'll get exactly half of the proceeds."

"And Charles?"

"His half will likely have to go toward repaying the Wishes Come True Foundation, but I can't be sure about that."

"And my half is absolutely safe. The courts or whoever can't change their minds tomorrow?"

"Basically, your house was a joint asset before Charles's fraud. You aren't guilty in that crime, and the courts agree that you shouldn't have to lose what is rightfully yours. Charles has victimized enough people. You can put your house on the market as soon as possible."

I blow out a shaky breath. "Wow. So this is over?"

"Not entirely."

My face drops. "No?"

"Your divorce still needs to be finalized."

"Oh. Right." I chuckle. Compared to getting over this hurdle, the dissolution of my marriage seems like a minor detail to deal with.

"And, to that end, I'm meeting with the judge next week. I'm going to ask that he expedite the process, given everything. You were married to a liar, a cheater, a thief. Clearly, you want the union absolved as soon as possible."

"Exactly."

"I think this will go our way."

"I wish it could be over tomorrow."

"Understandably. But at least we've gotten past the biggest hindrance."

"Thank God."

"Now, there's still the issue of Charles's other assets. Until the state has figured out what it's doing, I can't make you any promises. However, based on what I've been able to learn, it looks like much of his property and other assets were most likely purchased with stolen money."

"I don't care about the rest of it," I tell him, meaning it. "As long as my portion of the house is safe." I pause, happiness filling my chest. "Oh, Nick. Thank you."

"I'm just the messenger."

"Oh, you're more than that. I know you've been making calls on my behalf. Lobbying for me."

"You're a victim in this, just like the children from the foundation."

"Thank you." I reach across the desk and shake Nick's hand. "Thank you, thank you."

"You're welcome."

I can't stop grinning.

"Now, I can handle getting a real estate agent for you. Or you can do it. Whatever you like."

I'm already paying enough money per hour for Nick's services. There's no need to let him handle aspects I can deal with myself. "I'll call someone. Hopefully the house will sell right away."

"I have a friend who's a real estate agent, and I can put

you in touch with him if you like. He can deal with the legal issues of selling the house that are required in this situation, given its special circumstances. He can control the money and cut you a check for your half directly, minus his commission, of course."

Of course. People might have your best interests at heart…for a cost.

But I can't worry about that, especially since the reality is that, despite any commission I'll have to pay, I stand to collect a pretty penny. Charles and I bought that house when we were first married five years ago, and house prices in our neighborhood have gone up greatly since then. We paid off the mortgage after one of Charles's large class-action cases settled, which means I should walk away with some sizable cash. Likely a little over three hundred grand after the commission is paid.

Three hundred thousand dollars! With that kind of money, I can easily invest what's necessary into my business.

"Annelise?"

"I'm sorry." I know that, as I meet Nick's eyes, I'm grinning like a fool. "What were you saying?"

"I'll let you know what the judge says about expediting your divorce."

"Great."

"I don't anticipate any problems."

"I can't thank you enough for all your help, Nick." Of course, I'll owe him a pretty penny as well, but now I can afford to pay him! And it's money well spent.

"That's my job." He closes the folder. "Please, when you get an offer for your house that you want to accept, let me know."

"Absolutely."

I reach across the table and shake Nick's hand again.

When I turn to leave, I'm so high on happiness that I practically float out of the office.

Three

Lishelle

I have got The Headache from Hell. I rub my temples and groan as I stare at Linda Tennant, my station manager. She's sitting on the armchair in my dressing room, while I'm on the folding chair in front of the mirror. The makeup artist recently finished doing my face for the six-o'clock news.

"I'm just saying," Linda says, "you need to give me more than this. Some sort of concrete direction."

"All I know is that it needs to be a pledge drive."

"A *nationwide* pledge drive," Linda says, her tone doubtful.

"Yes," I respond without hesitation. "I'd really like to co-ordinate this with our sister stations across the country. That's what will make this fund-raising effort unique—as well as raise much more money for the Wishes Come True Foundation."

"I'm not saying it isn't a great idea…in theory. But a nationwide fund-raising effort—that's going to take time.

Honestly, by the time we all coordinate schedules, it could be a year before this event takes place."

"A year?" I all but gasp. "That's way too long."

"I'm giving you my opinion."

"But we need to do this *now*. Strike while the iron is hot. The embezzlement story has been big news across the country. This is when people will be more likely to give—a lot."

"I hear you. And we can definitely try to do something on our end. It's the coordinating it with our sister stations that's going to be tough."

"We'll work it out," I say confidently. How, God only knows. But I want to see this happen. Soon. Before everyone forgets about the tragic turn of events the foundation faced. Now is the time that people will happily dig into their pockets and give. But a year from now? Who knows?

"I'm open to whatever ideas you have," Linda says.

"I'll get you something." If it means I have to start making calls to all of our sister stations across the country, then I'll do that.

When Linda leaves my dressing room, I stare at my reflection in the mirror. I don't like what I see. Even with makeup, the dark circles under my eyes are noticeable. I haven't admitted this to any of my friends, but I haven't been sleeping well since Glenn screwed me over. And I've been far more stressed than I thought I would be.

I was able to exact some delicious revenge on my ex-boyfriend, but I realized after that, that the greatest reward would be doing something to benefit all those kids. My friends Claudia and Annelise agreed. Which is why I'm hell-bent on seeing this nationwide fund-raiser come to fruition.

I sigh and turn away from the mirror. Am I expecting too

much? Should I coordinate a local fund-raising drive and forget the grandiose plans?

But that's not what I want. This means a lot to me. I want more than anything to see something positive come of the heartache my girlfriends and I suffered at the hands of the men we loved. And I can't think of anything more positive than raising money for the terminally ill children who were robbed.

Of course, it also helps that every moment I spend thinking about how I'll make this fund-raiser happen is a moment I'm distracted from the memory of just how badly my heart was broken.

Two days later, I'm more than ready to get together with my girlfriends at our regular Sunday brunch spot. I arrive at Liaisons to see that Claudia and Annelise are already there, three mimosas on the table.

"Thank God," I say as I slip into the booth beside Claudia, already reaching for my drink. The mimosa goes down smooth, hits the spot inside me that needs to be soothed.

"And we're chopped liver?" Claudia asks playfully.

"Oh, hi, you two." I smile sweetly as Annelise rolls her eyes.

"It's been one of those weeks," I explain. "The planning for our pledge drive is stressing me out. My station manager is basically saying that we can't coordinate a nationwide effort—at least not in the time frame we want to do this. I want to prove her wrong, but I don't know if that's possible."

"It'll work out," Annelise says.

Her carefree attitude irritates me slightly. "That's very Pollyanna of you, but this shit is turning out to be harder than I'd hoped."

"And I understand that," Annelise tells me. "I guess I'm just saying that for today you should try to relax, put everything negative out of your mind. Things have a way of working out despite how much we fret over them."

I examine her then. Annelise has been looking really happy lately, despite the uncertainty in her life, but today she looks especially so. I ask her, "Something going on that I should know about?"

"Oh, yeah," Claudia chimes. "Annelise has some amazing news. And so do I."

"Well, spill it." I sip my mimosa. "I could use some good news, even if it's not mine."

Before Annelise can speak, a woman shows up at our table. I'm a little surprised that it's not Sierra, the cute Asian girl who has been our regular waitress for as long as I can remember.

"Have you made up your minds?" the stranger asks.

I glance at Claudia and Annelise, wondering if they feel the way I do—unhappy that there's this new woman at our table. They don't seem particularly perturbed, but I am.

"Um," I begin cautiously. "Who are you?"

Beside me, Claudia forces a chuckle. "Our waitress, silly. Lishelle, this is Apple."

"*Apple?*" I stare at the woman, a tall, skinny, dark-haired woman who looks too conservative to have such a ridiculous name. "Your name is Apple?"

Apple giggles as she nods. "According to my mother, she was drinking apple martinis the night I was conceived."

"So she got drunk and got knocked up," I comment dryly.

Annelise's eyes grow wide with horror. "Lishelle," she admonishes.

"I'm just saying…I thought only movie stars gave their kids names like 'Apple' and 'Orange' or 'Banana.'"

Claudia places a hand on my wrist. To everyone, it must

look like a subtle show of affection. But Claudia actually squeezes my wrist—hard. "Looks like you were already drinking before you got here," she jokes.

"I can go through our specials," Apple says. "Of course, we have the buffet—"

"Which is what we always have," I point out. "Sierra would know that."

"We're going to have the buffet," Annelise quickly says.

"What happened to Sierra?" I ask. "She sick or something?"

"That's something else we didn't get to tell you yet." Claudia's grin is far too syrupy. "Apple tells us that Sierra apparently fell hot and heavy for some guy, and she's moved to L.A. to be with him."

"What?" I practically shriek.

Apple shrugs apologetically, as though this is her fault. Or rather, as though *I* think this is her fault.

"I'm happy for her," Annelise comments.

"She just *fell* for some guy? Didn't we warn her? Didn't she hear us bitch enough about men and how you can't trust them?"

"Can we…not do this?" Annelise gives me a pointed look.

A frustrated breath oozes out of me as I look up at Apple. "It's just that…for the longest time, Sierra has been our waitress. She always knows what we want."

"Lishelle, it's okay." Claudia lays a hand on my arm. "Apple here is perfectly capable of taking care of us."

I glance up at Apple. "Of course. I just didn't…expect *you*."

Apple nods, seeming to accept my half-baked apology. "So, three for the buffet…can I get you anything else?"

"Coffee," Annelise answers.

"And another round of mimosas," I add. "Lord knows that one won't be enough today."

When Apple disappears, Claudia looks at me and scowls. "Could you have been any ruder to that waitress?"

"I'm sorry," I say. Then I rub my temples. "The thing is…" I don't finish my statement. I'm not entirely sure what I wanted to say.

"The thing is what?" Claudia prompts.

"The thing is…" My voice trails off on a sigh. "So much has changed lately. For once I'd like to see something stay the same. Something be…fucking consistent. Fucking reliable."

Annelise fixes me with a mothering look she's so good at giving, then says softly, "Oh, hon."

And I swear, that simple look is my complete undoing. I feel my eyes start to mist, and I have to look away before I start bawling like a baby.

"Sweetie." Claudia's touch is now gentle. "What's really going on with you?"

I don't answer right away. I can't. I feel foolish for even thinking what I'm thinking.

"You've always told us everything," Annelise says. "Same as we do with you. Don't hold back now."

"Okay. I'm just gonna to say this. And I know this will sound weird, but hear me out." I pause before dropping my bombshell. "I kind of miss Glenn."

Startled gasps explode from my friends.

"I know. I told you it would sound weird. And I don't mean that the way it actually sounded."

"Huh?" Claudia asks before she and Annelise exchange confused looks at my double talk.

"Let me explain what I mean," I go on. "Glenn screwed me over big-time, so there's no way in hell I miss *him*. What I miss is being with a man. I miss being excited about someone. Since my divorce from David, I didn't give a shit if I ever fell in love again. Then Glenn came back into my life. And he made me so many promises. He went to elaborate lengths to con me. That house he was supposedly going to buy—"

"Lies, Lishelle," Claudia says. "All of it. Glenn Baxter doesn't deserve to breathe, much less have you missing him."

"Honestly, I know how this must sound, but I don't miss *him*. I guess I miss being with someone. First my marriage fell apart. Then my relationship with Glenn spontaneously combusted. Glenn made me hope again. Want a man again. And now…" I sip my mimosa. "Suddenly I'm starting to wonder if I'll ever find someone I can trust, who won't fuck around." I down the rest of my mimosa. "You know what? Forget I said that. I have no clue what's gotten over me."

Claudia and Annelise are silent for a long moment, then Claudia says, "For what it's worth, I understand what you're saying. I was with Adam for four years. It's hard to accept that we're not together anymore," she confesses. "Not that I miss *him*—what he did to me effectively killed my feelings for the bastard—but the pain he caused? That's still there."

"This is getting way too depressing." I glance around for a sign of Apple, who I hope to spot with our second round of drinks. "We're clearly better off without these guys in our lives."

"But you're both grieving," Annelise points out. "And there's no shame in that."

"You're right," I say, the understanding of what I'm experiencing helping to chase away some of the sadness. "That's *exactly* what we're doing. Going through a grieving process."

"Totally," Annelise agrees.

"I never thought of it that way," Claudia adds.

"I'm lucky," Annelise continues. "I've had Dominic to help me get over any of the hurt Charles caused me. You two…I say you both need a palate cleanser—a hot fling or a new man. Someone to help make the memories of your relationships distant ones."

That's the last thing I need, but I don't say that to Annelise. I have no interest in getting into the sack with some new guy for a meaningless night of sex.

"You said you have some good news," I remind her, remembering that Annelise had mentioned that before I got all dramatic. "Are you and Dominic getting married?"

"No."

"Oh," Claudia says, the word full of sadness.

"I didn't mean that to sound so final, if it did," Annelise tells us. "We'll definitely wait until my divorce from Charles is finalized before thinking of that step. Which is fine with me. What I want to tell you is what my lawyer said when I saw him today."

I suck in a sharp breath. For the past few weeks, we've all been hoping and praying that she'll get good news regarding her house with Charles. That she won't lose her portion of it because her husband decided to rip off terminally ill children. "You said it's good news?"

A smile spreads across Annelise's face. "I can't believe it, but I get to keep my half of the house!"

"Oh, Annie." I clasp my hands together. "That's the best news."

"I know." She can't stop beaming. "I've been feeling a bit guilty, though. Wondering if it isn't fair for all the proceeds from the house to go to the charity. But it's not like I don't need to live."

"And you had no part in Charles's scam." I reach across the table to grip her hand. "Honey, take the money and run. Put some into your business, invest some, find a place to live."

"Oh, I don't think she and Dom will be parting ways anytime soon," Claudia says.

"Not likely," I agree. "But you keep some of that money under lock and key. Never let yourself be in a situation again where a man can fuck you over because he's got the money and you don't."

"I won't."

I shift in my seat, sitting a little higher. "That was truly good news. My spirits have lifted already."

"And you haven't even heard *my* news yet."

I turn to my right and face Claudia. "If you tell me that you've found another man, I will whoop you upside the head. I don't want to be the only single one."

"A man. Right." Claudia laughs sardonically. "That's a good one."

"Then what could possibly be your good news? Adam is going to jail, too? No, if that news had broken, I would have heard it."

Adam, Claudia's ex-fiancé, who formerly held the position of president on the board of the Wishes Come True Foundation, was investigated for any possible connection to the embezzlement but was found to have no involvement. Still, when the news of his drug use and sexual fetishes came to light—thanks to our plan of revenge—he resigned from the board amid great scandal.

"No, this isn't about Adam. But it is about the foundation."

"I'm listening," I tell Claudia.

"You know one of my cousins is a music producer, and as such, he obviously has lots of connections."

"Right."

"Well, I was talking about our desire to help the Wishes Come True Foundation, and he had an idea. He said that if we want to make this fund-raising effort work, we need to get some big names attached to it."

"Which is a great idea, yes," I agree. "But getting someone—"

"Let me finish."

I mime pulling a zipper closed across my lips.

"Well, Morgan talked to Rugged—you know, that hot new rap artist from Atlanta—about the idea of possibly participating, given that this is his home town, and—"

"And he said yes?" Excitement washes over me.

Claudia nods. "He wants to do it."

"Yes!" I pump a fist in the air. "This is exactly what we needed. Some celebrity to headline the event."

Across the table Annelise is grinning, too. "It gets better," she practically sings.

"Really?" My eyes flit from Annelise to Claudia. Then I notice Apple in my peripheral vision.

"Here are your drinks." Her face looks flushed as she deposits three mimosas and three mugs of coffee onto the table. "I'm sorry, I got busy with other tables. I didn't mean to bring them out this late."

She's looking directly at me as she offers this explanation, as though she expects me to bite her head off.

"That's fine," I tell her.

Nodding nervously, she tucks a strand of hair behind her ear. "You haven't gotten food yet."

"We've been gabbing," Annelise explains. "We'll get to it."

When Apple walks off, I say to Claudia, "Okay, what's this even-better news?"

"Right." She grins. "Well, Rugged likes the idea so much that he said he'd ask other rap artists, like 50 Cent, Ludacris and some others, if they'd like to get involved as well. Maybe do a 'rap artists support the cause' type of event."

"You know what, I will never feel sorry for myself again," I proclaim, smacking the edge of the table as I do. "I came in here feeling so shitty, but life is still good. There are still good people in the world."

"Exactly," Annelise agrees. "I told you things have a way of working out."

"Can you believe it?" Claudia's eyes are beaming with happiness. "We're gonna make this happen. And we'll raise a ton of money for the foundation."

"Lord, I hope so." I reach for my second mimosa. "I'm so passionate about this now, ya know?"

"We know," Annelise agrees. "And we'll do right by the children who need this money so desperately."

"Oh, and Rugged is getting into town tonight and would like to set up a meeting," Claudia goes on. "Talk to you at least, Lishelle, as your network will be hosting this. Or we can all meet him. Whatever you'd prefer."

"It'd be great if he could come to the station. Meet with me and my station manager." My mind races as I think of how this is exactly the boost we needed. "And you're welcome to come, too, of course. Or I could handle the preliminary meeting. Whatever you think is best."

"We'll figure it out by tomorrow," Claudia assures me. "In the meantime, my stomach is growling."

"Yeah, mine's pretty angry too." Annelise chortles. "And if I keep drinking on an empty stomach…"

"Say no more." I rise. "Let's head to the buffet."

I know the moment that Rugged enters the studio. I hear the excitement in the air. Even a couple of squeals.

I'm in my office, but I don't move. I sit casually at my desk, a current tabloid open on my lap. It's trash, I know, but I read it to escape the reality of the heartbreaking stories I often report on the news.

My door is ajar, but someone raps on it nonetheless. "Lishelle?"

"Come in."

It's Carmen, one of the production assistants, and she's grinning from ear to ear. "Rugged is here."

"Oh?"

"Yes. I took him to the green room. Is that where you want to meet him? Linda says she'll be at least ten minutes. I didn't want to leave him waiting."

I glance around. My office looks presentable. "Why don't you bring him here?"

Carmen disappears, but less than five seconds later, she pops her head back in my door. "Can I ask you something?"

I lower my magazine to my desk, but don't close it. "Of course."

"I know this is going to sound silly, but I'm a huge fan of his. I thought he was hot on television, but in person he's even more attractive. Wait till you see him."

"What exactly is it you want me to do?"

"Ask him for his autograph for me. Please, pretty please."

"I don't get it. You've met him. Why don't you ask him yourself?"

"Because I'll die!"

Whatever, I think. But I say, "Sure."

A few minutes later Carmen reappears with Rugged. Her face is flushed—clearly she's blushing. I'm completely shocked, since I never figured Carmen the type to listen to rap music, much less be a huge fan of Rugged's. Hell, I'm not a big fan of rap. I have caught glimpses of Rugged's videos featuring women in barely there bikinis on late-night TV, and I wasn't exactly impressed. But for the cause of raising money for charity, I'm happy to embrace the idea of working with him.

"Lishelle, this is Rugged. Obviously." She grins and nods, her unkempt bangs bobbing with her bouncing head.

My God, what has gotten into her?

"Rugged, this is Lishelle Jennings."

I close the tabloid and toss it onto my desk. Then I rise from my chair and cross the room with my hand extended. Rugged meets me, takes my hand in his and shakes it.

And surprisingly, when our hands touch, I feel a jolt of heat. Something about Rugged has sparked a sexual reaction in me, one I didn't expect.

"Hello," he says.

Swallowing, I pull my hand away. "Hello."

I don't miss the way his eyes skim over my body. How can I—the move is so bold.

And makes a sex-starved woman like me think about riding a large, hard cock…

I clear my throat and add, "It's a pleasure to meet you, I'm a fan."

"I'ma fan o' yours, too."

Behind us, Carmen is standing stupidly, like she's frozen in place. Of course, she wants an autograph.

"Rugged, would you mind signing an autograph for Carmen? She's one of your biggest fans."

Now Carmen's eyes widen in alarm. Rugged glances over his shoulder at her.

"She's much too modest to ask you," I go on. "Isn't that right, Carmen?"

"Um…well, I didn't want to bother you."

"No bother," Rugged tells her. "You got a piece of paper? Or do you want me to something else—like your shirt?" Rugged's eyes move to Carmen's breasts, which look bountiful beneath her thin, cotton T-shirt.

"Um." Carmen's response is shaky. "My…my shirt?"

"I've got a Sharpie." I go back to my desk, scoop it up, and pass the black marker to Rugged.

After Rugged signs his scrawling signature on her shirt, Carmen can't stop saying thank you as she backs her way out the door. When she's gone, I move to the door and close it.

"So," I begin without preamble. "You're interested in helping out with the pledge drive I'm planning."

"Definitely. When Morgan called to tell me about it, I was excited, man. The city of Atlanta's my home. And the people here, they been good to me. I wanna give somethin' back."

"Please, sit." I gesture to the leather chair at my desk. As Rugged settles there, I sit in my own chair on the opposite side.

"Have you had any thoughts about how to participate? I'm thinking you could come into the studio, join me on TV as we appeal to people to open up their wallets."

"That all you want? Yo, I was thinkin' of doin' a concert or somethin'."

I perk up at that. "A concert?"

"Yeah, a summer concert. Maybe Labor Day Weekend, or wheneva you want. I'll do a concert, and all the proceeds will go to the kids."

The idea is so brilliant I could kiss this guy. "That's fucking amazing." I cover my mouth and mumble, "Excuse my Spanish."

"And see, what I was thinkin' was that some of my homies

could hold concerts in other parts of the country. Maybe ten, fifteen major cities. One big 'Give back to da kids' event. Ya know? We could raise some serious fuckin' cash. 'Scuse my Spanish." He grins.

I am so excited by this idea, my heart is beating seriously fast. "You think it will work?"

"I'ma try my hardest to help out. We gonna do this, we do it big."

"I like the way you think."

There's a pause, then Rugged asks, "What else you like?" The question catches me off guard—but the slight upturn of the rapper's mouth, plus the way he's rested his thumb in the loose waistband of his jeans above his crotch, makes it clear I didn't misunderstand the inflection in his voice.

He's just propositioned me.

"Excuse me?" I ask. I try to sound appalled, but the truth is, I'm not. In fact, my panties just got wet at Rugged's words. There's something about a guy who goes for what he wants that is a huge turn-on.

"I'm a fan, Miss Jennings. I like you. *A lot.*"

"And how old are you?" I ask, my tone much like that of an adult questioning a child who's been caught throwing rocks at her window. "Nineteen? Twenty?"

"Twenty-fo'."

"Oh." I force a laugh, trying, I guess, to hide my sudden sexual anxiety. "Like that's old enough."

"It sho' is," Rugged tells me confidently."

My entire body flushes with carnal heat. My nipples ache and my pussy starts to throb. And I realize that the thought I had, that I wasn't interested in a meaningless fling with some guy, is a lie. I'm more than interested.

Suddenly, my body needs sex.

I steal a quick glance at Rugged's crotch, try to judge by the bulge how big his cock is.

I like.

"Old enough fo' what you need," Rugged adds, this time drawing his bottom lip between his teeth when he finishes his statement.

"And how do you know what I need?" I ask. My body is attracted to his, but I'm unwilling to let go. I don't know why.

"I heard about how that guy played you."

Great. "And you're offering me what? Your penis as a way to solve all my problems?"

I expect Rugged to be offended by my comment. Instead he says, "If that's what you want…"

Wow. This guy is really serious.

So I decide to call his bluff. Play with him a little. "What am I supposed to do? Suck it or drop my pants?"

"Whateva gets you off."

Either could get me off…

The knock on the door has us both sitting up straight. I clear my throat, then say, "Come in."

Linda opens the door, grinning. She enters the room, her hand outstretched. "Hello, Rugged. It is so great to meet you."

Rugged shakes her hand. "Same here."

"I guess I'll cut right to the chase," Linda says. "Have you come up with any great ideas?"

"Actually," I begin slowly. "We've come up with an excellent plan. I'm really excited about it."

I fill Linda in on Rugged's fantastic suggestion, and by the end of my spiel, she can hardly contain her enthusiasm.

"I *love* it!" she exclaims. "You think we can make this happen?"

"I'ma try my best. Rap artists are always gettin' bad press. We do this, it'll show America we got good hearts, too."

Rugged glances my way with that statement, like he's trying to prove a point to me. *Does* he have a good heart? Or is he willing to 'give back' just because that'll get him good press, and therefore sell him more records? Not that it matters to me. I just want people to support the cause, by whatever means necessary.

I tune out for the next few minutes while Rugged and Linda discuss possibilities, thinking of how he propositioned me and wondering if he was serious. And fuck, I can't believe how wet I am. How much part of me wanted to lock the door and offer him my pussy. It is still throbbing, so much so that I ache to stroke my clitoris.

I ponder the possibility of fucking Rugged when Linda's gone, because I'm pretty sure he won't reject that idea. A quick fuck, or a blowjob—guys don't say no to an offer like that, even if the woman is a stranger. Why would Rugged?

And that's exactly the problem. Because Rugged is a star, women probably line up to do that for him now, whereas before they'd have smacked him for daring to be so crude.

I don't want to be as pathetic as one of his crazed female fans.

He might have me thinking about sex, but I'll get myself off like I normally do. Or I'll find someone else to fuck.

I hear Linda say something about Rugged having his manager call her, that they can go over some preliminary details.

"How does that sound, Lishelle?" she asks me.

"Sounds like a plan," I say, though I haven't been paying close attention to their chat. I've been lost in my thoughts about Rugged.

"All right, then." Linda shakes Rugged's hand once more. "We'll be in touch. I'm really looking forward to this."

"Me, too," Rugged concurs.

When Linda disappears, Rugged gets up and closes the door, then turns his hot gaze onto me. One side of his mouth lifts in a grin. "Now, where were we?"

"Finished," I tell him, and smile sweetly when he looks a bit surprised.

"But I thought—"

"Thought you were gonna get some? You want to impress a grown woman, you have to step to her in a different way."

"Ah, you're gonna play hard to get."

"I'm not playing anything." I pause, let my rejection sink in. No, I've made up my mind. I'm not going to act like one of his groupies. "I hope this isn't going to affect your willingness to see this fund-raising effort through to its fruition."

"'Course not," Rugged tells me, but his voice is clipped.

Oh, he's not a happy man. Inwardly, I beam. Honestly, did he expect me to drop to my knees just because he's a star?

"Great," I tell him, and place my hand on his arm. He throws a quick glance at my hand, then meets my eyes—as though he's hopeful that my touching him means I've changed my mind.

I lead him to the door and waste no time in opening it. "Thank you so much for coming in to meet with me and the station manager," I tell him, all professional. "Now if you don't mind, I've got work to do."

Four

Claudia

"Mmm, baby." I writhe against the hot tongue licking my pussy. "Oh…that feels so good. Yes. Right there." My body grows warm all over, starts to tingle. *"Right there!"*

My eyes fly open, and I see darkness. My hand is in my panties between my legs, two fingers resting on my wet, engorged clitoris. For a moment I'm confused.

And then I realize I was dreaming.

I groan, disappointed to have been pulled from my dream at the best moment. Groan because I'm disappointed my dream wasn't reality, that there isn't a gorgeous man between my thighs ready to make me come.

I close my eyes, stroke my wet pussy and hope to recapture the sensations I was experiencing in the dream. I try to imagine Taye Diggs going down on me, then Shemar Moore, then a few other hot actors I like. But I can't hold a single image long enough, like my subconscious won't let me enjoy my carnal urge to get off.

After nearly a minute, I give up. My body is still aroused, but I can't get my mind to that place where I can reach orgasm.

I want a man, not my fingers. A man stroking my clit. A man's teeth grazing it. A tongue so far inside my pussy it's driving me crazy.

I might not miss Adam, but I do miss the sex. And with Adam the sex was frequent, and passionate.

My body craves that—with a real lover.

Rolling onto my side, I glance at the digital clock on my night table. It's 6:18 in the morning.

Once again I close my eyes, this time trying to sleep. But after five minutes of tossing and turning, I know that I can't.

I'm still aroused.

I need to fuck.

Slowly, I rise and turn on the bedside lamp. I open the drawer on my night table and reach down to the bottom, beneath various papers, until I feel my vibrator. I pull it out, and go back into the drawer for the DVD I want to watch.

When Adam and I were together, we watched lots of porn—at his suggestion. Most of it was simply raunch, one guy after the next getting sloppy blow jobs and spraying semen all over some woman's face. Those didn't appeal to me, and I suggested to Adam that he find something a bit more appealing to couples.

That's what this DVD is—a movie of various sexual scenes, all featuring couples.

I like this one because the women get just as much attention to their needs as the men do. Guys eat pussy—and lots of it. They suck on tits like they want to make a woman come that way.

I turn on the television, making sure the volume is low, then insert the DVD into the machine. As I make my way back to the bed, my clit starts to pulse, anticipating what it's going to experience.

Using the remote, I fast forward until I find a scene that will get me off. It's an up-close view of a vagina and the man's mouth that is all over it. The angle allows me to see every explicit detail.

I push my nightshirt up and my panties down, slip two fingers between my folds and settle them on my clit. But I don't start stroking myself—not yet. I want to enjoy the graphic visual, the way a woman enjoys the build up of foreplay.

So with my free hand I begin playing with a nipple, pulling it and tweaking it until it is fully aroused. Waves of carnal pleasure sweep through me. My eyes are glued to the television, taking in every delicious moment of that hungry mouth devouring pussy.

And when the man pulls the woman's folds apart, completely exposing her clitoris, I start to stroke my pussy in earnest. The man flicks the tip of his tongue over her again and again, until the woman starts to cry out. As she does, the man completely draws her nub into his mouth and sucks on it.

My heart rate picks up speed—and so do my fingers. I rub them over my clit in a circular motion, creating delicious heat. Now I am the woman onscreen. Her pleasure is my pleasure.

My lover pulls my clit deep into his mouth and suckles on my clit. The sounds of pleasure he makes excites my entire body. I'm breathless as he stops sucking on my clit and runs his tongue along my opening. The next instant, he slips two fingers inside, pulls them out and licks them, then moans happily and plunges his tongue into my vagina.

Fuck, that's so hot.

As the man's tongue goes deep into the woman's pussy, I insert two fingers into my own.

It's wet, and warm. I stretch my fingers inside, but it doesn't reach where I need to be touched. On the screen, the woman is screaming with the onset of her release. The man is fingering her now while sucking on her clit. After a moment, the man moves his body upward and starts to deep throat the woman—not what I want to see.

With one hand I grip the remote and rewind the scene, while with the other I grab the vibrator. It's shaped like a massive black cock, and for now, it is my lover.

"Eat that pussy," I say softly as I ease the cock inside of me. I don't turn it on. Not yet. For now, I enjoy every sensation this life-like cock brings me.

My pussy throbs out of control as I watch the way the man suckles on the exposed clitoris. Fuck, that guy knows how to go down on a woman.

"Eat that pussy…" I plunge the cock inside me, gasp as I wiggle it around. My God, that feels amazing. With my free hand, I play with my pussy, massage my nub until I have to bite down on my bottom lip to suppress my moans.

I continue to thrust the cock in and out, in and out. It's large, and fills me completely.

"Yes, baby…" I murmur, stroking my engorged nub. "Fuck, yeah…"

The woman on the television screen screams when she starts to orgasm, and I watch. Watch the guy draw the clitoris fully into his mouth as she writhes in ecstasy. Watch him thrust his fingers in and out of her pussy as he continues to eat her.

And then my body jerks, a sudden orgasm gripping me with its sharp talons. The walls of my vagina close around the cock, pulsate against it as my body explodes.

For the next minute or so, I simply lie there, my body spent from my release. The sound of my heavy breathing mixes with the faint sound of fucking emanating from the TV. I reach for the remote and turn the movie off.

Then I pull out the vibrator, head off the bed and go to my bathroom to clean up.

When I'm back under my covers, I snuggle against my pillow and try to summon some of the warmth I felt during my orgasm.

I can't.

Later that morning, after I eat breakfast alone in my kitchen, I decide that I must get out of the house. First, I call Annelise, but she doesn't answer, so I call another friend, Risha. We're not extremely close, but occasionally go to the spa or hair salon together where we can spend a few hours gossiping.

Risha is home, and we make plans to meet an hour later at the spa we frequent downtown. I tell her I'll call the spa to schedule pedicures, and that she'll hear from me only if we can't get an appointment.

An hour later, Risha is heading to the building's steps as I park in an available spot on the street. I toot the horn, and she glances over her shoulder. When she sees me, she smiles and waves.

I finish parking and get out of the car. Risha rushes toward me, her arms outspread.

We hug, air kiss.

"Wow, Claudia. You look amazing."

"I do?"

"Yes. Really amazing. Your hair—you put auburn high lights?"

"Subtle highlights. I was tired of the jet black."

"Well, seeing how happy you look, no one would know you so recently broke up with the love of your life."

It's exactly that kind of comment that irks me where Risha's concerned, and one of the reasons I'll never consider her a close friend. She simply doesn't get me.

I don't worry about it, because she fulfills a purpose in my life. I never have to go to the spa, or shopping for designer clothes, alone.

Risha opens the spa's heavy door, then gestures for me to enter. "After you."

I walk in. The hostess at the front greets me with a warm smile. "Hello, Ms. Fisher, Ms. Taylor."

"Hello," Risha and I say in unison.

"You can come right this way."

The long-haired brunette leads us around the corner and to the back of the salon, where the pedicure tables are set up. I recognize Alice and Bree, the women who will give us our pedicures, as they've worked on us before.

Alice, who's working with me today, instructs me to take my sandals off and slip my feet into the warm, bubbling water. I do, and beside me, Risha does the same.

"How's Ryan?" I ask Risha.

"He's great," Risha answers. "Passed the Bar, and he's interviewing with a few firms in Atlanta. Also some in New York."

"So he might be moving?"

"*We* might be moving."

"He popped the question?" I ask excitedly, my eyes already searching for the rock on her left hand I must have somehow missed.

"No, not yet. But once he accepts a position with a firm, I'm sure he will."

"Right." I nod, hoping for Risha's sake that Ryan is planning exactly that. That he doesn't turn out to be another Adam.

I glance at Alice, an attractive and plump woman in her mid-forties, who is scrubbing my feet. She grins at me like buffing people's feet is what she's happiest doing. I don't believe it is, though. I mean, it can't be. I wonder if she's aspired to greater things in her life, and why she settled on this career path.

The sound of voices has me turning to my left to see who is about to join us in this portion of the salon.

And that's when my stomach takes a nosedive.

Hell, no! What's that bitch doing here?

"Who?"

Risha's question lets me know I voiced my thought out loud.

"Ah, Arlene…" Risha nods in Arlene Nash's direction, who happens to be the woman who immediately got involved with Adam when our relationship ended—if not before.

Arlene sees me. Flashes me a smug look as she wriggles her fingers in the pretense of a warm greeting.

Risha huffs. "What is her problem?"

"Hell if I know."

To my horror, the hostess leads Arlene to the far back of the shop where Risha and I are.

"Oh, God," I mumble.

Moaning in frustration, I look to my right as Arlene is seated in the leather pedicure chair on my left.

Risha's lips twist in disapproval.

"Hello, ladies."

Arlene's nasally voice has always irritated me, that and the way she walks around with her head held higher than everyone else's, like she's extra special.

"Hello," Risha responds, in an exaggerated airy tone—the tone of fake affection she reserves for people she doesn't like.

For a moment I debate simply ignoring the bitch. I mean, why pretend we're friends when we're not? But after a couple seconds, I paste a sugary smile on my face and turn to her—the only greeting I can find it in my soul to give her. Arlene and I were never friends, but after I saw her at my fiancé's place in a serious lip lock with him only days after we'd broken up, I knew I could never keep up the pretense of being civil to her.

That decision was solidified when Arlene starting flaunting the rock Adam gave her shortly after our own engagement ended.

A minute passes. I pretend to be completely absorbed in the issue of *Black Hair* magazine I scooped up before I sat down.

"Have you heard from Adam?"

My head turns to my left so fast, it's a surprise I don't get whiplash. "Excuse me?"

"I hear he's spending time in D.C.," Arlene tells me in a tone that says she's proud to be sharing information I likely don't know. "He's apparently exploring work opportunities. I figure he'll make a permanent move there, given his political ambitions. Especially since he's got family there he can stay with."

"His cousin, Milton. Senate aid. Yes, I know. Adam and I were together for four *years,* remember?" My tone is testy, but I can't stop myself.

"Of course." Arlene plasters a fake smile on her face. "Look, I figured you'd want to know what he's been up to."

"Really? And why is that?"

The water sloshes around Arlene's feet as she shifts her

butt in her chair to fully face me. "Because we share a common bond—whether you want to accept that or not."

This enrages me. Arlene's gall at acting as if she and I have both suffered equally at Adam's hands.

As Alice begins to buff my feet, I say to Arlene, "We have nothing in common."

"He hurt both of us."

"And you seem like you still want to him back, even though the whole world knows he's a perverted freak. What Adam does with his life doesn't interest me in the least. He could be starring in gay porn in D.C. for all I care."

Arlene's jaw flinches at my words, and I know I've hit the nail head-on. Tsking, she shakes her head. "So bitter." She pauses. "Bitter enough to spew nasty lies?"

I slam the magazine down on my lap. "Tell me, Arlene—how long were you fucking my fiancé before we broke up?"

I expect shock from Arlene. Instead, her face fills with smugness. "If you'd been able to satisfy him, he wouldn't have ended up in my bed."

"You bitch. I *more* than satisfied Adam."

Risha grips my arm. "Claudia—"

"Adam was a freak, okay?" I feel everyone's eyes on me—Alice's, Bree's, the stylists' at the other end of the salon and their patrons—but I don't stop. "A pathetic freak who liked all kinds of disgusting sex. When I found out about that, I knew I could no longer be with him. But you—how many times have you been engaged again? Three? Four? At least I'm not desperate enough to settle for anyone."

Arlene glances around uneasily, though her eyes flash fire. "Adam was right about you. You're bitter because he dumped you, and you started those rumors about him to ruin our relationship."

I laugh out loud at that. "Yeah, *that's* how it happened. And here I thought you were just desperate to finally get married, why you were so willing to settle for my rejects. But you're really as much of a freak as Adam, aren't you? You two really *should* get married. You deserve each other."

Arlene's gaze is venomous, but she doesn't respond.

I pull my feet away from Alice, apologizing as I do. "I don't think I can stomach sitting here any longer. Something foul in the air is getting to me."

Arlene quickly stands and steps out of the bubbly water soaking her feet. "I'll save you the trouble. I'll leave."

As Arlene slips her wet feet into her sandals, I casually lift the magazine off my lap. But I don't open it. Instead I face Risha.

She offers me a "You go girl!" smile, then squeezes my hand in support.

When I arrive home—which happens to be an apartment within my parents' very large house—I kick off my shoes, then head straight into my bedroom. I fluff my down-filled pillows and settle my back against them, sighing as I do. That's the only moment of repose I allow myself, because I need to seriously bitch to my two best friends about Arlene Nash. Hopefully I can get both Annelise and Lishelle on a three-way conference call.

I reach for the phone on my night table, but it rings before I can pick it up.

I lift the receiver to my ear. "Hello?"

"Claudia?"

My back straightens at the faint sound of the male voice on the other end of my line. Surely, it couldn't be…

"Adam?" I ask cautiously.

There's a pause, and in that moment of silence, I almost hang up. But then I hear, "No, this isn't Adam. It's Greg. Greg Rutherford."

Greg Rutherford? I frown, wondering why the name sounds familiar, but not recognizing who it is. Then it dawns on me. Greg Rutherford is a guy in my social circle whom I see out at various charity events.

"Oh, hello," I say, relieved. "Greg, how are you?"

"I'm good. Good."

"To what do I owe the honor?" I ask, though I already have a sneaking suspicion.

Another pause, long enough that I have to wonder if he heard my question. "Greg?"

"Um, sorry." I hear some nervous laughter on his end. "Didn't your mother tell you?"

"Tell me what?"

"She gave me your number. Said you were, uh, interested in getting together. With me."

"She said what?" I practically shriek. I know my mother has been desperate to marry me off, but how could she?

"I'm sorry. I thought…"

I want to tell Greg to stop apologizing, just be a man and express what he wants. But I see an image of his face and the brown eyes he hides behind thick glasses, and suddenly feel sorry for him. Almost sorry enough to spare his feelings, lie to him and tell him that yes, I did want to get together.

But that would accomplish nothing.

So I go for the truth.

"Greg…I don't know if my mother told you or not, but I recently ended a relationship."

"I know. You were engaged to Adam Hart."

"Right. And…and I'm not anymore. The last thing I'm interested in doing is dating." I don't add that even if I weren't nursing a broken heart, I wouldn't be interested in dating him.

In short, I'm letting him down easy. Giving him a way to save face.

"Say no more," Greg says.

"You understand?"

"I went through the same thing when my marriage ended. I know what you're going through."

"Of course." I suddenly remember hearing the surprising news that he and his wife parted about a year ago.

"That's why I thought…well, I wondered. You know, if you ever wanted to get dinner sometime. Do something to take your mind off your troubles…"

I appreciate the gesture, even if he isn't my type. "Maybe in a couple months," I tell him.

"Why don't you take my number? Call me. Whenever. If you want, of course."

Greg rattles off his number, and I jot it down.

We end the call, and no sooner do I drop the cordless handset on my bed, than I shoot to my feet. I head out of my apartment through the door that connects to my parents' house by way of their kitchen.

I find my mother upstairs in the laundry room, standing at the counter folding towels. Seeing me, she smiles brightly.

"Hello, sweetheart."

I walk into the room, saying, "I just heard from Greg."

"Oh, he called." Her hands rest on the pile of unfolded bath towels and face cloths. "Did you make a date for dinner?"

"What were you thinking?" I ask her. "*Greg?* He is totally not my type."

"Which is exactly why I thought he'd be perfect for you. You haven't exactly chosen wisely before."

My mouth falls open. "How can you say that? You liked Adam! You couldn't wait for me to marry him!"

"That's not exactly true. I always had reservations about your union. His father is a womanizer, and that's a trait I believe runs in the family."

"You never said—"

"I was hopeful, but proven wrong. I've come to terms with that now."

I eye my mother skeptically. I'm not sure I should believe her. She was helping me plan the most lavish wedding Atlanta's black society would ever see. Why would she do that if she didn't think I'd be happy with Adam?

"But Greg," my mother goes on. "I've never heard a bad thing said about him, nor his father or his uncles. And from what I can tell, they absolutely adore their wives."

"That's because they have no choice," I quip. "They aren't exactly the most attractive guys in Atlanta."

My mother stops folding a large white towel to gape at me. "Claudia Fisher. I did not raise you to judge people by their looks."

"Mom, it's true."

"It's also true that Greg is a well-respected doctor."

"A plastic surgeon. Hmm, I wonder if he's ever thought of going under the knife himself."

"That's awful!"

"I'm sorry. It's just…"

"Just that you like all the pretty boys—boys like Adam Hart?"

"Well. Yeah," I answer honestly. "Besides, Greg's divorced."

"With no children. No baggage to tie him to his ex. For a man his age—"

"I'm not interested," I stress. "The truth is I'm not really interested in anyone."

Now my mother moves toward me. "If you tell me that you still have feelings for Adam—"

"That's not what I was going to say."

"Good. Because given everything you learned about Adam, you need to count your blessings that the two of you didn't marry after all."

"I know that. Hell, I was the one who was engaged to him."

"My point is that Adam is the kind of man you cut out of your life with a clean slash—and you don't look back. And you certainly don't shed any tears over him."

"I haven't." Okay, so that's a bit of a lie. I'm only human. I was in love with Adam for four years. When you really care for someone, it's not easy to turn off your feelings for him overnight. That said, it took me about a week to really move past him, come to the realization that the motherfucker was a piece of shit I was better off without.

"I'm not saying Greg's not a nice guy," I go on. "Clearly he is. But…but I'm not attracted to him. You're attracted to Daddy, aren't you? You don't want me to marry someone simply to say I'm married?"

My mother meets my eyes with a steady gaze. "You're not getting any younger."

Wow, that floors me. Renders me speechless.

But only for a moment.

"I'm not going to settle," I tell my mother, my anger toward her barely contained. "I will never do that."

And then I turn and walk out of the laundry room. I am

seriously tempted to run, but I don't want to give my mother the satisfaction.

When did my marital status become her biggest concern? What about my happiness?

I know she means well. But still.

When I reach my apartment, I make sure to lock the door behind me.

I'm not sure what rattled me more—my run-in with Arlene or my chat with my mother. I only know that I need to vent, so I grab my cordless handset off my bed and call Annelise. I put her on hold while I call Lishelle, hoping to connect her on a three-way call. But Lishelle doesn't pick up, which means I can't have a serious bitch session with both of them at the same time.

"Annelise, you still there?" I ask when I press the link button to connect back to her.

"I'm still here. You okay?"

"I'm pissed." I take the next few minutes to fill her in on the chance meeting I had with Arlene Nash. "Do you believe that bitch's nerve? I'm not sure what she was trying to do."

"Rattle you, obviously. And it worked."

"What pisses me off is that she admitted she was sleeping with Adam while we were still together. While we were *engaged*. That *whore*."

"She's that kind of woman. Some are simply like that. They get off on thinking that they can steal your man. People like her make it their life's mission. What they don't get is that if they can steal a guy from someone he supposedly loves, he's not worth having. Trust me, I think Charles's lover has learned that the hard way."

"I know." A sigh escapes my lips. "I shouldn't let her even

get to me. And then there's my mother. It's like she thinks I'm a failure because I don't have a man in my life."

"She didn't say that?" Annelise asks, a hint of horror in her tone.

"Well, not exactly. And I know she doesn't really think that. But she's trying to set me up with this guy who is so dull…" I blow out a frustrated breath.

"You want to get together?" Annelise asks me.

"I want to get out of town." It burns me to know that Adam is in D.C., getting on with his life like he never hurt me. He was never charged with embezzlement in the scandal surrounding the Wishes Come True Foundation, but I hope he can't outrun the tainted brush of scandal. And secrets have a way of coming to light in a town like D.C.

"Out of town, hmm?"

"It'd be nice. Get away from Atlanta and do something fun. Everywhere I go in this city, I feel like people are staring at me. Pitying me because I didn't get to walk down the aisle."

"I'm sorry."

I run a hand through my hair and groan. "I'm the one who's sorry. Here I am going on and on about my problems, not even asking you how you're doing."

"I've been great since my visit to your uncle's law office. Hey, why don't we get together? We can have a drink at some happening spot. Listen to some good music, maybe even dance a little. Liven up our Tuesday night."

For a moment I seriously consider Annelise's offer. "It's not that I don't want to, but I'd be really bad company."

"No you won't," Annelise protests.

"Yes," I insist. "I'm in one of those moods. I'm gonna stay in and stuff my face with junk food. Rain check?"

"Of course," Annelise agrees.

When I end the call, I sit on my bed and inhale several deep breaths. I try to center myself, to de-stress.

But after five minutes, I don't feel any better. I feel glum, listless.

Kind of like I've lost my groove.

Part Two

Gettin' our groove back

Five

Annelise

After talking to Claudia, something clicked. The reality that not only did I *need* to do something to uplift my friends and my sister, but that I *could*.

Dominic and I are getting along well, and I'm in love. For me, life is good. But it's hard to share my excitement about him with my friends and sister when they're all suffering from broken hearts.

Life can change in an instant, and in my case, it definitely did. First, for the worst—when I learned Charles was cheating on me. Then, for the better—when I learned I would be getting the money I deserved from my house. And even though only five days have passed since the house has been listed, there are already two serious offers, which has driven the price up beyond what I was asking.

The point is, I have *money*. Well, very soon I will. And I'm going to use some of it to surprise Samera, Claudia and Lishelle with exactly what they need.

A vacation.

It's high time that my friends and I go away. Get out of Atlanta and do a girlfriend trip. Someplace fun, like Mexico. Or maybe the Bahamas. Or Vegas.

The very idea of planning this—especially as a surprise— has me giddy. I head to the kitchen to grab the phone book and start looking up travel agents. But as my fingers skim the heavy book, I decide against making calls.

I'm going to head out to the mall and walk into an actual travel agency, have a live travel counselor give me glossy brochures and lots of suggestions.

Dominic is at work, so I jot a note and leave it on the kitchen table in case he gets home before I do. Then I grab my purse and head out the door, determined to change the course of the future.

If Stella could get her groove back on the sun-drenched beaches of Jamaica, why can't we?

By the next week, I have everything all planned. I've booked a surprise getaway to Las Vegas at the beautiful Venetian Hotel. I've splurged, but I figure my friends and sister are worth it. And considering my house just sold for over $800,000, I can afford the expense, which I charged to my credit card until my cash comes in.

My sister isn't working, and neither is Claudia, so I know they can leave with only a moment's notice, but I had to call Lishelle's television station and secretly book her some time off. Thankfully, her station manager agreed, stating that Lishelle could use some R&R. And Lishelle won't be able to give me any excuses about why she can't go.

I'm excited. Not only did I book the trip to Vegas for this Thursday, two days from now, I got us tickets for the Thunder from Down Under our first night there—a popular touring show from Australia featuring the hottest male strippers. It'll be a fun way to start the trip, to help us let loose. I've got a few other ideas in mind as well—some sinful ideas along the line of "What happens in Vegas stays in Vegas." In a way, I can't believe the scandalous ideas I've come up with, considering I grew up as a prude, but those days are behind me.

I wasn't kidding when I told Lishelle and Claudia that they need a palate cleanser to get over Glenn and Adam. They need to get laid. And I can't think of a better place than Las Vegas to help make that happen.

I'm beaming as I hold the telephone receiver to my ear.

"Hello?" my sister says.

"Sam, hi."

"Annelise?"

"Yes, it's me."

"You sound incredibly happy. Of course. Dom."

"And you sound…like you need a break."

"I had a break in Costa Rica. I came home feeling worse."

"How does Las Vegas sound?"

"Like an expense I can't afford right now. I've got a bit of savings in the bank but until I find another job, I've got to be frugal with my money."

"You don't have to worry about the money. I'm paying."

"Like you can afford that."

I take a moment to fill Samera in on the great news that I'll get even more money than I expected from the house. "See, so you have no excuses."

Samera hesitates before saying, "I don't think I'd be much fun."

"You're going," I inform her. "I've already booked your flight."

"Annie!"

"I did. I had a feeling I'd have to. Non-refundable. So, you can't say no."

Samera moans. "Annie, you shouldn't have."

"But I did. Hey, you're the one who insisted on going to Costa Rica with me. Said we needed to bond as sisters. That trip was the best thing we ever did. Vegas…we'll bond even more."

"You sure know how to drive a hard bargain."

"We leave bright and early on Thursday."

"Thursday!" Samera exclaims.

"Actually, we don't have an early-morning flight. We're booked on Delta, scheduled to leave at close to 1:00 p.m. We'll arrive in Vegas around two in the afternoon—"

"*This* Thursday?" Samera interjects. "As in two days from now?"

"That's the date. July twenty-sixth."

"You're serious about this."

"Absolutely. Start packing!"

Next I call Claudia, who resists the idea at first, until I tell her that the trip is paid for—and that Lishelle is going, too. I don't mention that my sister is also going, because the truth is, Claudia doesn't know her well, and I don't want to give her a reason to turn me down. After about five minutes of arm twisting, Claudia agrees to the impromptu getaway, though she sounds somewhat reluctant.

I expect the most resistance from Lishelle, and when I call her at the station, she cuts my suggestion off midsentence.

"I can't. Gotta work."

"Actually, you don't have to—"

"You know I always work weekdays. I can't book off Thursday and Friday last minute. I'm free Saturday and Sunday, which would barely give me time to fly to Vegas and back."

"Lishelle?"

"Yes?"

"You didn't let me finish. You don't have to go to work because I booked you off from Thursday to Sunday."

"What?"

"Okay, I'll be clearer. You don't have to go in on Thursday. And your next day at work will be Monday—July thirtieth."

"How—"

"I spoke with Linda Tennant last week because I didn't want you to have any excuse to say no. Plus, I wanted this to be a surprise."

"And Linda said yes?" Lishelle asks, her tone saying she's surprised.

"She did. And quite frankly, she sounded relieved that I was taking you away somewhere. According to her, you've been moping around, not at all like your usual self."

"Moping around?"

"Her words."

"I ought to smack her. But, if she says I can go, then fuck, I'm outta here."

"Oh, Lishelle. We're gonna have a blast," I tell her, relieved that she's down with the idea of getting away. "Sin City, watch out!"

"I hear that. Four days of drinking, gambling…"

And a little something extra, I think.

"You're a doll. How much will I owe you?"

"Nothing! This is my treat."

"No, I can't accept—"

"You can and you will. I've got an excellent chunk of change coming my way, probably in the next couple weeks."

"All right, girl. If you insist." She still sounds uneasy.

"You can buy the drinks," I tell her.

"You're on. Look," Lishelle says, "I have to get going. But we'll talk tomorrow at least."

"For sure."

I squeal with happiness, and so does she.

"So much to do," Lishelle says. "So little time."

"I know, I know. Talk to you later."

No sooner do I hang up with Lishelle, than I head to the kitchen and snatch up the Yellow Pages. I flip through until I find listings for limo services, and I book one for early Thursday that will pick each of us up.

"Okay," I say to the person who has confirmed the pickup. "Thursday morning at 8:00 a.m. Thanks a lot."

"You sound happy."

I whirl around at the sound of Dominic's voice. He's leaning against the wall at the entrance of the kitchen, holding his blazer casually over his shoulder.

He looks sexy as hell.

"Hi, sweetheart." I get up from a chair at the small kitchen table and float toward him, my arms outstretched. "I didn't hear you come in."

Our lips meet first before we fall into a warm hug. Dominic kisses the top of my head before releasing me.

"What are you up to?" he asks.

"Booking the limo for our ride to the airport Thursday morning." I told Dominic about my plan for the trip last week. "And I told all the girls today. Everyone's onboard."

Dominic settles onto the chair I vacated. "So that means

you're leaving me." He reaches for me and pulls me onto his lap. "For four whole days."

"Four *long* days. I know."

Dominic brushes my hair over one shoulder, his fingers skimming the back of my neck as he does. The gentle touch sends shivers of pleasure down my spine. "What am I going to do? All by myself?"

I gyrate my hips against his crotch. He's already hard, and that makes me wet. "I wish I could take you…"

Dominic cradles the back of my head with his palm and urges my face closer to his. I think he's going to kiss me, but instead he leans his mouth close to my ear. "Guess we're going to have to fuck our brains out until you go. Then pick up where we left off when you get back…"

As his teeth graze my earlobe, I moan with pure pleasure. My ear is a definite hot zone on my body, as Dom knows very well. He adds his tongue, flicking it on my earlobe slowly.

"Are you going to miss this?" he whispers.

"You know damn well I am."

"Know what I love about your ear?" He nibbles on it briefly. "I love how the lobe is so much like your clitoris. It's fleshy." *Flick.* "Soft." *Nibble.* "And when I suck on it—" Dominic does exactly that, suck on my earlobe until I am whimpering, and he groans excitedly. "When I suck on it, your body quivers the same way it does when I suck on your sweet pussy."

Now, Dominic picks up his game, alternately sucking and nibbling my earlobe the same way he does to my pussy. My sex is instantly moist and pulsing with need and anticipation.

His mouth is pressed right to my ear when he whispers, "Are you taking your vibrator?"

"Forget my vibrator." I ease my body up and stroke

Dominic's hard cock through his pants. "This is what I want to remember while I'm in Vegas. This is what will get me off at night when I think of you."

I rain hot kisses all over Dom's face as I lift my skirt up to my waist and straddle his lap. My vagina presses against his erection, and it feels so good. I cover his mouth with mine, immediately prying his lips apart with my tongue. Heat swallows us whole.

I tear at Dominic's shirt, letting him know I want it rough. He covers my breasts in response, squeezing them hard before he pushes my cotton shirt up and my bra down in two quick actions. He draws first one nipple into his mouth, sucking it urgently, before doing the same with the other.

"Jeez, Annelise…"

I rub my hand over the hard length of his cock, taking pleasure in the guttural sounds emanating from his throat. I could so easily give up control, throw my head back and let him continue to tease me with his mouth. But I want to give Dominic extra-special attention tonight, show him how much I love having my mouth all over his body as well.

I ease my butt off his lap and kiss his jawline. Dominic's eyes meet mine in question. He's wondering why I pulled away from him so hastily. I answer the question when I lower myself onto my knees before him. I make quick work of unfastening Dominic's belt and undoing his pants, and we both sigh when I free his cock.

Taking it in both my hands, I raise my gaze to his. With our eyes locked, I run my tongue over the tip of his penis. I watch his expression as I cover him with my mouth.

God, I love looking at Dominic's face as I give him head. The way his eyes narrow and his mouth forms a perfect *O*.

I moan as I move my mouth over him, up and down his shaft. I suck on the tip of his cock, and Dominic rakes his fingers through my hair. Some of my blond strands have fallen over my face, and Dominic moves them out of the way so he can better see what I'm doing to him.

I take him into my throat, hold him there for a few seconds while I massage his testicles. Dominic throws his head back and groans in delight.

Very gently, I graze my teeth along the length of his cock, and now a rush of breath escapes Dominic's lips.

"Your cock is magnificent," I tell him, then fervently suck on the tip.

"Fuck!"

I trail my tongue from the tip of his penis to its base, where I suck on his balls. Dominic tightens his fingers in my hair, and I think he might come, but instead he urges me upward. His lips are on mine in an instant, his hot tongue tangling with mine.

"I need your cock," I murmur against his mouth. "Right now. Inside me." I hastily brush my panties aside and spread my lips with my fingers. "Touch me, baby. See how much I want you."

Dominic groans when he slides a finger over my opening. Then his fingers enter me, stretch me, move in and out of me with hurried thrusts. Dominic pulls his fingers out and licks at them greedily, and the sight of that makes my nub tremble.

I gasp when Dominic moves upward in one fast motion, lifting me off my feet as he does. He carries me to the kitchen counter and perches my ass on it. Then he spreads my legs, making it clear that this is where he wants to fuck me.

I lift my right foot onto the counter so I can better balance myself. Dominic helps me with my left leg. The next instant, Dominic moves my panties out of the way and fingers my pussy until I'm whimpering.

"Please fuck me," I beg. "Put that big cock inside me—"

My plea dies on a moan when Dominic's mouth covers my pussy. Holding my legs apart, he flicks his hot tongue all over my clitoris before fully taking it into his mouth and suckling it until I'm screaming his name.

Then finally, blissfully, Dominic thrusts his magnificent cock deep inside me.

I cry out and grip Dominic's shoulders. He pulls out, then drives his cock into me again, deeper this time, eliciting a long, raspy moan from me. He withdraws and thrusts, again and again, gaining momentum with each stroke. Soon, he's ramming my pussy mercilessly, hitting my G-spot every time, making me heady and breathless.

My fingers dig into Dominic's shoulders through his shirt as I hold on for the ride. "Oh, baby." My words float on a moan. "I'm gonna…gonna *co-o-o-ome!*"

At my words Dominic picks up speed, pounding me furiously until he forces my orgasm. It thunders through me, electrifying every nerve ending in my body.

As my body trembles with my release, Dominic's groans grow louder. I tighten my vaginal walls around him, determined to steal his orgasm the way he did mine.

Dominic pulls out, pumps his cock as he spills semen onto my belly. I mewl softly as he does, a subtle sign of my disappointment.

When it comes to sex, I want all of him.

Our mouths meet for a tender kiss, the kind that speaks of our love for each other.

I want to ask Dom why he pulled out, especially since he knows I'm on the Pill.

But I don't.

I'll admit, the fact that Dom pulled out when he normally comes inside me has had me a tad bit insecure. But on Thursday I'm not thinking about that as our plane touches down in Las Vegas at 2:02 p.m. Sitting in the tenth row with my sister, I'm simply excited about being in Sin City. Samera and I both stretch our necks to gaze out the window. In the distance, I can see the high-rise hotels on the strip, and I marvel at how different the city looks from the last time I was here, just five years ago.

"You excited?" I ask Samera.

She glances at me and smiles. "Yeah."

The moment the *Fasten Seat Belt* sign turns off, accompanied by the traditional pinging sound, everyone on the plane collectively throws open their buckles. I ease my body upward and turn to look at Lishelle and Claudia, who are a couple rows behind us on the opposite side. Lishelle shakes her head in mock chagrin as she stares back at me, then her face erupts in a grin. I've known her long enough to understand that the first look wasn't entirely false, and I know what it's about. When she got into the limo and found my sister there, her eyes registered total surprise. She doesn't know my sister, and Lishelle's the kind of person who doesn't like to let loose with acquaintances. She's probably a little perturbed that I decided to bring my sister on this trip.

Well, she's just going to have to get used to it. To paraphrase Rodney King—we're all going to have to get along.

Minutes later we're all off the plane, commenting on the extreme heat as we head toward the baggage claim. I notice that Samera stays on my left side, away from Lishelle and Claudia, who are on my right. This remains our formation even as we get our luggage, then head outside to catch a taxi.

I decide not to worry about this. At least not yet. They're kind of like kids in a playground on the first day of school—cautious yet curious. But by the end of the day, I'm sure everyone will be chatting and laughing over a round of margaritas. Bonding as we ogle hot, naked men.

"Whoo, and I thought Atlanta was hot." Claudia fans herself with her ticket envelope as we stroll outside. "Where's a taxi?"

"Costa Rica wasn't even this hot," Samera comments, the only thing she's said by way of conversation. The weather—always a safe topic.

"This is the desert," I say. "And humidity or not, 120 degrees is hot. Period."

"I need to get in a taxi before I melt." Lishelle looks from left to right. She starts dragging her luggage to the right. "Thank God, there's the taxi stand."

By the time we get a taxi, which can't be more than two minutes after we've stepped outside, we all sigh loudly with relief.

"Where to?" the taxi driver, who appears to be East Indian, asks.

"The Venetian," I reply and climb into the backseat, followed by Claudia. Samera enters the backseat from the car's opposite side, which leaves me sandwiched in the middle. Lishelle sits in the front.

"The Venetian?" Samera asks me. "Why did I think we were staying at Bellagio?"

Shrugging, I face her. "I don't know. I did consider Bellagio, but decided against it."

"You staying a couple weeks?" the driver asks.

"Four days," Lishelle answers.

"Four days!" the cabdriver exclaims, mirth in his voice. "And so much luggage!"

That gets a chuckle from all of us. "Hey, we're women," is my simple explanation as to why, between us, we have filled his trunk to capacity with eight pieces of luggage, not including our large handbags.

"I go away with my wife for a weekend, she packs like we're staying a year." The cabbie shakes his head as he smiles. "I don't understand."

We make small talk during the short drive to The Venetian, but mostly we gawk at the impressive, gold-colored high-rises. We get a taste of New York and Egypt and Paris—all in one drive down the Vegas strip. When the driver pulls up to the Venetian, with its bridges and waterways that already make me think we're in Italy, we all gasp in awe. The building is majestic, stunning. Pale in color, it also boasts the gold-tinted windows that are popular on the strip. Seeing the pictures of the place online is nothing like seeing the hotel in person.

Once the cabdriver helps us get our bags out of the trunk, Samera says to me, "This place is gorgeous. How much is this costing?"

"Yeah, I'd love to know that, as well," Lishelle adds.

"None of your business," I answer flippantly. I head toward the driver to pay him, but Claudia is already giving him cash.

A bellhop appears and begins piling our bags onto a trolley. He follows us inside, where I lead the way to the front desk. A red-haired clerk who looks far too pale to be living under the Nevada sun smiles warmly at me.

"I'm checking in," I say, and give her my name.

Claudia, Lishelle and Samera all crowd around me, listening as the woman behind the counter asks the standard questions, and then for my credit card.

When the woman turns her back, Claudia says, "Wait a second. Did I hear her say *three* rooms?"

I wave a hand to shush her. This is part of my surprise. When I booked this, I went all out. Booked three lavish suites, but I got them at a forty percent discount.

"Here's your credit card, Mrs. Crawford." I cringe slightly at the clerk's words. They imply I'm a happily married woman, not one on the brink of divorce.

Her gaze floats over all four of us. "Now, all three suites are on the thirty-fifth floor. One is the Venetian Prima, which is slightly larger than the two others, the Piazza suites. Who will be staying in which suite, and how many keys do you want?"

I shrug. Behind me, Claudia and Lishelle start to whisper.

"Are the rooms connected?" I ask.

"They're not connected, but the two Venetian Piazza suites are side by side, and the Venetian Prima suite is directly across the hall."

More whispering behind me. I make out "I can't believe she did this."

I say to the clerk, "Why don't we get two keys per room for the Piazza suites, four for the Prima, and we'll sort out who's sleeping where when we get upstairs."

"Certainly." The clerk complies, her smile never leaving her face. She hands me the keys and points the way toward the bank of elevators before wishing us a grand day.

I start for the elevators, and the questions start.

"You booked three rooms?" Samera asks.

"No, not rooms. The clerk said *suites*," Lishelle clarifies.

"Annelise, we know you wanted us to have a good time," Claudia says, "but there was no need to spend a fortune."

I face them all when we get to the elevators. "What's done is done. And remember, I wanted to do it. Because I love you all, okay? So no worrying that I spent too much. No fussing over anything, all right?" My eyes volley back and forth between my friends as I wait for them to answer.

"All right," Lishelle agrees after a moment. "We just hope you didn't go overboard."

Their worry that I've spent too much is confirmed when we get to the thirty-fifth floor. I head to the left, in the direction of the suites. I stop at the Prima suite, which is on the right side of the hallway, and open the door.

There are more gasps, then stunned silence, and we haven't even stepped beyond the massive foyer which boasts marble floors.

Samera is the first to venture forward, around the slight corner into the room beyond. "Holy shit," she calls out. "How the fuck are you affording this?"

I lower my purse to the floor, then head into the suite. I have to admit, I gape at its beauty. The colors are warm—the carpet beige, and the walls a pale peach. The wood detail on the walls provides a sophisticated touch. There is a large bar area to the immediate left with a black marble counter, complete with a sink, three bar stools, and what appears to be a bottle of champagne chilling in a carafe.

Samera turns to face me. "Sis, how much did you spend on this?"

"None of your concern," I respond.

"Seriously," Lishelle says. "This suite is fucking gorgeous." She pokes her head into the bedroom, then whistles. "And you got *three* of them?"

"This only has one bed," I point out.

"The sofa's got to be a pull-out," Claudia comments. "You

and Samera could have shared one bed, and Lishelle and I could share the pull-out. There's definitely enough room for all of us in here."

"Yes, but…" I pause for effect. "We might need some privacy."

Lishelle's eyebrow shoots up.

"Dom showing up?" Samera asks, but I can tell the question isn't sincere.

"This isn't about Dom. It's about you. All of you. And the possibilities of Vegas."

Claudia crosses her arms over her chest. "So you've put a small fortune into renting three rooms so we…so we can…"

"Get lucky?" I smile. That's exactly what I was thinking. "I already told you, I'm about to get a ton of cash from the sale of my house."

"Which you should be putting into your business," Lishelle pipes in, ever matter-of-fact. "Not spending it on a lavish trip."

I sigh softly as I face each of them in turn. "Look, this is an investment. An investment in the people who matter the most to me. You already agreed not to get upset over how much I've spent. So, please, no more arguments."

Claudia snakes an arm around my waist. "I can't argue with that. And, girl, I love you for caring."

I press my cheek against hers.

Lishelle makes her way to the bar's counter and the bottle of champagne chilling in a silver bucket. "Cristal. Very nice. You really are in the mood to celebrate."

"That really is champagne?" I ask. "Not a prop? Because I didn't order any."

"It's the real deal," Lishelle answers.

"When you pay for three suites, you get the VIP treatment," Claudia explains.

"Not only is it a nice touch," I begin, "but it's absolutely perfect. We're all fabulous women. We deserve to celebrate that—and the fact that we are no longer tied to scumbag men."

"Here, here," Samera says.

"And this trip is also about getting your groove back," I explain. "Because quite frankly, I miss all our talks about sex—which have been totally lacking since you guys stopped getting any."

Samera howls at that. "Who'd have thought it—*you* talking so frankly about sex. And I used to think you were a prude."

"I was a prude. But I've seen the light."

Claudia shakes her head. "You, a prude? You never heard your sister during our weekly brunches. I wouldn't call her a—"

"Okay, ladies."

I turn to see Lishelle wrestling with the cork on the champagne bottle. It pops open with a bang, and a plume of bubbly smoke spews out of the bottle.

She holds up the bottle and smiles. "I don't know about the rest of you, but I'm ready to have a good fucking time."

Samera steps up to the table beside Lishelle, lifting one of the champagne flutes already placed on the table. "Girl, I hear you. Pour me a glass."

Less than a minute later, we all have our glasses filled.

"Now I know this is corny," I begin, "but I don't care. We're in Vegas, and we're damn well gonna live by the slogan this city is famous for. What happens in Vegas stays in Vegas. Girls, let's get our freak on!"

Six

Samera

Get our freak on?

I stare at my sister in disbelief. Seriously, is this the person I've known all my life? As I watch her laugh and chat with her friends, I can't help noticing that she's as bubbly as the champagne she's sipping. And I realize then—really realize—that she *isn't* the person I knew growing up. Hell, she's not even the woman I knew last year. Sexually, she's grown by leaps and bounds. Finally she seems to have escaped the fire-and-brimstone guilt my mother drummed into her about anything pleasurable in life. And if I have Dom to thank for that, then I am forever grateful.

In fact, I wish I were in a better mood. That way I could laugh airily as I sip my champagne and entertain the idea of what my sister is suggesting.

Because I'm fairly certain that Annelise is suggesting we find some hot men and have a passionate fling.

Normally it's an idea I'd be hip to. I'd at least be into the idea of serious flirtation. But here I am in Las Vegas in a gorgeous hotel suite, and all I want is to be back at home, curled up on my sofa watching a movie.

The truth is, I've been pretty bummed out since I got back from Costa Rica. I don't even care about looking at other men.

Yeah, I'm still missing Miguel. Which is so unlike me. Every day I've been trying to figure out why he's gotten so completely under my skin.

Maybe I'm missing him simply because Reed fucked up our last days together. Having your ex show up on your vacation and telling you he still loves you can throw a girl for a loop.

A bout of excited laughter pulls me from my thoughts.

"Love it, love it, *love it!*" Lishelle exclaims.

"And I don't know about you," Annelise begins, "but I could use a new outfit. Did you know that some lucky women get to go up on stage with those hotties?"

"Wait a second," I say. "What are you talking about?"

"Tonight," my sister answers. "Didn't you hear what I said? I got tickets for the Thunder from Down Under," she explains, her eyes dancing with excitement. "That all-male revue from Australia."

"We're going to see strippers?" I ask for clarification.

"I figured you'd get a kick out of that." Annelise wiggles her eyebrows at me and squeezes my hand. "We'll be right up front, and who knows—maybe we'll be lucky enough to get picked to go on stage."

"Before I see any men without their clothes on, I need to eat," Claudia proclaims.

"Let's see what room service has to offer." Lishelle glances around, then heads into the large living room. She scoops up a slim, black leather-bound binder from the coffee table before sitting on the beige-colored sofa near the large bay window. "Here's the menu."

"I need a cigarette," I comment.

"I don't smoke," Lishelle quickly says.

"Neither do I." This from Claudia.

Then my sister approaches me, looking a little uncomfortable. "You're not planning to smoke in here, are you? It's a nonsmoking room, and none of us smoke. Maybe you could—"

"You want me to go downstairs? I could just open a window."

"Do you know how bad secondhand smoke is for nonsmokers?"

"All right." I'm not going to fight with her. As a smoker, I'm used to having to go out of my way in order to get my nicotine fix. "I'll head downstairs. I'm sure smokers still dominate the casino floor."

"What about food?" my sister asks.

"Order me whatever you want. Where's the room key?"

My sister strolls to the dining room table, finds a plastic key card and passes it to me.

Downstairs I head outside. A blast of hot air hits me in the face.

Maybe this isn't the smartest idea. Smoking a cigarette in one-hundred-degree heat—I may as well light myself on fire.

But I do need a dose of nicotine, and the first drag I inhale is like heaven.

I smoke only half of the cigarette, and am about to ground it out in the ashtray when I notice an attractive beefcake of a guy with sandy-blond hair. He's with a dark-haired guy about half a foot shorter than he is, both carrying luggage, and I notice him because he slows when he sees me, and his mouth turns upward in a smile.

I turn away.

Normally, I would flirt with a guy like that. But God, I'm just not into it.

I linger as the guys head into the hotel, taking the time to finish off my cigarette. A few minutes later, my craving fully satisfied, I head back up to the suite.

"Yes, French fries," Lishelle is saying into the phone. "And give me a second." She covers the receiver's mouthpiece. "Sam, what do you want? I ordered a burger for you, but if you want something else…"

"Do they have a chicken Caesar salad?"

Lishelle asks the person on the phone, then nods.

"Okay, I'll have that. And…French fries on the side."

As Lishelle relays my request, I turn to face Annelise. She smiles brightly at me.

"After we eat, we're gonna head downstairs to shop. The Venetian's got a bunch of trendy and upscale stores, like Jimmy Choo. I could use some new shoes. And maybe something tiny and black. Think you can help me pick out something really scandalous?"

"Sure."

"Don't sound so excited," Annelise jokes.

I glance over my shoulder. Claudia and Lishelle are talking quietly. I don't want to be paranoid, but I'm pretty sure there's disdain in Lishelle's gaze as she looks my way. I don't know why my sister invited me along on this trip. I don't belong in her crowd.

I take Annelise by her upper arm and lead her into the very large bedroom. "What is the sleeping arrangement?"

"We're going to share this suite," she explains. "One of us can sleep on the pullout."

Now that we're out of view—and out of earshot—of her friends, I ask her, "What's up with Lishelle and Claudia?"

"What do you mean?"

"Do they even want to be here with me? Because Lishelle keeps giving me dirty looks—"

"Don't be ridiculous. They just don't know you. It wouldn't hurt for you to try and be a little friendly."

"I have nothing in common with those two. Claudia— she's some sort of debutante. Doesn't work but Daddy provides her with a shitload of money to play with. Lishelle—some high-profile anchorwoman."

"And me—the sister you haven't seen eye-to-eye with most of your life." A soft smile forms on Annelise's lips. "And look at us now. Finally being sisters in God knows how long."

I smile as well. "This is true."

Annelise places her hands on my shoulders. "Don't judge my friends, and they won't judge you."

"I hope not."

"Sammy, I want you to have fun on this trip. Honestly, ever since you got back from Costa Rica, you've been sulking. I want to see you smiling again."

"Thanks. That means a lot."

"Promise me you'll try to have fun," Annelise says.

"Okay. I promise."

When the food arrives, my chicken salad doesn't look nearly as appetizing as the burgers that Annelise, Lishelle and Claudia ordered. And it doesn't smell as good, either. The charbroiled scent entices me enough to ask my sister for a bite of hers, and I swear, it's the best burger I've ever tasted.

We gorge on the food as if we haven't eaten in days, then head downstairs to the Venetian's Grand Shops.

We stroll the long corridors with the various shops until we reach a large court. There are people dressed in historic costumes. A woman in a stunning gown, a jester who must be on stilts. There's an elevated stage area with a man in all white— white clothes, completely white face—who I first mistake for a statue. It's when I see people snapping pictures and placing money on the stage that I understand it's a real person.

Annelise links arms with me. "Isn't this fun? An ancient Venetian court, and all these real waterways with gondola rides, just like in Venice!"

"And look at that ceiling," Claudia says. "It's so blue, and those clouds make it look like a real sky."

"Amazing what people can do," I comment.

"Ooh, there's Jimmy Choo!" Annelise releases me to hurry in that direction. "I know I brought a ton of clothes, but I want something ultrasexy. Something that says I'm a free woman, one who's getting laid regularly."

"You sure you want that kind of attention?" I ask. "You've got Dom waiting back at home for you."

"Yes, but that doesn't mean I can't look sexy, does it? For the first time in a long time, I feel really free. Liberated."

"Watch out, Vegas!" Claudia says, then chuckles.

Half an hour later, my sister has a pair of seriously hot shoes. Black, with a clear heel, and jewels on the straps that cross over the foot and up around the ankle. I picked out a pair of thigh-high boots. Since I've generally been frugal with my money after quitting my job, I decided to join in the fun and splurge a little. The great thing about having worked as a stripper is the money I've made. As a result, I have a very healthy bank account. It's money I have no desire to squander, but I don't feel too guilty about the boots since they were last year's design and therefore half-price. A little shopping spree once in a while is good for the soul.

We meet Claudia and Lishelle at Max Azaria, on the second floor of the store.

Annelise heads to Claudia. "What do you have?"

Claudia holds up a black dress that could be called conservative—except for the plunging neckline.

"How sexy is this?" Annelise asks. "But if you bounce around too much in this dress, you might just show off more than you bargained for."

"You like?" Claudia asks.

"Very much so," my sister tells her. "It's totally hot."

I chuckle at those words coming from my sister's mouth. She sounds like Paris Hilton, and I tell her so.

"Seriously, that *is* hot," my sister repeats. "Wait a minute—is that see-through?"

"I've got a black bra to wear underneath," Claudia explains. "I can't believe I'm going to buy this. I already packed enough clothes for three weeks. Oh, and I found out that Gucci and Fendi are at the Bellagio's shops. And there's a mall down the street."

Lishelle approaches us carrying a gorgeous, barely there black halter. She holds it up to her chest. "I think we can find all we need right here."

Annelise reaches into her Jimmy Choo bag and lifts the lid off the box to show off her shoes. "I need something to go with these."

Lishelle whistles. "Fucking gorgeous. Well, I'll just have to help you shop. And I think this halter will look great on you."

Annelise stares at the scrap of material on the hanger Lishelle holds up. "That is so…risqué. Normally, I'd never wear anything like that. Except when I was trying to get Charles's attention, of course. And then, only in the bedroom "

"Are you gonna try it on?" Lishelle interjects.

"Absolutely." Annelise snatches the halter from Lishelle. "But I need a skirt to wear it with."

I wander off while Annelise begins searching for a skirt. There are a lot of gorgeous clothes in this store, but I packed enough clothes. I do stop, however, when I see the bathing suits. I pick up what I guess is *supposed* to be a one-piece—considering the top and bottom are attached—but between the breast cups and the bottom are gaping holes in the fabric.

"That's a bathing suit?" Claudia asks. I turn to see her about a foot away.

I nod. "I'm gonna buy this."

"I like this one." Lishelle holds up a dress that's almost a gray blue. With a V-shaped neck and back, it's sexy while still being elegant.

Claudia examines the dress. "I don't know. Too long. You should see what I'm wearing tonight."

"But the neckline is definitely not conservative. It's below the knee but flirty. I like it."

"Try it on," Annelise tells her. Then she gasps as though she's found a bucket of gold among the clothes.

"What?" I ask, making my way to her.

Annelise holds up a stunning dress. It's a mix of reds and oranges and browns in subtle swirls. The dress is soft and delicate, pleated and has beaded detail. The top straps go around the neck like a halter.

"That is gorgeous," I tell her, and look at the label. It reads: Chili Chai Printed Silk Chiffon. It's got a killer V-neck, something I wouldn't expect my sister to wear. Heck, I've seen her

Kayla Perrin

mostly in baggy clothes. I'm still trying to get used to the liberated woman she's become.

Now I'm the one who gasps when I spot a dress in a leopard print. I hold it up, and it's very similar in style to the one Annelise just picked up, except for the fabric and the more conservative neckline.

"You get that one," I say to Annelise, "and I'll get this one."

"You can tell you're sisters," Lishelle comments. "You picked out pretty much the same style of dress, only different colors."

Annelise and I share a smile. Then she says, "I think this one will look better on you. The V-neck will fit your breasts better."

"You're probably right. I always have trouble finding dresses to fit my bust."

"Well, they *are* very large," Annelise points out. What she doesn't say, although I can tell she's thinking it, is that they're very large because I had them augmented. Maybe she doesn't elaborate because she doesn't want to embarrass me in front of her friends, but it's not like it isn't obvious. I'm not trying to hide the fact that I got them enhanced. You want to survive in my business, and it's just something you do.

"I don't know about the leopard print," Annelise goes on.

"You kidding?" I ask. "This will look gorgeous on you. And it will go better with your shoes."

"I wasn't even thinking about that," Annelise says. "And you're absolutely right. Give me the dress."

We swap dresses. Then all of us rush to the dressing rooms to see what fits.

Seven

Annelise

Later that evening, we're all dressed in our newly purchased outfits, wearing come-fuck-me heels, and ready to see hot, naked men strut their stuff.

"Where is this show?" Lishelle asks. Though we have three suites, Lishelle and Claudia are in mine, using the powder room to finish the last of their makeup.

"Excalibur," I answer. "We drove past it in the taxi coming from the airport. It's that medieval-looking building."

"All I saw were lights," Claudia confesses.

"I've been there before," Lishelle says. "I was in Vegas once—for my twenty-first birthday. Wow. I can't believe almost ten years have passed!"

"You're smarter, and more beautiful, and you've still got it going on," I tell her. "So don't sweat that you're older."

"Thank you, darling."

Ready to party, we head downstairs to the lobby, and the

four of us turn heads as we march across the marble floor in our designer shoes and slinky outfits. Two men with olive-colored skin stop and stare. One of them whistles, then speaks in a language I don't understand, though it sounds like Italian.

We head outside, where the bellman smiles and heads toward us. "Where are you ladies off to tonight?"

"Somewhere scandalous," I answer.

"Let me guess?" the attractive black man asks. "Thunder from Down Under?"

"That's the plan," Claudia replies. "How far is the Excalibur Hotel?"

"You're not walking," the bellman tells us. "Not in all those pretty shoes."

I'm feeling flirtatious and fun, so I do a twirl, lifting my foot behind me, showing off my gorgeous new shoes. My sister and girlfriends join me, then we all laugh.

"Taxi or town car?" the bellman asks.

"Whatever's faster," Lishelle replies, ever practical.

The bellman blows his whistle, and a taxi heads up the circular drive. He opens the door for us and we all climb in. Lishelle is the last in, and the first to pass the bellman a tip.

The man raises his eyebrows at her. "If you want, I can do a private striptease for you later."

"We'll see." Lishelle winks.

The bellman's eyes linger on her as he closes the door, but the next moment, the taxi surges forward and we all start to laugh. We're all a little bubbly from finishing off a second bottle of champagne, the one from Claudia's suite. Samera is in the front of the taxi, chatting with the driver, while the rest of us are in the back. I notice the driver's gaze dropping to Samera's chest—her nipples barely covered by the two triangle-shaped pieces of fabric that make up the dress's top. If she weren't so large-chested, the dress wouldn't be nearly as risqué.

I only hope the driver doesn't crash and kill us all.

"You think we'll get to go onstage?" I ask.

"What is it with you and this obsession with getting on stage with the strippers?" Lishelle asks. "You have a man at home."

"Because it'll be fun," I answer.

"They might pick us to go up if Lishelle flashes them," Claudia says. "Or your sister."

I lean forward and poke Samera on the shoulder. "How about it, sis? Want to flash those double D's?"

"Only if I'm getting paid."

When we arrive at Excalibur, Lishelle, Claudia and I are still giggling like schoolgirls about to see a man get naked for the first time. Samera pays the driver before I can.

And then we're off.

The show starts with an explosion of light and sound. Then the men charge onto the stage, and the women go wild. Frenzied screams fill the air, and I could very well win the prize for the loudest female in the room.

Our table near the front affords us a perfect view of all the hot bodies—their rock-hard abs, muscular legs and killer smiles. These guys don't just take their clothes off. They dance and do acrobatics. And the way they move their bodies… Just watching them, I can't help getting hot.

Beside me, Claudia puts her fingers in her mouth and whistles when a fireman comes on stage. Lishelle leans close to me and says, "Is that a hose, or are you just happy to see me? Mmm, is he fine or what?"

The thrill of this show isn't just that the guys take their

clothes off—it's the high energy, the feeling that this show is larger than life.

And it is. In many ways.

The guys don't take it all off, but beneath their g-strings it isn't hard to tell they're well-endowed. And if their penises are anything like their bodies, then I can only imagine they are very beautiful.

Man after hot man entertains. The guys strip out of all the prerequisite uniforms—cop, naval officer, G.I. And there are pirates and knights. This show is fun as well as sexy.

Both Claudia and Lishelle are giggling, hooting and howling, and dancing to the upbeat music as the guys perform. Exactly like a girl in a male strip club should. But every time I glance Samera's way, she's not reacting at all. She stays seated the entire time and nurses a glass of scotch.

In fact, she looks absolutely bored.

Considering she takes her clothes off for a living, I figured she'd be the one out of all of us to appreciate this most.

I scoot my chair closer to hers. "Hey, Sammy. You all right?"

"I'm fine," she answers in a tone that is totally unconvincing.

"I don't think you've smiled once. And there's been plenty to smile about."

She cracks a fake smile.

"You really hate this?" I ask. "I thought you'd find this fun."

"I know, and normally I would. This is totally me." She finishes off the last of her drink. "But I don't feel like me these days."

I wonder what's going on with her. I've asked her more than once if she misses Miguel, if it's possible she has stronger feelings for him than she realized. But she's told me no so many times that I have no choice but to believe her.

"Want another drink?" I ask her. "Another scotch, or something more exciting? The apple martinis are really good."

"Another scotch," she replies. "Straight up."

I flag down our waiter, a buff guy dressed in black slacks and a bowtie. Every time I see him, a sexual charge runs through me. And not just because he's got a body to die for, but because with his dark hair and dark eyes, he reminds me a lot of Dom.

There's been so much sexual stimulation tonight. I'll definitely be unpacking the vibrator.

Better yet, I can use the vibrator while I have phone sex with Dominic.

When Samera's drink arrives at the table, I pay for it, then push my chair back and stand. There's a woman sitting on a chair on the stage, getting up-close and personal with a Zorro look-alike who has stripped his shirt off. I would love to stay and see the rest of the show, but I'm suddenly missing Dominic horribly.

"You know what, ladies? I'm gonna get out of here."

"You're leaving?" Lishelle asks, stunned.

I nod. "Yeah."

"Where are you going?" Claudia asks.

I glance at Samera, who has a look of unease on her face. It's an expression that says she doesn't want me to leave her alone with my friends.

"I...I'm not feeling well."

"Liar," Lishelle quips, but she's smiling.

"Okay, so I'm going back to the room to call Dominic. Don't wait for me to get back here. I might be a while."

"Anyone know what happened to my sister?" Samera asks. "Because if I'm not mistaken, she's about to go back to the room to have phone sex with her boyfriend."

"Like I said. Don't wait up."

I wink at Samera and my friends before I hurry out of the room.

"Dominic, hi." A shuddery breath oozes out of me when I hear his voice on the other end of my line.

"Hey, babe."

"I am missing you *so* much."

"I miss you, too."

"I wish you could see me right now. I'm wearing this dress you would want to rip off of me."

"Really?"

"Yeah. And I spent a small fortune on it."

"Describe it for me."

"Hot. Halter-style top, leopard print."

Dominic makes a meowing sound.

"The skirt is wispy and flirty. Very sexy."

"Wispy and flirty?"

"Trust me, it's hot."

"Hopefully not too hot. I don't want all the guys in Vegas going after my woman."

"They can look all they want, but I only want your cock," I tell him. "I'm not sure I can go four days without fucking you."

"It's been a rough fourteen hours for me, too."

I lie backward on the bed. Spread my legs. "My pussy misses you." My voice is breathy. Sultry.

"How much?"

"Enough that I want have phone sex until I get off."

"Oh?" The question is a deep whisper.

"Mmmm. My pussy's already so wet, just from hearing your voice."

"Nothing like a woman touching herself on the other end of the line to get a guy hard."

"Do you have your cock in your hand?"

"Yes…"

"If you were here right now, do you know what I'd do?"

"Tell me," Dominic says.

"I would take your cock in my hands, taste the tip with my tongue. Then I'd suck on the tip, nice and slow, just the way you like."

Dominic moans.

"That's right. Then I'll take you deep in my mouth, to the back of my throat…"

Now I can hear the sound of Dominic jerking off. He's pumping his shaft with hard strokes.

"Yes, that's it. I'm taking you so deep. You want to come. But not yet. I want you to come when you're deep inside me." I crawl onto my knees. "I'm on my knees, baby. My ass is sticking in the air. I want you to take me this way."

"No, I want to eat you first," Dominic rasps.

I play with my pussy. "Ooh, baby. I'm thinking about your tongue on my clitoris. I'm so wet." I make the sounds I normally make when Dominic is sucking on my clit and swallowing my juices.

"Can you come?" he asks.

"Yes…"

"I want you on your back."

I ease onto my back. "I'm on my back, baby."

"Spread your legs. And play with your pussy. Stick your fingers inside, get them really wet."

I do as Dominic tells me. I whimper as I play with myself.

"Are your fingers wet?" he asks me.

"Yes."

"Fuck, I'm so hard I could explode. I want to taste you so badly."

"I know, baby."

"You have your vibrator there?"

"Uh-huh. It's right here."

"Put it inside you."

I reach for the vibrator, which I put on the bed before I called Dom. I turn it on, play the massaging tip over my clitoris. And when I slip it inside me, I cry out in pleasure.

"That's right, babe. Right now, that's not your vibrator. It's my dick. I want you to play with that sweet pussy of yours until you come."

"Dom…"

"Ride me, sweetheart. Ride me until you scream my name."

"It feels so good…"

"I'm sucking on your tits, I'm sucking on your earlobe. And I'm grinding my dick into your sweet pussy. Going so deep."

"I love it when you're deep inside me…" I push the vibrator deeper, moaning loudly as I do.

"Oh, yeah. I love those sounds you make. I can always tell when you're getting close, and I go faster, harder…"

"I'm riding you, baby." The little tentacles attached to the vibrator that play over my clit bring me ever closer to orgasm. I twist my nipple with my free hand. Every delicious sensation, plus Dominic's heavy breathing, brings me closer and closer to orgasmic bliss.

"Annelise, are you gonna come? 'Cause I'm almost ready to blow…"

"Come, baby," I urge. "I'm ready." The vibrator works its magic inside me and out. As I hear Dominic grunt at the onset of his release, I let myself go. Let myself ride the wave of pleasure with him.

When my orgasm subsides, my entire body is tingling. My heavy breathing mixes with Dominic's, even though we are three thousand miles apart.

"Love you," Dominic murmurs.

"Oh, baby. I love you, too."

"Me or that vibrator of yours?" Dominic jokes.

"You, of course. I wish you were with me right now. We'd fuck all night long."

"I know." A beat passes. "Babe, I've got to get cleaned up, here."

I chuckle. "I can imagine."

"I'll call you later, okay? Actually, it's pretty late now. I'm gonna shower and head to bed."

"Right. I forgot about the time difference. We'll talk tomorrow."

"Have fun, babe. And be safe."

"I miss you."

"Miss you, too. And don't lose too much cash!"

I giggle, then hang up the phone.

Eight

Claudia

Lishelle, Samera and I make the slow trek out of the theater with the rest of the crowd when the Thunder from Down Under finish their ninety-minute performance. The night is still young, only ten-thirty, and though I should be tired because of the time difference, I'm nowhere near ready to go to bed.

"You want to stay here and hit the slots?" Lishelle asks.

"We can do that back at the Venetian," Samera says. "And be closer to our rooms if we want to freshen up. Or if we get bored."

I dig my cell phone out of my purse. "You think we should call Annelise?"

Lishelle rolls her eyes. "Are you kidding? She went off to have phone sex."

"Forty-five minutes ago," I point out. "She's got to be finished by now. Hell, this is Vegas. There's no point sleeping the nights away. What do you think, Samera?"

"Sure," she answers. "Tell her to meet us in the bar."

Lishelle gets a cab while I make the call. Annelise doesn't answer, so I tell her to meet us downstairs in the lobby in ten minutes, and that if she doesn't show, we'll go up and get her.

When we arrive at the hotel, there's no sign of Annelise in the lobby. I take the time to ask the concierge about the entertainment options, and he tells me that the Venetian's Tao Nightclub is the spot if we want high energy with a variety of music. It has the added feature of a large terrace that allows club-goers to view the Las Vegas strip.

I glance at my watch as I head back to Lishelle and Samera, who are both waiting near the bank of elevators. "The happening place here is the Tao Nightclub. So, do we go up and get Annelise?"

"I'll just call her," Samera volunteers. "The Tao Nightclub?"

"Yeah."

Samera heads to the far edge of the front desk, where she uses a house phone to call upstairs. She returns in less than a minute, saying, "She said she just got out of the shower, but that she'd meet us there."

"All right, then," Lishelle says. "Let's go."

Five minutes later we're in the club. The music is loud and pulses not only through the club, but through my body.

"I like," Lishelle says.

"Yeah, this place is hip," I agree. "Look—go-go dancers."

"Should we head to the bar?" Lishelle asks.

"Yeah. I'd like a drink. Samera?"

"I can definitely use a drink."

Lishelle leads the way, and we find a spot where two seats are available. I take one, and Samera gestures to Lishelle to take the other.

As soon as Samera gets her drink, she wanders off to the edge of the dance floor.

"She totally doesn't want to hang with us," Lishelle comments. "And I can't say the feeling isn't mutual."

A funky old school tune starts to play, and I sway my upper body while I sip my cosmopolitan. Standing by herself, Samera also starts to dance.

Well, she's not exactly alone. A small crowd formed around her the moment she started to twist her hips. Mostly guys, of course, and they're brazenly ogling her as she moves her body in a way that screams she takes her clothes off for a living.

She's moving far too slowly for the upbeat tune, gyrating her hips, slinking down onto her haunches and then back up again. The longer the song plays, the less inhibited she becomes. She runs a hand over her breast, through her hair, then down between her cleavage. Considering her breasts are so big and the dress doesn't cover much of them, the guys surrounding her are probably hoping she'll have a wardrobe malfunction any moment now.

I'm not frigid or anything, but I wonder why the girl's got to show herself off like that.

I'm not sure I like her. Yeah, she's Annelise's sister, but that's the only thing she's got in common with her. Annelise is sweet. She's vulnerable. She's real. She cares about others, which I'm not sure I can say about her sister.

Annelise went to the trouble of planning this trip for all of us, and Samera hasn't said much to Lishelle or me. The least Samera can do is crack a friggin' smile.

I turn to Lishelle, asking, "You think she's as much of a bitch as she looks?"

"She doesn't give a shit about us, that's for sure. Personally, I don't care, but I'll be damned if she ruins this trip for Annelise."

"Yeah, I know. Annelise went all out. If her sister sulks for the whole trip, Annelise will be crushed."

"Don't worry. If she keeps up with that stand-offish routine, I'll just have to kick some sense into her."

At the sound of a collective gasp, I quickly whirl around. I'm shocked at the sight of Samera standing over a guy who's flat on his back, one of her fists raised.

"Keep your fucking hands off me, you creep!"

I turn back to Lishelle. "Did you see what happened?"

"No. But my guess is, she decked him. Something good."

"Maybe we should go over there."

Lishelle shrugs, but the next second gets off her barstool.

We meet up with Samera as she's storming toward us. "Hey, girl." I hold up a hand to block her path. "What the hell happened?"

"That asshole stuck his hand up my dress. Fucking pervert!" she yells in his direction as the guy is getting to his feet.

I share a look with Lishelle, and I read in her eyes what I'm thinking. What did Samera expect, dancing the way she was?

But there was something else that struck me, and it doesn't take long for my own thought to disgust me. There was a part of me that figured because she was dancing so suggestively, and because she takes her clothes off for a living, that she wouldn't mind if some guy felt her up. In fact, I'd have figured that she'd like it. Especially considering the guy she flattened is seriously cute.

But not only is that stupid, it's highly judgmental. So what if Samera was dancing in a very sexual way? Does that mean she wanted some stranger to touch her body?

Yeah, I think I've judged Samera unjustly. Lishelle and I both. I know that a guy should never put his hands on you, no matter how hot he is, but if I hadn't seen how Samera handled him with my own eyes, I would think she's the kind of girl who gets off fucking strange men.

And lots of them.

"You want to leave?" I ask her.

"Yeah, I'm tired of this place. Where the fuck is Annelise?"

"She didn't show," I explain.

"We can call her," Lishelle offers. "Tell her we're leaving in case she's on her way here."

"I doubt she's on her way," Samera says, "but I guess leaving a message can't hurt."

"So, what now?" I ask.

"I'm kind of tired," Samera says. "I'm ready for bed. But you two feel free to hang here."

"No, we'll leave with you," I tell her.

We all head out of the club, none of us speaking. By the time we reach the lobby, I'm starting to wonder if Samera is ever going to try to get to know me and Lishelle on this trip, or if she'll stay in her shell the entire time.

Samera heads for the elevators without looking back. I'm debating what to say when Lishelle speaks. "So, that's it? You're not even going to try and get along with us on this trip?"

Samera turns. "Excuse me?"

"You heard me," Lishelle continues. "Okay, so you don't really know us well, and maybe you don't like the idea of being on a trip with us since we're your sister's friends, but we're here, and we may as well make the most of it. Don't you agree?"

"You think I'm lying about being tired?"

"Yeah, I do," Lishelle says, not even bothering to sugarcoat her answer. "But I understand why." She pauses. "There was a place called the V Bar that we passed on the way to the lobby. It looked quiet and intimate. A good place to talk. Why don't we go there for a drink? My treat. We can just shoot the shit. Break the ice, ya know?"

"Great idea," I say. "We can call Annelise, tell her to meet us there."

"Annelise is probably sleeping," Lishelle says. "No, it'll be just the three of us."

My eyes volley back and forth between Samera and Lishelle. For a minute, I think Samera is going to say no. Tell us that we're wasting our time trying to get to know her. But then she begins to bob her head up and down.

"All right. No point heading up to the room to mope. This is Vegas, after all."

"Exactly," Lishelle says.

And I think, *Maybe Samera isn't all that bad.*

"So why would you say 'go upstairs and mope'?" I ask Samera when we're seated in the V Bar. The place is sophisticated, with sleek lines, warm colors and subdued lighting that adds to its intimate appeal. Lishelle, Samera and I have gotten comfortable on one side of a double-sided leather lounge chair, our drinks resting on the table before us.

I reach for my cosmopolitan before speaking again. "Of all the things you can do in Vegas, moping isn't what typically comes to mind. I'm just curious."

Samera shrugs. "I don't know why I said that."

"Okay," Lishelle begins in a frank tone. "I'll start. Just in case your sister didn't tell you all about the sleazeball I almost married."

"I know some vague details," Samera admits.

"My guy's name was Glenn," Lishelle goes on. "And let me tell you, this guy rocked my world in every way possible."

"Good and bad," I interject.

"Yeah." Lishelle shakes her head sadly, as if remembering both aspects about her ex. "Glenn was…well, I thought he was my soul mate. When we fucked…girl, my toes would curl. Glenn had a dick that made me melt every time, come for days."

I'm a little surprised that Lishelle is being so honest with Samera. And so graphic. But Lishelle has never shied away from explicit talk, and I suppose she doesn't expect Samera to be offended by it.

"I thought the man loved me," Lishelle goes on. "We dated in college, and I should have known after what happened then that he couldn't be trusted, but you figure when a guy contacts you after nearly ten years, that he's grown up. That he's past playing games."

"I'm not sure they're ever past playing games," I say, thinking about how Adam screwed me over. I sip my cosmo and wince.

Samera clinks her glass of scotch against mine. "Here here."

"You want to know how my guy fucked me big-time?" I ask.

"Let me finish my story," Lishelle says.

And she does. She gives this long account of how Glenn started wooing her again, promised her the world but really tried to fleece her of nearly a million dollars.

"Fuck." Samera shakes her head. "And I thought what I went through in Costa Rica was bad. At least Reed didn't try to take my money as well as my heart."

"*And* the motherfucker was married and had two kids," Lishelle goes on.

"Ouch." Samera winces.

Lishelle brings her apple martini to her lips and takes a liberal sip. She's clearly finished her story, so I begin mine.

"And Adam, as I'm sure you know, was president of the Wishes Come True Foundation."

Samera nods. "He claimed he knew nothing about the charity fraud, right? Are the authorities buying that, or is he up on charges?"

"One thing about Adam, he was born with a silver spoon in his mouth and a horseshoe up his ass. He was charged, yeah, but the charges were ultimately dropped. The only two found to be involved in the charity fraud were Annelise's husband and his law partner, Marsha Hindenberg. But at least Adam's reputation was shot to hell, which was priceless revenge for me."

"How'd he screw you over?" Samera asks.

"You mean, after I did everything sexual under the sun to please the freak? Well, he dumped me. Of course. I was such a fool. But I'd loved the man for four years, and we were engaged and…" My voice trails off as I think of how stupid I was, how I lost myself with Adam. I love sex, yes, but I was never comfortable trying all the kinky things he wanted to do. Maybe I knew in my heart that he wasn't really into me.

"And I didn't want to lose him," I say quietly, finishing my thought.

"What did your guy do?" Lishelle asks Samera.

"If you can top my story or Lishelle's, drinks are on me for the rest of the night."

"All right." Samera sips her scotch, then looks at me and Lishelle in turn. "I'm not sure my story's worse—"

"But it's bad nonetheless," I say. "Go on, girl."

"You both know I was in Costa Rica with Annelise when she went to find evidence against Charles. And I'm sure you heard that I met someone."

"Yeah, some hot Spanish guy," I say. "What happened with that? Annelise sounded so hopeful when she talked about you and this guy."

"Miguel, right?" Lishelle asks.

"Yeah, Miguel."

Samera says his name softly, and it's obvious there's pain there. It's the first time I'm seeing any emotion from her.

"He hurt you something good, didn't he?" Lishelle asks. "Men. I swear."

"No, Miguel didn't hurt me." Samera sighs. "I liked him immediately. He was really hot. And I may be a stripper, but I'm not a whore. I didn't go down there to find some man. So if either of you has any bullshit misconceptions about me, I'm setting you straight right now."

"I didn't think so," I tell her, but I can't say it with total conviction.

"I'd just come out of a relationship with the manager at the club where I worked," Samera goes on, "after I found out he was screwing another dancer."

"Typical." Lishelle *tsks*.

"Talk about doing everything sexual for a guy." Samera meets and holds my gaze for a moment. "And then Reed fucked someone else? The timing of the trip to Costa Rica was perfect for me. And when I met Miguel, he was a nice—"

"Hard body?" Lishelle supplies, chuckling.

"That, too," Samera says. "But I was going to say he was a nice diversion. He helped me forget about the fact that I'd sworn off men. And the more I got to know him, the more I realized what a sweetheart he was. Suddenly I found myself thinking I might possibly have a relationship with him."

"And then you found out he was married." Lishelle slurs her words slightly. "And let me guess—he had a couple of kids."

"Nothing like that. Reed showed up and fucked every-thing up. Said he realized he'd messed up, but that he loved me and wanted me back in his life. And I bought it."

"Uh-oh." My body sways a little when I reach for my drink. Now that we're not dancing and not watching hot men, all the alcohol I've consumed is catching up with me.

"The thing is, it didn't take me long to realize Reed was full of it. He didn't love me. His ego was hurt because I'd dumped him. But still, I fucked him. Miguel was in love with me, yet I fucked another guy."

"You were duped," Lishelle says. "Reed came back into your life and made you promises. Trust me, I know what that's like."

"I was duped, yeah, but if I really cared about Miguel the way I should have, I wouldn't have fallen for Reed's lies so easily. Miguel didn't deserve that. He deserves someone better than me."

"You sound pretty smitten," I tell Samera. "And he sounds like a winner."

"He'll make some other woman very happy someday."

My eyes narrow as I stare at Samera. "How can you say that? If you like the guy as much as it seems—"

"I have to let him be happy," Samera says.

"Wow. You're a better woman than I am. I'd be back in Costa Rica, knocking on his door. Wouldn't you, Lishelle?"

When Lishelle doesn't answer, I glance past Samera to look at her. Lishelle is out cold, her head tipped back against the top of the chair, her lips slightly parted.

"Okay, time to go." I get to my feet, the sudden movement helping to clear my head a little. I step past Samera and reach for Lishelle's hand. "Lishelle, come on."

Her eyes fly open. "Huh?"

"We're going upstairs, party animal. Time to call it a night."

"Oh, man." Lishelle leans forward and drags her hands over her face. "You shouldn't have woken me up. I was in the middle of a very hot dream. There was a guy between my thighs, going down on me. I think he was from Costa Rica."

"Right." I smile sheepishly at Samera. "Okay, you're definitely drunk."

"Annelise was so smart, thinking to get separate rooms," Lishelle goes on. "Because I'm gonna pull out the rabbit."

"Too much information!" I exclaim.

Samera starts to chuckle.

"Or maybe I should just find a guy and bring him upstairs." Lishelle's gaze volleys around the room, as though she's looking for a candidate. "Damn, I want to get laid. I don't want to dream about it anymore. Maybe the bartender over there." She veers in his direction. "He's kind of cute, don'tcha—"

"Absolutely not." I push Lishelle toward the door, but she fights me. "Samera, help me out please."

Samera can't stop laughing as she takes Lishelle by her left arm and helps me get her out the door. "I get why my sister loves you two so much," she says. "You're cool. Fun."

"If not a little sex starved." My grin is syrupy. "But honestly, Lishelle went without sex for two years until Glenn came back into her life."

"And, fuck, was he ever great in bed," Lishelle comments. "He could make me—"

I cover Lishelle's mouth, saving her from blurting out more of her personal business as we pass a group of women.

A few minutes later, Samera and I have Lishelle safely tucked in bed. She won't be using the rabbit. At least not tonight.

But with all this talk about sex, I'm suddenly feeling that familiar longing. The proverbial itch that needs to be scratched.

Yes, I want a real man to replace the fantasies. But for tonight my dildo will have to do.

Nine

Lishelle

My eyes fly open, and it feels like a nuclear bomb has gone off inside my head. For a moment I'm disoriented. I don't know where I am, or what's going on.

And then I realize that the phone in my room is ringing.

It all comes back to me in that moment. That I'm in Vegas. The numerous drinks I consumed the night before.

I roll over clumsily and grope for the phone on the night table beside the bed. I hold the receiver to my ear. "Hello?"

The voice on the other end of the line is faint, so faint I can barely hear it. I pull the receiver from my ear, narrow my eyes as I stare at it, then notice that it's upside down.

I turn it right side up and repeat, "Hello?"

"Rise and shine, girlfriend."

"Annelise?"

"The one and only."

"I am so fucking tired right now, you have no clue."

"You need to get up," she tells me. "I have a surprise for you."

"What kind of surprise?"

"The kind that's due here any minute."

I grumble. "I just want to sleep."

"You won't want to sleep through this. Trust me."

I can't imagine what Annelise is talking about, but it's obvious she won't take no for an answer. "All right."

"Come to my suite as soon as you can, okay? Claudia's on her way as well."

"You had better damn well be making the coffee." Lishelle asks.

"I'm brewing a pot right now. But you shouldn't need it. My surprise will wake you right up."

Five minutes later, I'm dressed and standing outside Annelise's door. Before I can knock, Claudia appears, dressed in a beautiful sundress, her hair pulled back in a ponytail and her makeup done.

"Holy shit, Claudia. What time did you get up?"

"Annelise called about ten minutes ago."

"And you look this great already?" I'd only thrown on my gym shorts and a T-shirt.

"Well…Annelise said some people are coming over. Some sort of surprise."

"People?" I ask. "What people?"

"I guess we're about to find out."

Claudia steps up to Annelise's door and knocks. A few seconds later, the door swings open.

"Morning," Annelise sings.

I sweep into the room. "Okay, where's the coffee? And I couldn't find my Advil, so I hope you have some."

"The coffee's on the bar, and I do believe I've got Motrin in my luggage."

"Praise God." I plop myself down onto one of the bar stools. Then I raise a hand in a wave at Samera, who's sitting on the sofa holding a mug of coffee to her lips.

Annelise takes two mugs from the cupboard and fills them with java for me and Claudia. Then she disappears in her bedroom and reappears with a bottle of Motrin. I reach for it like she's offering me a stash of cash.

"So," Claudia begins after I've downed a couple pills. "What's this surprise?"

"You'll see in a minute." Again, she speaks in a sing-song voice.

"My God, you're chipper," I say. "You sound like a fucking bird—" I stop cold, lower my mug of coffee and shoot to my feet as the reason for her secrecy and excitement hits me. "Annie…oh, Annie." I walk toward her and grip her hands. "Are you…getting *married?*"

Claudia gasps, then squeals. "Oh my God. Of course. No wonder you've been so giddy. No wonder you insisted that we all come to Las Vegas! You and Dom…Samera, did you know about this?"

Samera stares at us stupidly. "Annie, is Dom here?"

"Hush, all of you," Annelise tells us. "You're way off base. First of all, I'm still legally married to Charles. Hopefully for not much longer, but still, I can't get married to anyone else. Yet."

"Ohhh…" Claudia frowns, clearly disappointed.

"I promise, you'll know exactly what's in store for you very shortly." Annelise barely finishes her statement before the doorbell rings. Her eyes light up. "That's got to be them now."

Them? I sip more of my coffee and try to erase the frown from my face. I don't want to disappoint Annelise, but I'm not up for seeing anyone.

"Okay, ladies." We hear Annelise before we see her round the corner in the foyer. "Here they are!"

Three guys who look like bodybuilders step forward, grinning. Two are white, one black. Each is carrying a large black bag over his shoulder. And they're all dressed in black jeans and white T-shirts. Almost like they planned it to look uniform.

Perhaps they did, I realize, remembering the strippers last night.

"Hello, gentlemen." Claudia shakes each man's hand. "I'm Claudia Fisher."

"What you are is gorgeous," the shorter, blond-haired guy tells her.

I mumble a quick hello to the guys, then take Annelise by the arm. "Will you excuse us a moment?"

I lead her into her bedroom, and before I can close the door, Samera rushes in.

I ask, "Annie, what is this? A private strip show?"

Samera says, "We already saw the Thunder from Down Under, which I pretty much slept through."

"If you sleep through this, then you're not the sister I've known and loved for years."

"So it is a strip show?" I ask. "At eleven in the morning?"

"Am I the only one who was disappointed that the guys last night didn't take all off?" Annelise asks, looking from me to her sister.

My eyes widen. "Annie!"

"This *is* Sin City." Annelise laughs.

"You really have changed," Samera comments.

Annelise takes one of my hands and one of Samera's. "You two can relax. I didn't book strippers. I booked masseurs!"

"They're masseurs?" Samera asks skeptically.

"And whatever else you'd like them to be…Come on. I don't want to keep them waiting."

Annelise opens the door and heads back into the living room. I want to protest, but she's so excited, I hold my wary thoughts in and follow her.

Claudia is chatting happily with the guys, ever the great hostess. I take a seat on the sofa, and Samera sits beside me.

"All right." Annelise claps her hands together. "This is my surprise. Three hot guys to give each of you a massage." Annelise wanders toward them. "This is Marcus," she says, introducing the tall, light-skinned black guy. "And this is Arnold."

"Hasta la vista," the tanned beefcake says, in a pretty good impersonation of Arnold Schwarzenegger. He's the tallest of the two white guys, with dark brown hair pulled back in a ponytail.

"And Luke, right?" Annelise asks of the blond guy.

"That's me."

Oh, he's got a killer sexy smile and piercing blue eyes. To me, he's the cutest of the three. Even Annelise must think so, because she squeezes one of his biceps.

"These guys are here to give you massages, to pamper you. Give you whatever you desire. What better way to get over stress than to have a hot guy work the kinks out of your body? And maybe kinks out of other places as well…"

"Did my sister just say what I think she said?" Samera whispers.

"Uh-huh," I reply.

"Their bags are filled with exotic body oils and creams. Everything you need to leave you feeling beautiful. So, indulge."

That explains the black bags each has over his shoulder. And here I thought they had some sort of costume in there.

"And remember our mantra—what happens in Vegas stays in Vegas. So, do whatever your heart tells you."

"Assuming these three guys are for me, Lishelle and Samera," Claudia begins, "what about you?"

"I'm in a committed relationship," Annelise responds easily. "Maybe I'll call Dom and we can have some more phone sex."

"She did *not* just say that in front of three strangers," Samera says. "Has she lost her mind, or has Dominic released the sexual monster within her?"

Yeah, Annelise has morphed into a different person. I've never seen her so bold when it comes to sex. Hell, I've never seen her so bold, period.

"Go ahead, girls," Annelise says. "Pick a guy you like. Then take him to your room and get comfortable."

I'm the first to step forward. "I'll take Marcus."

Samera gapes at me, and I shrug. "What the hell?"

"I guess I'll take Luke," Claudia says.

"I don't know, Claudia," I say. "Luke hasn't been able to take his eyes off Samera."

"Me?" Samera asks, sounding completely stunned. She looks at Luke as though seeing him for the first time. And I see definite sizzle between them.

"Then I'll take this hunk." Claudia approaches Arnold and trails a finger down his impressive arm.

"Am I the only one who'd rather just go for breakfast?" Samera protests. I look at her, and she seems to wither on the sofa. I get the distinct feeling that she'd like to run screaming from the room. The girl is full of surprises, especially for one who works in the sex industry.

Luke starts toward her, his slow gait sexy as hell. "Sweetheart, when my hands touch that beautiful body of yours, you'll forget all about breakfast."

"Just a massage," Samera tells him. "Nothing more."

Luke takes her by the hand and pulls her to her feet. "Whatever you wish, sweetheart. Whatever you wish."

A short while later, I'm facedown on the king-size bed in my suite. Marcus is sitting on a chair placed beside my bed, and his hands are working over my back, massaging lightly scented coconut oil into my pores. The way he's touching me feels utterly amazing.

Amazing enough that he's got me thinking about sex.

Hell, I'm not gonna lie. I considered fucking him the moment we got into this room together. But so far, Marcus has been all business. I don't know if he'll make a move on me, or if he'll be offended if I proposition him.

I sigh as his hands work the kinks out of my shoulder blades. I'm topless, my breasts flat against the bed. There's a towel covering my behind, beneath which I'm wearing a thong.

Marcus's fingers press into my back and move down, toward my butt. I hold my breath, wondering what he's going to do. His fingers move beneath the towel, but only for a moment. I moan softly in disappointment.

"How often do you do this?" I ask him.

"Perform a private massage on a gorgeous woman?"

"So you think I'm gorgeous," I ask, dangling bait.

"Hell, yeah. You're hot."

"If you think I'm hot, then how are you maintaining your cool?" I ask brazenly.

"You think I'm maintaining my cool?"

"If you're not, you're a damn good actor."

"Turn over," Marcus instructs me.

I pout a little, but don't voice my disappointment. If he's not into me, he's not into me. I'm not going to beg for a little play.

I reach for my towel and pull it forward, careful to cover my breasts as I shift onto my back.

Marcus says nothing, just starts massaging my neck. I close my eyes and enjoy his skilled hands.

"You sure you want this towel here?" he asks after a moment.

My eyes fly open. A sexy smirk is pulling at the corners of Marcus's mouth.

"Is it in the way?" I ask coyly.

"For what I want to do, yeah."

He holds my gaze, nice and steady, leaving no doubt as to what he wants. And in that moment, I decide to take Annelise's advice. To go with the flow, wherever this may lead.

"Then let me just toss this right over here." I scoop the towel off my breasts and throw it to my left.

"Wow." Marcus lets out a low whistle. "Lie back."

I do, and Marcus continues his massage, still working my neck. He tells me to close my eyes, so I do. His fingers move lower, below my collarbone, but he doesn't touch my breasts. I'm beginning to wonder if removing the towel was simply a way to give him more access to my body.

Until his finger brushes one of my nipples.

I inhale a shuddery breath and open my eyes. Marcus begins kneading the soft tissue of my breasts, something I'm sure is not part of the normal massage routine.

"Can I ask you something?" I say. "And don't be offended."

He tweaks my nipples now. "Sure."

"Are you really a masseur?"

"I am."

I eye him skeptically, trying to ignore the sensations shooting through my body at his touch.

He works his hands around my breasts and downward, toward my navel.

"Another question," I say.

His hands work over my stomach. "Go ahead."

"How many of your clients do you…get this close to? Honestly?"

"Most of my clients are older women. Fifties, sixties."

"Meaning?"

"Meaning I'm not into women that old."

"But they must be into you. I'm sure they offer you extra money for some extra special treatment."

"Some, yeah. But I'm a professional. I do my job, then leave."

"So that's what you're going to do today—give me a massage, then leave?"

"You—" Marcus shakes his head slowly "—are making it very hard for me to remain professional."

Now, I take one of his hands and lower it to my vagina. I can't believe I'm doing this, but damn, I need to get laid.

"I like you," I tell him. "And I really love the way your hands are making me feel right now."

Marcus cups my pussy. "Do you like that?"

"I'd like it even more if my thong was gone."

His eyes locked with mine, Marcus moves onto the bed. Then he skims my thong over my hips, leaving me completely naked.

And completely turned on.

Marcus runs his hands slowly back up my legs, strokes my belly, then my breasts. My breathing grows heavy as he settles between my thighs. And when he plants the first kiss on the skin below my breasts, I moan from the sheer pleasure of being this close to a man again.

"What do you want me to do?" Marcus asks.

I ponder the question, unsure. Part of me wants to fuck him. In the worst possible way. But another part of me questions how smart that is.

"Do you have a condom?" I ask him.

He kisses the soft area between my breasts before answering. "No."

"No?" I hear the disappointment in my voice.

"No." Marcus eases his body backward. "Now what?"

I think about that for a moment. "Maybe…maybe you could still touch me. Get me off, even if we can't fuck." When Marcus doesn't speak, I sit up. "Or maybe not. I'm sorry."

Marcus places one of his large hands on my stomach and urges me backward. "Don't be sorry. I'm here to please you."

And then Marcus kisses his way up my left leg. He keeps going, along my hipbone, then up my stomach. His lips ignite my skin, but my erogenous zones are thrumming. I want his tongue on my breasts, on my clit…

Finally Marcus's lips close over one of my nipples, and I sigh long and loud. He sucks on it reverently, draws it deep into his mouth. Soon, I have completely let go of the last of my inhibitions and am panting shamelessly as Marcus sucks on one nipple, then the other.

"Oh my God, I could come like this…"

"You don't want to come in my mouth?"

"Fuck, yeah."

Marcus moves quickly to settle his face between my thighs. The next instant he draws my clitoris completely into his mouth and sucks on me hard. He moves his tongue over my clit the way he did over my nipple.

I lift my head. Watch his mouth as he suckles me. And that's all it takes to push me over the edge.

My entire body convulses as I come. Marcus laves my clit hungrily, sucks my juices. I squeeze my legs around his face and savor every bit of this illicit pleasure.

When my orgasm finally subsides, Marcus lifts his head and grins at me. "How was that?" he asks.

I reach for his hand and smile. Marcus will never know it, but he just set me free.

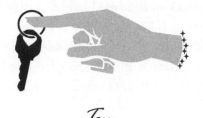

Ten

Claudia

A few hours after Annelise's surprise, I'm sitting in a café with Lishelle. Samera and Annelise decided to head to the pool, which was fine with me. I want some alone time with Lishelle to find out exactly how far she went with her masseur.

Lishelle sips her glass of red wine and eyes me. I tap my fingers on the table and stare at her. We're both wondering which of us will be the first to speak about what happened— or didn't happen—earlier.

"Is this place stunning, or what?" Lishelle asks.

"Yep," I agree.

"I want to go swimming, but I think I'll wait till later. It's too damn hot in the day."

I fold my arms onto the table. "So we're gonna talk about the weather?"

"Hmm?" Lishelle sips more wine, playing dumb.

"You know what I'm talking about," I say in an urgent whisper. "Lishelle, how far did you go?"

A grin spreads on her face. She glances left and right, as though trying to make sure that no one will hear her. She doesn't have to worry about that. I specifically asked for a table near the back of the café because I didn't want anyone within earshot.

"How far did *you* go?" Lishelle counters.

"You first." I take a quick sip of my mimosa. "And I promise not to hate you if you tell me you were a total ho." I smile sweetly.

"Okay, then. I was a total ho."

I gasp. "You were?"

"Well, not *totally*. We didn't…we didn't fuck. But we did have a very good time. I hope you did, as well."

Now I frown. Ever since Arnold left my room, I've had a million regrets. I'm not convinced I made the right decision.

"Well?" Lishelle prompts.

"I had a great massage, but I didn't have as much fun as you had. In fact, I think I made a fool of myself."

Our waitress arrives with the chicken Caesar salads we ordered. Lishelle digs in. Not really hungry, I pick at mine.

"What happened?" Lishelle asks around a mouthful of lettuce.

I draw in a deep breath. "I was naked. Facedown. And the way Arnold was touching me… Trust me, I knew where things were going to lead. And I wanted that. Hell, I need a palate cleanser. But when Arnold asked me to roll onto my back, I sort of freaked."

"Why?"

"Because." I pause. "I don't know why, but I suddenly started thinking about everything I'd done to please Adam sexually, and I felt like this evil, dirty person for even considering sleeping with Arnold."

"Claudia! You're not evil, and you're certainly not dirty."

"I know that. Logically. Then I started worrying about what Arnold would think of me if I *did* have sex with him. I didn't want him to think I was a slut."

Lishelle dabs at the sides of her mouth with her napkin, then tosses it onto the table. "See, this is what I don't understand. If guys fuck a hundred women, they're heroes. They feel no shame in bedding a woman they've just met. But if a woman has a one-night stand, my God, she's a dirty whore. How dare she like sex? This is the twenty-first century, honey. It's high time we women embrace our sexuality and bury the shame. We have needs, the same as men do. Why do we feel so friggin' bad about going after what we want?"

Listening to Lishelle's spiel, the truth of her words hit me in the face. "You absolutely hit the nail on the head," I tell her. "You couldn't be more right."

"Or maybe you didn't want to fuck him."

"No. That's the thing. I did. I didn't think I would, but the way he was touching me, I was really turned on. And then I let shame take control of me."

"You know what's really amazing? All my life, I've heard about how a palate cleanser can really help you move on. But until I allowed myself that today, I didn't believe it could really work. And it did. I had the most incredible, freeing orgasm with Marcus between my legs, and I swear, I'm a different woman."

Why didn't I take advantage of the opportunity presented to me? A no-strings-attached fling with a hot guy who wanted to please me?

"Damn," I say. "I blew it."

"Not necessarily. We can get the number from Annelise and you can call him. Or who knows? You might meet someone else you like tonight."

"Arnold gave me his number."

"Then there you go. Problem solved."

"It's not that simple. Yes, he gave me his number. But I didn't get to tell you how I freaked out."

"You didn't really freak out, did you?"

"Pretty much, yeah. When Arnold told me to turn over, I did. Of course, he checked me out. He told me he loved my pussy, the way it was so naked and exposed. Then I grabbed my towel, covered myself, and told him to leave the room while I got dressed."

"Uh-oh."

"He was a perfect gentleman about it, but I felt I owed him an explanation. So I told him about Adam. Went on and on about it, actually. Said Adam had been the love of my life, that he'd broken my heart, that I wasn't sure I could trust another guy."

"Ouch."

"Basically, I treated him like he was my shrink. It was pathetic."

"When did he give you his number? Before or after that?"

"After," I reply.

Lishelle grins. "Then there's still hope."

Back in my room, I ponder Lishelle's words. That there's still hope for me to have a rendezvous with Arnold. Honestly, it's something I didn't even think I'd consider, but I've certainly done more scandalous things. My trip with Adam to a swinger's club, the threesome with a stranger, sex in public places.

All this I did to please him. Isn't it time I indulge my own fantasies?

And I'll be honest. I have definitely fantasized about having a sensual massage turn into something more.

I collapse onto the bed, groaning softly as I do. Lying on my back, I stare around the room. It's gorgeous. Everything about this suite is gorgeous. The king-size bed has a canopy that can be pulled around it to enhance a romantic mood. The bathroom is very large and boasts a huge Jacuzzi tub. It's the kind of tub where lovers indulge their every fantasy. The entire suite is.

My vagina thrums. Damn, I have so much sexual tension built up inside me. Ever since Arnold left my room, my body has craved sexual release.

I get off the bed and dig my vibrator out of my suitcase. I used it last night, but I need it again. I've needed it a lot these days.

I pull my dress up, and my underwear off. Then I make myself comfortable on my bed and close my eyes. As I touch myself, I think about Arnold, about what should have happened this morning.

I imagine that when he told me how much he loved my pussy, I slowly spread my legs. Let him see my hairless pussy in all its splendor.

"You like?" I ask him.

I look up at Arnold's eyes, fogged with his obvious desire for me, and know his answer before he speaks.

"Oh, yeah. I like."

I reach for his hand then, bring it to my mouth and kiss each finger. Slowly. My gaze holds his while I close my lips over his thumb and suck it gently.

"You're gorgeous. *Fuck*."

"This is what I want to do to your cock," I tell him. I flick my tongue over his finger, coaxing a moan from his lips.

"You have no clue what I want to do to you."

Arnold gets onto the bed beside me and rolls me onto my stomach. Then he sweeps my hair to one side and plants his moist lips on my neck.

"Mmm."

Arnold's lips move over my neck and shoulder blades as skillfully as his hands did earlier. But he keeps going, running his tongue down my spine. When he gets to my ass, he sucks on my flesh. Sucks on it as his fingers skim my vagina.

Grunting, Arnold grips my hips and jerks me to my knees. He fingers and eats my pussy from behind. Spreads my folds and tongue-fucks me until I am panting and screaming his name.

"Fuck me," I beg. "I want to feel your cock so far inside me…"

I hear the rustling of Arnold's pants. And then he enters me fast and hard, giving me no mercy. This is pure ecstasy, and I lean forward so that Arnold's penis has no trouble reaching my G-spot.

Arnold pounds his cock into me, over and over. I brace my hands on the bed as his shaft goes deeper and deeper with each stroke.

I'm growing weaker. My breathing is getting shallower. I feel my orgasm building with each merciless stroke of his cock.

I plunge the rabbit deep inside me, imagining that it's Arnold's cock. And when the little ears on my vibrator play over my clit, I implode. A shock wave of pleasure rips through every inch of my body.

I bite down on my bottom lip to stifle my cry. For

several seconds I don't move. Not until I enjoy every last drop of my orgasm.

But when it's over, I feel…I feel ambiguous. Nowhere near as satisfied as I should be.

Kind of hollow, really.

Fucking my vibrator is fun while it lasts, but it's no fun lying next to it after you've come.

I reach for the card Arnold gave me and scoop it off of the night table. And as I stare at his phone number, I wonder if he'll be as good in bed in reality as he was in my fantasy.

Eleven

Samera

I had a major blow-up with Annelise at the pool. With a wink, wink, nudge, nudge, she asked me how I enjoyed my massage. I point-blank told her that I didn't appreciate her hiring some guy for me to sleep with.

"I hired them to give *massages*," my sister explained. "But I did ask if they'd be open to the idea of…of a little more."

"Why would you do that? And where the hell did you find them?"

"I did it because you need to get laid."

I shot to my feet inside our poolside cabana. "I need to get laid? I got laid plenty in Costa Rica, thank you very much."

"And ever since then, you've been miserable—"

"You don't know *shit*," I told Annelise. Then I gathered my belongings and stormed out of the cabana. I went to the room, changed, then hit the Fashion Show mall.

It's where I spent the next four hours, trying on cute outfits, beautiful shoes, and in the end buying only a pair of flip-flops with glitter on the straps for $12.99. I also called my friend Maxine back in Atlanta, who still works at the strip club where I used to. Before I left for Vegas, I told her about the trip my sister had planned. I was really hoping to chat with Maxine, but her voice mail picked up. Instead I left her a message to let her know I'm having a good time.

I was doing everything in my power to avoid thinking about why I'd gotten so mad at my sister. Hell, I've never been prudish when it comes to sex, especially the idea of a hot, fun fling. But Annelise was right when she said that I've been miserable since returning from Costa Rica, and it really struck a nerve.

I am miserable. Because I'm still missing Miguel.

Oh, I've tried to put him out of my mind. Told myself that he's no more special than the other guys I've fucked and forgotten in the past. He certainly didn't have as large a cock as Reed's, something I've assured myself over and over since leaving Costa Rica that matters to me. The truth, however, is that regardless of the size of Miguel's penis, he never failed to please me in bed. In fact, every time I fucked him, it seemed like more than just sex.

Maybe that's why, when I lie in bed at night, I remember him. Remember his soft mouth on mine. Remember the way his eyes lit up every time he looked at me. The way there was such reverence and love in his touch. Remembering him makes me feel warm inside in a way I've never experienced before, not even when I thought I was head-over-heels in love with Reed.

I force Miguel out of my mind when the taxi driver pulls up to the hotel. My stomach tightens as I think of my sister.

I've avoided Annelise for hours, but in just a few minutes I'll see her, and I don't know if our fight has ruined this trip for us.

And the strides we've made as sisters.

I thank the taxi driver, pay him, then get out of the car with my one small bag. A couple minutes later, I'm standing outside the suite. I sigh heavily before I open the door.

I don't immediately see my sister. "Annie?" I call, walking farther inside.

There's no sign of her, so I step into the bedroom and look around. "Annie?"

Hearing the sound of a toilet flush, I whirl around. A moment later the bathroom door opens and Annelise appears.

"Annie."

"Hey." She speaks but doesn't meet my eyes. But then she starts to move forward. "Are you still mad at me?"

"No." I hurry across the room and wrap her in a hug. "I'm sorry I got mad. It's just…I didn't expect…"

"I only wanted to do something nice for you. You know? I didn't hire those guys to sleep with you. I just thought if there was an attraction there, you could. If you wanted. But that wasn't why they were there."

"I know. I overreacted." We pull apart and I stroke her hair. "The truth is—and this is going to sound weird coming from me—but I just didn't want to go there because…well, because I'm still thinking about Miguel," I finish hurriedly." "There, I've said it. And I know it's crazy, because obviously it's over between us. He was a vacation fling, for God's sake."

"That's not what you said when I left Costa Rica. You told me you thought you were in love."

"I know what I said then, and Miguel is a great guy. But the truth is, he lives thousands of miles from where I do. Even if I wanted to…" I don't finish my thought.

"You really have it bad for him," my sister says, tenderness in her voice.

"It's probably because he's off-limits," I quickly say. "I can't have him, therefore I'm obsessing over him."

"Or maybe it's something more," Annelise suggests. "Maybe you *did* fall in love and would still be in Costa Rica if Reed hadn't shown up and messed things up for you."

The very words make my heart accelerate, but I don't want to acknowledge that she could be right. That if it hadn't been for Reed, I would still be with Miguel. My feelings for Miguel were incredibly strong, but when Reed showed up in Costa Rica claiming he still loved me, I foolishly believed him, gave him another chance, and ruined things with Miguel.

"But if I really loved Miguel, why did I give Reed another chance?" I ask, but my heart knows the answer isn't a simple one. "Whatever I think I'm feeling for Miguel, I have to get over it. The guy's out of my life." I pause, then say, "Let's talk about something else."

Annelise nods her understanding, for which I am grateful. "Where did you go?" she asks me.

"Shopping," I tell her. "More window-shopping, really. I didn't buy much. What did you do?"

"I couldn't find Claudia or Lishelle, so I hung out for a bit. Watched some TV, then talked to Dom. Went downstairs and gambled a little. I lost three hundred bucks on the slot machines, but I'm gonna win that back."

"That's how they get you." I wag a playful finger at my sister.

We're both silent for a few seconds. Then we smile at each other. "I really am sorry," Annelise tells me.

"No, I'm the one who's sorry. I guess I just have to get used to the new you. The one who's not afraid to go after what she wants sexually. It's not like I didn't preach that to you for years."

"This is true."

"Want to get something to eat? Or did you make plans with your friends?"

"I was going to," Annelise says. "But why don't we get dinner? Just the two of us?"

"You sure?"

"Of course I'm sure. You're my sister. That's what sisters do."

A feeling of warmth spreads through me. "Are we gonna dress up or go casual?"

"Dressy. Let's show this town what we're made of."

It's while Annelise and I are eating dinner at a restaurant called Postrio that I see him again—the man who first caught my eye yesterday, when I was having a smoke outside the lobby. And it's clear by the way he's not-so-secretly stealing glances at me from the table where he's sitting that he's definitely interested.

I hold his gaze for a second, then turn away.

Annelise lowers her fork as she stares at me. "I am either boring you to tears, or someone has caught your eye." She twists in her chair to look over her shoulder.

"No! Don't do that!"

She faces me again, grinning. "So there *is* someone."

"No," I protest. "Well, sort of."

Annelise leans across the table and asks, "Who is he?"

I glance at the sexy stranger, and he smiles. "Why is it that guys haven't mastered the art of how to check a woman out without being noticed? I think a guy's cute, I can steal glances of him all night without him knowing."

"Maybe he *wants* you to notice that he's checking you out."

"I think you're right. I saw him when we first got here. When I was having a cigarette outside the lobby. He walked by me. Definitely checked me out." Annelise starts to angle her head. "Don't! Seriously. If you do that, he's gonna think I'm interested."

"I'm dying to see him. Is he cute?"

I shoot a quick glance his way, though I already know what he looks like. "Yeah. He's cute."

"Are you gonna talk to him?"

I shake my head.

"Why not?"

"I don't know. I just—"

I stop short when the man gets up. He's with the same guy I saw him with yesterday, and both of them head our way.

"Oh, shit. I think he's coming over here."

I reach for my glass of water and busy myself putting it to my lips. From my peripheral vision, I see the sexy stranger. I fully expect him to stop.

But he doesn't.

I shift around to look at him, but all I see is his back as he heads out the restaurant door.

"Was that him?" Annelise asks. "Which one?"

"The taller one. With the sandy-blond hair."

"The well-built one. Oh, I wish I'd seen his face."

"No big deal," I say. "Ready to blow this joint and hit the slots?"

Annelise chortles. "I'm always ready to hit the slots."

Annelise and I make the rounds on the casino floor, dropping quarters into various slot machines. We win a few quarters here and there, but mostly we lose.

"All right," Annelise announces as she sits down at a Lucky 7 machine. "This is the one. Right here."

"You've said that about how many machines now?"

"But this is it." Annelise grins at me. "I can feel it."

"If you say so."

Annelise puts three quarters into the machine, pumps the handle and yells, "Big money, big money!"

"Why don't you just put a twenty in and press maximum bet until you run out of money?"

"Because I have a system," she replies, then puts one, two, three quarters into the machine.

"You really think it makes a difference?"

"Shh! Big money, big money!"

Lights flash, music plays, and a dinging sound fills the air. I quickly look at the display. The number of credits rapidly increases.

Now I'm getting excited. "How much did you win?"

"Looks like eighty credits."

I quickly do the math. "Twenty bucks? That's all?"

"It's better than a slap in the face." Annelise presses a button to release all the coins, then scoops them up and puts them in her bucket. "I want to try another machine."

"I'm going to wander, find my own lucky machine. If we lose each other, let's meet at the bar. Say in half an hour?"

Annelise doesn't even look at me as she sits in front of a nearby machine. "Sure."

Famous last words. I chuckle and walk away. But I don't get far. My eyes spot a Wild Cherry dollar slot machine. The thing about Las Vegas is that everywhere you turn is potential fortune. Is it this machine or that one? Make the right choice and you'll be happy. But make the wrong one…

Kind of like men, really.

I sit in front of the machine, but before I start to play, I reach into my purse and dig out a cigarette. I perch it between my lips and look for my lighter.

"Looks like you need a light."

My eyes fly to my left. And there's the guy. The sexy stranger I've sort of been flirting with since I got here.

"Allow me." He takes the cigarette from my hand. I watch as he presses the tip of his lit cigarette to mine. He passes it back to me and I take a long drag off of it.

"We keep running into each other."

"We're staying at the same hotel. It's bound to happen."

"Have you got your mind set on gambling, or can I lure you to the bar?"

I stare at the Wild Cherry symbol, and decide to take a different gamble. If only for tonight, I'm going to live in the here and now and put the past out of my mind. I get to my feet. "Actually, I would love a drink."

It dawns on me as we enter the Tao Lounge that I still don't know this sexy guy's name. He heads to an empty leather lounge chair, and I follow him there.

As I sit and cross my legs, he whistles. "Have I told you that you are fucking gorgeous?"

I roll my eyes. "Please tell me you're not into lame pick-up lines."

"Pick-up line? Babe, that's just the truth. From the moment I saw you…" His unfinished statement hangs in the air between us.

I realize immediately that I've gambled and lost. This guy doesn't want to get to know me. He wants to get to know my pussy.

I start to rise. "You know—"

He grabs my hand. "Hey, where are you going?"

"I'm not sure a drink is a good idea."

"What are you talking about? We just got here."

"I know, but."

He urges me down beside him. "What—you think I'm a creep? I assure you, I'm not. I'm just a guy who finds you fascinating. C'mon. Let me buy you a drink."

I eye this guy skeptically. "All right," I say after a moment. "I'd love a glass of Cristal."

It's a test, of course. To see if he thinks I'm worth a glass of such expensive champagne. "Of course, you have to buy the whole bottle to get one glass."

"Sugar, I know that."

"Actually, you can buy me a scotch."

"Why Cristal?" the guy asks. "I've always loved Veuve Clicquot."

My eyebrow shoots up. "Oh?"

"Yeah, it's not as trendy, but I like it better."

So the guy knows his expensive champagnes. And is he really going to buy a bottle just to give me a glass?

"But if you want Cristal—"

"No, I've been meaning to try Veuve Clicquot again. The first time I tasted it, it was sour, but friends swore it had to be a bad batch, or worse, counterfeit."

"Veuve Clicquot it is." He raises his hand to flag a waitress.

Okay, so this guy has me intrigued. Not interested, but intrigued.

But I don't care how much money he spends on me. I'm not about to spread my legs for any price.

He is attractive, though. The body of The Rock and a face that's pleasant to look at. Certainly not the kind of guy who has to pay for sex, at least not in a town like Vegas.

So does that mean he likes me?

A dark-haired waitress finally approaches us. "Bottle of Veuve Clicquot," my date tells her.

"You didn't just do that," I say. "You didn't just order a bottle of one of the most expensive champagnes."

"Maybe you're worth it."

"And maybe you're a drug dealer." I smile sweetly to soften the accusation.

The guy laughs. "Yeah, I get mistaken for that a lot at my restaurant."

"Your restaurant?"

"Uh-huh."

"You know what's crazy?" I ask.

"What?"

"How long have we been talking and I don't even know your name?"

The guy laughs. "Rusty. My name is Rusty."

"Rusty." I run the name over my tongue. It's a nice name.

"And you are?"

"Samera."

The waitress reappears, and I can't help thinking that she was super fast. She presents us with the bottle of champagne and asks if we'd like her to open it.

"I'll open it," Rusty tells her. But before he does, he withdraws his wallet from his blazer and passes her a Platinum American Express card. "Charge it to this."

"Absolutely." The waitress grins as she strolls away.

Rusty now turns his attention to the bottle of champagne. He wrestles the cork open, and the popping elicits cheers from those around us.

Rusty reaches for one of the two champagne flutes on the tray the waitress brought to our table. He fills it, passes it to me, then fills his own.

He grins at me as he clinks his glass against mine. "Cheers."

"Cheers," I echo.

The fruity taste plays over my tongue. "This is delicious," I tell him. "I definitely had a bad batch the first time."

"I figured you'd like it."

"So." Once again, I cross my legs. "So, you're in the restaurant business."

"Five establishments in the state of Illinois."

"Really." Is this guy bullshitting me?

"Tex-Mex joints."

"Wow. I'm impressed."

"Thanks."

"Why'd you decide on Tex-Mex?"

"I grew up in Houston, practically the home of Tex-Mex. When I moved to Illinois, I didn't see a lot of places like that in my town."

"Which town is that?"

"Springfield."

"Haven't been there."

"Lucky you." Rusty grins. He really does have an attractive smile.

"How'd you end up in Springfield? Considering you were from Houston."

"Love," he answers honestly. "But I don't live there anymore. I'm in Chicago now."

"The love thing didn't work out?"

"Oh, it worked out. I married her."

"I see." My stomach clenches. So this son of a bitch is married.

"My wife died six months ago."

"*Oh.*" My eyes widen in horror. "Oh my God. I'm sorry." Now I feel like a fool for judging him.

"Thanks. It was an awful time. She was my soul mate."

It strikes me as odd, this beefcake of a guy talking about

his soul mate. But he's clearly not just a guy in Las Vegas to get laid. He's a guy capable of emotions, capable of love.

I should know better than to judge someone based on their appearance, considering people do that to me all the time.

"I can't imagine what it's like to lose someone," I say.

"It was the worst thing I ever had to go through," he goes on. "But it was for the best, you know? She had cancer. God, that's one bitch of a disease."

"Oh, that's awful."

Rusty nods solemnly, and for a moment, I wonder if he's going to get emotional.

"Yeah. What can ya do? Life hands you something like that…"

Rusty lowers his eyes and breathes in heavily. Despite the fact that we're in this bar with music playing and many people mingling and laughing, I feel like it's only him and me in the room. I reach forward and gently rest my hand on his.

"Rusty…" I really don't know what to say.

His smile is faint but appreciative. And then he pulls away.

He downs his champagne, a deliberate gesture as far as I'm concerned. I think he needed to break the intimacy between us.

When he faces me again, he seems totally normal. Not at all like a guy who just got lost in emotional memories.

"I feel like dancing," he announces. "Maybe we can go to the club. It's a little more upbeat than this place."

"Sure," I agree. "No…I have a better idea. Why don't we go to Bellagio?"

"Bellagio? Why?"

"Because when I got to Vegas, I thought that's where my friends and I were staying. And when I found out we weren't…well, I was a little disappointed."

"Disappointed? This place is gorgeous."

"I know. But I kind of want to check it out before I leave. Why not with you? They've got to have a nightclub there."

"All right. Why not?"

"Oh, shit," I say suddenly. "The champagne."

"We'll take it with us. Sneak it into the club like a couple of teenagers." He winks at me. "Wait here while I go find the waitress and get my credit card back."

As I wait for Rusty, I drink more champagne and sway my body to the R&B tune filling the lounge. A few guys look my way and smile, but I ignore them.

"I have to tell you," Rusty begins when he returns. "I feel like the luckiest guy in this place. Every man in here is looking at me with envy."

Rusty helps me to my feet, then lifts the bottle of champagne off the table. I loop my arm through his and together we head for the door.

Ten minutes later we're entering the Fontana Bar, Rusty not-so-discreetly hiding the bottle of champagne beneath his blazer at his side.

We search around until we find a table near the terrace, from which we can see the impressive fountains. A range of colors illuminates the water as it shoots into the air in a dazzling show.

"You sit here," Rusty tells me. "I'll get a couple of glasses."

With Rusty gone, I check the place out. There's a dance floor and large stage to my right, but the red curtains are drawn, meaning there isn't an act performing tonight. At least not right now. Instead, a DJ mixes the music. The dance floor is packed with people bouncing their bodies to the electric techno beat.

Rusty returns and fills two wineglasses with champagne.

We both drink a little. Then he places his glass on the table and sweeps me into his arms.

"Ready to shake that beautiful body of yours?"

He doesn't wait for my answer, just leads me to the dance floor and finds an empty space for us. I immediately throw my hands in the air and sway my body. I move my hips a beat slower than the music in a way that is designed to seduce.

Rusty raises his eyebrows as he dances toward me, matching my moves.

Slowly I turn, positioning my butt against his groin. His hands lock on my hips, hold me against him. When the music changes to a salsa tune, I ease my upper body forward and gyrate against him in a much bolder sexual movement. I'm not sure, but I think I hear Rusty growl as he runs his fingers over my ass.

What I am certain of is that he's got a boner. A big, impressive boner.

I stand fully and turn around so that I'm facing him. I reach for Rusty's hands, hold them as I twist my hips and lower my body. Lower and lower I go, until I'm on my haunches, my head positioned in front of his crotch.

Rusty pulls me upright. "Naughty girl. Naughty, naughty girl. You should be spanked."

I laugh, turn again, and jiggle my ass against his cock. The champagne has worked a number on me. My head feels light, and I'm in a especially flirtatious mood.

Leaning against Rusty, I grip his thighs. They're muscular. Firm.

Just the way I like it.

Rusty breathes hotly against my ear. "Do you have any idea what I want to do to you?"

I laugh again. Then I grab his hand and lead him off the dance floor.

"You don't want to dance anymore?" he asks.

"I'm thirsty."

Hanging on to Rusty's hand, I zigzag through the crowd until we're at our table. I'm not sure where I want my association with him to lead, but for now I'm having a ton of fun.

So much fun that I push Rusty onto the soft leather chair. He stares up at me, a look of pleasant shock on his face. My eyes don't leave his as I lower myself onto his lap. From this position, Rusty's head is very close to my breasts.

I know I'm torturing him, but I can't seem to stop myself.

"You have me seriously hot and bothered—"

"Shh." I place a finger on his lips to shush him. I let it linger in a deliberate sexual gesture.

Should I fuck him? I wonder.

He can be an easy Vegas fling. Given the story he told me about his wife, I'm sure he's got to be grieving. In other words, he might be up for a fling to distract him from his sadness but nothing more than that.

We're on the exact same page.

I reach beyond Rusty's head to lift one of the wineglasses off the table. First I take a liberal sip, then I put the glass to Rusty's lips so he can do the same.

A bit of champagne drips down his chin. I scoop it up with a finger, then put that finger in my mouth and suck on it slowly.

"You're fucking killing me."

"Want to go back to the dance floor?"

He thrusts his groin upward, I suppose to make sure I feel his erection. "Is that what you want to do?"

A moment passes before I answer. "Yeah."

Before we head back to the dance floor, I pour myself another glass of the Veuve Clicquot. It's meant to be savored, but I finish the glass in a few large gulps.

When I look around, I catch Rusty's eyes lingering on my ass.

"Want some?" I ask.

"Oh, yeah." With his gaze fixed on my behind, there's no doubt what he's referring to.

I hold the bottle of champagne toward him. "I was talking about this."

Rusty takes the bottle from me and drinks straight from it.

"Come on, baby." I tug on his hand. "Let's dance."

I'm already moving my body to 50 Cent's "In Da Club" as we head onto the dance floor. My hands are in the air. The rhythm of my body is slow and sultry. Rusty can't hide the lust in his eyes as he stares at me.

I kick the seduction routine up a notch, running my fingers through my hair, gyrating my body in an even more explicit manner. Around me, I hear some catcalls, but I tune them out. All I care is that I'm turning Rusty on.

He wraps his arms around me and holds me close. "Anyone ever tell you that you dance like a stripper?"

I howl at that, but don't answer him.

"I know you're not mine," he goes on. "But I'm feeling a bit possessive right now. So many guys are lusting after you. Even some of the women."

"What's your point?"

Rusty locks his hands on my hips and holds them in place as he rubs his cock against my pelvis. "That's my point."

"You expect me to fuck you?" I whisper in his ear. "What kind of girl do you think I am?"

"Oh, don't play coy. You know your way around a bedroom."

I walk away from Rusty and don't look back. Let him wonder what's going on.

If I fuck him, it'll be on my terms, not his.

Back at our table, I fill my glass with the last of the Veuve Clicquot. But I suddenly have an odd feeling—as though among the crowd in this club, someone is watching me.

Maybe I've had too much to drink. Forgoing the champagne, I reach into the small purse that's hanging off my shoulder and withdraw a cigarette.

"Wanna cigarette?" I ask Rusty, who has joined me at our table. I wobble a little, and he slips an arm around my waist.

"Here." I offer Rusty the cigarette.

He takes it from my hand, and the next moment, leans forward and covers my mouth with his. I'm completely caught off guard, but I don't pull away. His tongue is hot and hungry as it plays over mine, igniting my body completely.

After several seconds I'm breathless, and I pull away. I turn slightly as I take another cigarette from my purse as well as my lighter.

A feathery light touch on my leg. It goes higher, and higher until it reaches the hem of my skirt. I glance over my shoulder. Make eye contact with Rusty when his fingers skim my ass.

I blow a plume of smoke through my mouth and nose. Then I grab my glass of champagne and drink it all, my own fingers trailing up my thigh now.

I have to stop myself from touching my pussy right here in front of Rusty. I have to remind myself that I'm not on a stage being paid to take my clothes off.

I lower myself onto Rusty, not too gracefully, considering the alcohol is now getting to my head. "I think I'm drunk," I tell him.

"What you are is hot."

God, the way the deep timber of his voice resonates in my ear makes my clit start to pulsate. I can quickly get used to the idea of this guys hands and mouth all over my body.

"What now?" Rusty whispers in my ear.

"A drink." When his eyes bulge, I say, "Water. Do you mind getting me a glass?"

"Not at all." Rusty gives me a lingering kiss before he heads for the bar. It seems like a good five minutes pass before he returns.

"I was starting to worry," I tell him. "Thought you decided to leave me here."

Rusty hands me the glass of water. "As if."

I down the water in seconds.

"Thank you for taking me to Bellagio."

"Does that mean you're ready to leave?" Rusty asks hopefully.

I rise to a standing position, wobbling slightly. Rusty shoots to his feet and places his hands on my shoulders to steady me.

"Okay, let's go get a cab," Rusty says.

I cling to him as we leave Fontana and cross the casino floor. I see eyes look me up and down, something I'm used to. I'm used to scornful looks from women, lustful looks from guys.

A couple minutes later, we're in the lobby. As we step outside I tell him, "I'm not going to fuck you." My words slur.

Rusty doesn't reply.

We're silent as we get into a taxi, and I even close my eyes as we're driven back to the Venetian. It's a short drive, and thankfully Rusty is with me, because the alcohol has hit me hard.

He helps me out of the car, leads me into the hotel. When the elevator door opens, I stumble onto it.

"Easy, baby," Rusty tells me.

I press the button for the thirty-fifth floor, but it doesn't light up. It takes me a moment to remember that I need to insert my room key to access that floor.

"What about you?" I ask. "What floor are you on?"

"I'll see you to your door," Rusty says. "Make sure you're okay."

The elevator comes to a stop, and the door opens. I walk off without waiting for Rusty.

"Hey," he says, grabbing my arm. "You messing with me? Or do you want to fuck? It's been a long time since I've been on a date."

An airy laugh escapes me. "You call this a date?"

"I don't know what it is."

"I think—"

Rusty silences me with an urgent kiss. But it's over quickly, and he steps backward. "I like you. Really like you. But if you're not feeling this—"

"Maybe I ought to go to bed."

The disappointment in Rusty's eyes is palpable. But he says, "All right."

"Thanks for everything," I tell him. Then I start to walk off. I'm not really sure why I'm playing with him the way I am, except that I'm testing how far I can push him.

After I've taken several steps, I glance over my shoulder. Rusty is standing in front of the elevator watching me go.

I keep going. And my God, I get that weird feeling again. Like someone is watching me. Which is absolutely crazy, considering only Rusty and I are on this floor.

The pinging sound of the elevator arriving has me

spinning around. And in that moment I know that it's time to put up or shut up.

"Wait!" I yell.

I dash down the hallway to meet Rusty.

Twelve

Lishelle

"I wonder where the hell Annelise and Samera are."

I'm with Claudia at the Tao Nightclub, and currently we're sitting at our table, taking a break from all the dancing we've been doing the last hour. "I thought for sure we'd see them here."

"Maybe they're gambling," Claudia suggests.

"Maybe," I agree. "Or maybe they checked out another casino."

Claudia leans her head on my shoulder. "At least we have each other," she jokes in a fake-sad voice.

"Yes, darling." I pat her hand and giggle.

Though the club is crowded, the music and chatter loud, I notice the sudden excited squeals and cheers.

"Something just happened," I say.

Claudia glances around. "There's a bit of a crowd over there." She points in the direction of the entrance. "Some star must have entered the club. Ooh, I wonder if it's Taye Diggs. Or Will Smith."

"You think so?"

"A girl can dream, can't she?"

Yes, a girl can dream, and now I'm curious. The crowd is moving our way—mostly women—so I know that at the center must be a guy. As it nears our table, I notice four very large black men first. Clearly, they're bodyguards. And then I get a glimpse of the star, who's stretching this way and that to shake hands.

"I don't believe it," I say to Claudia.

"Can you see who it is?"

"It's Rugged!"

Claudia whips around. "Rugged?" Her voice is tinged with excitement. "You're sure?"

"Yeah, I'm sure." I knew it had to be some big star, but what are the chances it'd be Rugged, of all people? I can't help remembering what happened with him in my office, and I feel vindicated by my assessment of him. If we'd gotten involved, I would have simply been a number to him. Considering the flock of groupies around him now, I can only imagine how many women he's slept with.

"We should go say hi."

I gape at Claudia. "Are you kidding?"

"Of course not. The guy's working with us to make our fund-raiser a huge success. It only stands to reason—"

"I'm not in the least interested in fighting all those groupies to get to him."

"Lishelle, you're a star in your own right."

"He probably won't even remember me."

"Why are you suddenly playing Miss Insecure? That's not like you."

"Maybe because he wanted to fuck me in my office."

Claudia gasps.

"Exactly. Now do you understand?"

"He actually came right out and asked you that the day you met him?"

"Pretty much. Guys like him expect women to drop to their knees or spread their legs." I snap my fingers. "Like *that.*"

"Wow." Claudia shakes her head in disbelief. But the next instant her eyes light up. "Are you interested?"

"No!" I exclaim. "Yeah he's cute, but, Claudia, the guy's a baby."

"He's twenty-four."

"How do you know that?"

"Duh. I read."

"Oh. All those magazines on celebrities."

"You're not quite thirty-one. He's certainly old enough."

"That's what he said."

"And you know what they say about younger guys. They're like the Energizer Bunny when it comes to sex—they keep going and going."

I whack Claudia's arm. "Shut up!"

Claudia stands. "I'm going to say hello."

"Like you'll get through his entourage."

"Please." Claudia rolls her eyes as if to say that won't be a problem. And with the way she's dressed—jewel-encrusted clutch, jewel-encrusted shoes and a form-fitting black dress with a scoop neck—she looks like an heiress. All she's missing is the tiny pooch under her arm—the current signature of many starlets.

Claudia works her way out of the booth.

"Claudia!" I say urgently. "Claudia, wait!"

But off she goes before I can do a damn thing to stop her.

Well, I'm not going anywhere. I sip my cosmopolitan and shake my shoulders to the funky beat blaring in the club.

Now I really wish Annelise were here, as well. Because sitting alone in a crowded club, you kind of feel like a loser. Like a woman who's been stood up or deserted.

Two songs play before Claudia finally heads back to our table, beaming. "He's invited us to his table."

"What?"

Claudia grabs my hand. "Come on."

"I'm not going anywhere."

"Don't be a sourpuss."

"If I go over there, he's going to think I'm desperate to be with him."

"I don't think so. By the way, he's with Baby J. And Baby J said we can also count on his support for the fund-raising effort."

Despite that great news, I roll my eyes.

"Come on. Be a good sport. No one's going to force you to have sex with him in a public bar."

I suppose she's right. It's just that I'm not exactly thrilled about the idea of hanging with a couple young guys and dealing with all the barely legal groupies who will be vying for their attention.

"They're waiting," Claudia says.

Grudgingly I get to my feet. "All right. But I'm not gonna kiss his ass. And if he paws me, I'm gone."

Rugged's smile is as bright as a neon light when I arrive at his table with Claudia. He rises, and so does Baby J. I expected to see a throng of nearly naked women draped all over them, but it's just Rugged, Baby J, and five bodyguards who look like linebackers.

"Hey," I say casually.

"You stalking me?" Rugged asks.

"Funny. Ha ha."

Rugged puts his hand on my back and guides me forward. "This is Baby J," he explains.

"I know who he is." I offer the rapper my hand.

"You're right, G," Baby J says. "She's hot."

I smile stupidly. I'm really not in the mood to hang out with young guys I have nothing in common with. I want desperately for Claudia to be tired of this already, but instead, she makes herself comfortable on the plush chair beside Baby J's.

"So how is it you're in Vegas?" I ask when we settle into our chairs. Rugged inches his chair closer to mine, and slings an arm across the back of my seat.

"Just here with my boy. Hangin' out. Doin' some gamblin'. You?"

"Here with my girls. Hanging out. Doing some gambling."

We both smile at that. And here's a shock—Rugged's warm smile actually gets to me. Endears me to him a little. He is like his rap name implies—rough around the edges. But while he's dressed in baggy jeans that hang below his waist and an Atlanta Falcons jersey—not at all the kind of style that would attract me—he's very handsome. His boyish face says he's not as rough and tough as the image he wants to portray to the world.

"So, Rugged—"

"Actually, my mama named me Roger. My close friends, that's what they call me. So, call me Roger."

"We're close friends now?"

"We could be."

I mull that over as I sip my drink.

"Cosmo, right?" Roger asks me.

"Yep."

"Want anotha?"

I shrug. "Why not?"

"All right. Gimme a minute."

Roger gets up from the table, and two of the linebackers do as well. Rugged starts off, and almost immediately, several young women follow his movements with their eyes. A couple even head after him.

Groupies. For them, any rich man will do. They hope to seduce with their good looks and loose pussies. And if they get pregnant, even better. Because even if the relationship doesn't last, they've at least snagged a huge cash settlement for their child.

Pathetic.

Well, he's not my man, so I don't let myself worry about the women. Until Roger takes a seriously long time to return to the table. I'm talking ten, fifteen minutes. As I glance at my watch, I actually start to get a bit pissed.

What's he doing—fucking some groupie in the bathroom?

About a minute after the thought pops into my mind, Roger appears. Once again he flashes a smile that he must think will get my panties wet.

He passes me my new cosmopolitan. "Sorry 'bout that. Didn't think I'd be so long."

"Some pretty young thing distract you?" I can't help asking.

"*You* distract me."

I make a concerted effort to not roll my eyes, and instead concentrate on sipping my new drink. Claudia's loud burst of laughter causes me to look her way. She's got a leg draped over one of the linebackers, who is also laughing, as though the two of them have known each other for years and are sharing some private joke.

Now I roll my eyes. "Looks like my friend has gone and lost her mind."

"Why—cuz she's havin' a little fun?"

Before I can answer the question, I notice a woman approaching our table. She has a huge bouquet of roses. If not for the fact that she appears to be in her midfifties, I'd assume she was a groupie out to impress the rap stars at our table. Instead, I figure she's got to be one of those people who peddles roses in clubs just like this one.

"Lishelle Jennings?" The woman looks from me to Claudia.

I'm completely shocked that the woman has mentioned my name, but recover after a couple seconds. "That's me."

"These are for you." She's beaming as she presents me with the roses. "Courtesy of the flower shop here at the Venetian."

I accept them. "I don't understand."

But the woman is already walking away.

"Read the card," Roger tells me.

I lift the card from the bouquet, open the envelope and read aloud, "I hope you find this a better way to approach a woman."

Looking at Roger, I laugh.

"Well?" he asks.

"It's definitely better," I tell him. "If not a little typical."

"Ouch."

"Hey." As if my hand has a mind of its own, it places itself on Roger's leg. When he meets my gaze, I say, "I didn't mean to sound so ungrateful. The flowers are beautiful. Thank you."

Roger leans forward so fast I don't have time to react. He kisses me—a soft, teasing kiss that goes on for several seconds. Never once does his tongue enter my mouth, but I can taste the passion.

"What was that for?" I ask. I'm a little breathless.

"Ever drop water into a pan of hot oil?"

"Uh-huh."

"You see how it sizzles? Well, that's me and you." Roger links fingers with mine. "The passion between us is like that sizzle."

"You think there's passion between us? You're jumping to a lot of—"

Damn, Roger kisses me again. He draws my bottom lip into his mouth and suckles it. The sensual movement has my body tingling.

When he pulls away from me, I lean forward to reach for my cosmopolitan. But Roger grips my arm, stopping me. "No, no. I ain't gonna let you avoid what's happening between us."

"What exactly do you think is happening?" I ask him. But I know. And, honestly, I couldn't be more surprised.

Maybe it's the friggin' cosmopolitans. Or maybe it's the seductive power of Sin City.

Roger runs the tip of his finger over the top of my hand and says simply, "Sizzle."

"Okay," I admit. "Maybe there is some *sizzle* between us."

"So what we gonna do about it?"

I don't answer, not with words. Instead, I snake my hand around his head and pull him close. This kiss isn't gentle or reserved. It's full-blown passion, and by the time we're done, we're both panting.

"Do you want to fuck?" I boldly ask.

Roger takes my hand, puts it on his crotch. Through his baggy jeans, I can feel his erection. It's as hard as a slab of granite.

"Very nice," I tell him. "I'll bet lots of young groupies have sampled it."

"You keep talkin' 'bout young. Like you're too old for me or sumthin'. Or like you think I like 'em young." He pauses. "Think I can't appreciate a beautiful, mature woman like yourself?"

"Pussy's pussy, right?"

Roger releases my hand as though he's just been burned. "This ain't just about pussy. I can get pussy anywhere." He gestures to the club at large. I take a good look at the people around us. Suddenly it's mostly women. Young women in cute little outfits.

"Max," Roger calls out, and one of the linebackers turns. Roger beckons him over, and the man comes. What Roger says to Max, however, I don't know, because he whispers it in his ear.

I watch as Max heads toward a very attractive girl in a short orange dress. She looks part black and part Asian.

My breath snags in my chest. Has Roger sent Max over to her to invite her to our table?

I get my answer a moment later, when a stricken look streaks across the girl's face. I'm not sure what Max has said to her, but she juts her chin out, defiant. Almost like she's ready to do battle. But the friend who is with her takes hold of her arm and pulls the girl away. The young beauty storms off.

I turn to Roger. "Okay, I'll bite. What was that about?"

"Everywhere I went today, that girl was there."

"And you don't like attractive young girls following you around?"

"Not when they start stalkin' me and shit. Know what she said to me?" Roger leans close, and his warm breath tickles my ear. "She came up to me and whispered, 'I wanna taste your dick. Give you the best blow job of your life.' You believe that?"

"Uh, yeah. That's typical, isn't it? Don't you get that kind of offer everywhere you go?"

"It don't make me feel good, if that's what you think."

I eye Roger suspiciously. "Most guys would be in a bathroom with her so fast…"

"Naw."

"Really?" I ask, wondering if he's trying to pull my leg.

Roger shakes his head. "Girl like that—she dangerous. She ain't into me. She's into any guy with some fame. A girl like that'll cry rape an' try to take you for all you got."

"I understand that," I tell him. And I do. As much as I'd like to believe that a guy in his position would take advantage of all the sex offered to him, I know firsthand that as a person in the public eye you have to be careful what you do and with whom you associate. You can't accept all favors people offer you, because some of them come with strings you didn't bargain for.

The music switches from an upbeat dance tune to a heavy hip-hop bass. Frenzied cheers erupt in the club. And then I realize that it's one of Rugged's songs. They know he's in the house.

I look at him, and we both chuckle. Then he extends his hand. "This is my song. If I can't dance to it, I can't expect anyone else to."

I accept his offered hand, and Roger leads me to the dance floor, where we move our bodies to the rhythmic beat. The guy really knows how to get down. In fact, he gives me a run for the money with all his hip swaying and fancy footwork.

I find myself laughing. A lot. I never would have thought it, but Roger is a lot of fun. Along with his dance moves, he makes these silly faces that have me cracking up. God, I'm laughing like I'm young and carefree again.

When the second Rugged song begins, I kick off my slingbacks so I can really get down. My hips go into high gear and I thrust my hands in the air. My entire body is feeling the magnetic beat.

It's not hard to understand why Rugged is so popular.

I do a half spin so that my back is facing Roger. And now I get a little more seductive, running my fingers through my hair, and tossing coy glances over my shoulder at him.

When his body touches mine, I feel a zap of pleasure. I can no longer deny the truth—something about the guy turns me on.

He grips my hips and pulls me close. His cock presses against my ass, and I get this tantalizing visual of Roger pushing my skirt up to my waist and fucking me from behind.

I think of Claudia's words, that young guys in bed are like the Energizer Bunny. And I can't help wondering if Roger would be able to keep me satisfied all night long....

His hands slowly move higher, to my rib cage, and stop there. But I'm feeling frisky so I link my fingers with his and guide his hands even higher—to the swell of my breasts, then over my nipples. My clit is pulsing wildly. It needs to be stroked. Licked.

"Girl, you got a brotha on fire!" Roger exclaims.

I let my head fall backward onto his shoulder. He glances at me, and our gazes lock. I read in his eyes what I know I'm feeling—that we're ready to fuck.

As he turns me around in his arms, I have to hold myself back from running my tongue along his neck. I love his scent. It oozes strength and sexuality.

I'm almost about to whisper something in Roger's ear when Claudia comes up to us.

"I'm gonna go upstairs," she tells me.

"You're leaving?" I excuse myself from Roger and walk

with her a few feet away. "What about that bodyguard? It looked like you two were getting very cozy."

She shrugs. "I'm not feeling it."

"No?"

"No."

"Oh." I honestly feel bad for her. I'd like to see Claudia let go of her reservations and have a fling.

"You're gonna be okay with Rugged?" she asks me.

"I'm fine," I tell her. "I can't believe I'm saying this, but I'm feeling it. Maybe I'm just feeling the effects of too much alcohol!"

"So you're cool?" Claudia asks. "You're going to stay with him?"

"Uh-huh."

She winks. "Enjoy yourself."

"I plan on it."

At the door to his suite, Roger says to his bodyguards, "I'm cool for the night. You guys can take off."

Cool for the night…the implication that we'll be fucking all night long makes me flush. I can't believe I'm upstairs with a rapper, but what I experienced with my masseuse was simply foreplay. My body needs so much more.

Roger closes the door and turns around. My breath catches in my throat as he walks toward me.

"Want something to drink?" he asks me. "I've got Cristal in the fridge."

"I kinda just want to fuck," I admit. Brazen, I know, but what's the point in beating around the bush?

"We'll get there," Roger tells me. "Trust me. We don't have to rush."

"All right."

My answer seems to satisfy him, and he heads to the kitchen area and opens the fridge. A minute later he returns to me with a champagne flute filled with champagne.

"Having another drink is probably not a good idea," I tell him. My head already feels like it's stuffed with cotton balls. "And, hey, where's your glass? Still trying to get me drunk?"

Roger places a finger over my mouth to quiet me, then he takes a sip of the champagne. "I wanted to share this with you. One glass. Symbolizing how tonight we'll be one."

I can't help it, I laugh. It's so…so damned corny.

But the look of hurt on Roger's face tells me he's entirely serious about the romantic gesture.

"You don't take me seriously, do you?" he asks.

I don't answer right away. Then I say, "I feel like I'm in the middle of a rap video."

"That so?"

"I don't know. What do you expect me to say? That this is about love? You and I both know that's not the case."

Now Roger lowers the glass onto the coffee table. "I see."

I get a weird vibe…a vibe that tells me he's pissed. "What do you see?" I ask him.

He faces me and says, "You know—maybe you ought to go."

For several seconds I don't say a word. I'm not sure what to say.

"You want me to go?" I finally ask.

"According to you, I could have any girl up in here, right? It's not about you. It's about getting off."

Now I really don't know how to respond.

"That's what I thought." Roger starts walking away from me. "Suddenly I'm feeling kinda tired. You can see yourself out."

Oh my God. He's kicking me out.

I hurry toward him, stepping in front of him and placing a hand on his chest. "So that's it?"

"You think I live and die by my cock? That I don't care who I sleep with as long as she's got a pussy?"

"I didn't say that." I don't dare admit that I certainly thought it.

"You didn't have to."

"I'm sorry, Roger. It's just that…at my age, I've heard a lot of lines. I've been through a lot of bullshit."

Now Roger grips my shoulders. "When will you stop throwing the age thing in my face? I'm not a boy." He takes my hand and forces it onto his penis. "Trust me, this is all man."

His eyes lock on mine, and I'm left breathless at what I see in their depths.

"You really like me?" I ask softly.

"Why the hell you think I came to Vegas?"

"For the same reason anyone comes to Vegas. To hang out, do some gambling, maybe see some strippers."

"Fuck that shit," Roger says. "I came 'cuz of you."

That shocks me. Totally. "You're telling me that you came to Las Vegas because…because of *me*?"

"Yeah."

I'm not sure I should believe him. If he's lying, he's damn smooth.

"But how'd you know?"

"Your girl Claudia. Her cousin told me y'all would be here. Mentioned it in passing. And I figured…" He shrugs.

"I'm sorry," I apologize, meaning it. If he's lying to me, then he's one of the best damn liars alive. Next to Glenn. But I believe him. Believe that he likes me enough to have tracked me down.

"What're you sorry for?" he asks me, not like he's curious, but in a tone that says he wants to hear me explain that I understand how I've misjudged him.

"I'm sorry for being judgmental. For being a bitch. Like I said, I've dealt with some guys who have been less than honest."

Something changes then. Roger touches my face, a delicate gesture that tells me he no longer wants me to leave.

"I'm not like most guys," he tells me.

I smile. "And I bet you'll prove it to me, too." I kiss his palm. "All night long."

"Maybe some day." Roger pulls his hand from my mouth. "But not tonight."

My eyes widen at that. "Not tonight?"

"Nope. Not tonight."

I pause for a second, wait for Roger to laugh and say the joke's on me. But he doesn't.

"Are you telling me," I begin, "that we're not gonna fuck?"

"In the future—maybe. But tonight—uh-uh."

"You're still mad at me."

"Naw, I ain't mad at ya."

"Then why—"

"'Cuz I know that there's a part of you, even if it's a small part, that thinks I'm playin' you. A part that doesn't trust that I'm into you."

"I thought we were past that."

"Tell me I'm lyin'."

I stare up at Roger and, God help me, I can't tell him he's lying. *Fuck.*

"That's what I thought."

"Do I trust you the way I would some guy I've known for years? No." The hypocrisy of my statement, given that

I trusted Glenn and he royally screwed me over, slaps me in the face. "But that doesn't mean I don't trust you enough to fuck you—"

"Ain't gonna happen."

Now I place my hands on Roger's chest. I'm suddenly desperate to get him naked, to fuck him wildly and end my body's suffering.

He takes my hands into his and removes them from his chest. "Look, if we stay in touch, and things change…" He shrugs.

"Things like what?"

Roger kisses me on the forehead, a chaste kiss that lets me know we definitely won't be getting naked. "You get some sleep, okay?"

Though I'm crushed, I do have some pride. I'm not about to beg.

"Okay," I say softly.

Roger puts his hand on my lower back and guides me to the door. "We'll be in touch," is all he says as he sees me out.

And I'm left standing in the hallway not quite believing what just happened.

Thirteen

Claudia

When I get upstairs, I knock on Annelise's door. Then knock again.

There's no answer.

Resigned to the fact that I have no one to talk to, I head into my suite, plop down on the living room sofa and turn on the television. I channel surf for about five minutes before I wonder why the hell I'm upstairs alone.

I think about what Lishelle said to me about Arnold—that if he left me with his number, there's still hope we can connect. I'm not sure why I'm still thinking about him, other than the fact that I regret a missed opportunity.

Maybe all I really need is to bring out the rabbit. Give myself an orgasm and then go to bed. I head to the bedroom area determined to do just that. But as I look at the king-size bed with its canopy covering, I suddenly realize that I don't want to be alone.

I go to the night table and find the card Arnold gave me. Fingering it, I contemplate what to do. It's not like I expect him to be free right now, not on a Friday night in Las Vegas. He could be admiring some other woman's pussy right now, making her private fantasy a reality.

He won't be around, I tell myself as I punch in the digits to the number he gave me. *I'm only humoring myself by calling.*

I truly believe that, which is why I'm stunned when a male says hello. "Arnold?" I ask.

"Yeah. Who's this?"

I pause. "Arnold, it's Claudia. We met this—"

"Hey, Claudia." I can hear a smile in his voice. "I didn't think you were going to call."

"I almost didn't. I figured you'd be busy. You probably have plans, right?"

"Actually, I don't."

"No massages scheduled?"

"If you want me tonight, just say the word."

If I want him…

"I want you." I blow out a shaky breath, unable to believe how easily those words came out of my mouth.

"Then I'm on my way. Want me to bring anything over? Beer or wine?"

"Just yourself." I run my fingers down my neck, to the area between my breasts. "How long will it take you to get here?"

"If I take a shower now—"

"Take it here. With me."

There's a pause. Then Arnold says, "Give me ten minutes."

My heart thunders in my chest when there's a knock on my door exactly ten minutes later. I'm not sure why. Arnold has already seen me more exposed than most people ever will. Why the heck should I be nervous?

But I am, and I hesitate a few seconds before I get up from the sofa to head for the door. By the time I reach the hallway there's more rapping, this time louder. I take a deep breath and swing open the door.

And there stands Arnold, dressed in a form-fitting black T-shirt that shows off his beautifully defined torso, and complements his deep tan. And, Lord, the man smells incredible.

He smiles at me. "Hello, sexy."

"You look…" My voice trails off on a breathless sigh.

I can see the edge of a tattoo on his arm, but I can't make out what it is. All I know is that everything about Arnold oozes bad boy.

And I love it.

He steps forward, placing his hands on my waist as he does. It's as though his hands are a live wire, sending an electrical charge through my body.

He wastes no time running his lips along my neck to the sensitive spot beneath my ear. I moan softly, right before Arnold gently pulls my earlobe between his teeth and nibbles on it.

Yeah, this is a guy who knows how to fuck. A guy who knows exactly how to please a woman.

My hands find his chest. They rest somewhat tentatively on his hard pecs. Part of me wants to pull his shirt off, push him onto the floor and ride him wildly all night long. The other part is unsure that I should even be doing this.

Arnold moves his mouth to the other side of my neck, walking forward as he does, moving me further into the suite. I hear the door click shut.

Arnold must sense my hesitation, because he's gentle as

his lips travel down my neck. He pauses briefly, as though waiting for permission. When I say nothing, he continues, kissing a path down to the area between my breasts.

"Can I tell you something?" I ask. My voice is breathy.

"Sure." He continues to kiss my skin.

"This is going to sound stupid, and I'm not sure why I'm saying it, but I've never...never been with a white guy before. Well, never fucked one."

Arnold suckles on my neck. "Then you're in for a pleasant surprise."

"Oh, I don't doubt that." If he can work his cock as well as he's working his mouth, I will be very satisfied.

"And those myths about white guys and size?"

"Uh-huh?" I ask.

"False." Arnold takes my hand and places it on his crotch. "At least where I'm concerned."

"I can feel that."

"How do you want it, baby?" he asks me. "Nice and slow? Hard and raunchy?"

"I want it hard. And I want it over and over and over again."

My answer seems to please him, if the megawatt smile on his face is any indication. That I can ask for what I want and he's willing to give it empowers me.

And turns me on big-time.

The best part about this suite, aside from the king-size bed, is the extralarge Jacuzzi tub. And that's where I lead Arnold for the first part of what I hope will be an all night fantasy turned reality.

"You said you needed to shower," I begin as we enter the bathroom. "But I set a bath instead. With lots of bubbles, as you can see. Is that all right?"

"I love bubbles."

The way he says that is as erotic as if he's just told me that he wants to eat my pussy.

"Good to hear."

I pull my dress over my head. Arnold just watches me, and man if I don't get a rush from that. There's something thrilling about taking your clothes off in front of a guy for the first time. One you know will become your lover in a matter of minutes.

"I know I saw it this morning," Arnold begins, "but your body is perfection."

I shoot him a coy look. Without my dress, I'm wearing only my thong and my sexy-as-hell Jimmy Choos. Knowing how sinful I must look, I turn slowly, neatly folding my dress as I do. I lay the dress on the bathroom counter.

When I spin back around, I gasp. Arnold is right there, not more than half a foot directly in front of me.

"Rich girl, right?"

"Excuse me?"

"The way you folded your dress so nicely. The expensive watch on your wrist."

"You mean my timepiece," I correct him.

"Rich folks. They always have fancy names for ordinary things."

"Is that a problem?"

He runs his palms over my flat belly, his sensual touch telling me it isn't. "I'm just trying to figure out if I should do all the things to you I'd like. If you can handle it."

I think of Adam, all the freaky sex acts he introduced me to. Then I forcefully pull the snap open on Arnold's jeans. "You have no clue what I can handle. And that's the truth."

I force his jeans down his hips and run my fingers up one leg as I bite his thigh.

"Fuck, the way your ass looks when you're squatting like that. You are mad beautiful."

I lift his T-shirt and dip my tongue into his belly button, then slowly rise. As I do, Arnold pulls his shirt off. My eyes slowly roam over his upper body, noting the large tattoo of a scorpion on the right side of his chest. Now I see that the tattoo on his left arm is that of a topless woman on her haunches.

Slowly I finger the tattoo of the scorpion. "I'm a Scorpio," he explains. "Guaranteed to please," he adds whispering hotly in my ear. "Every time."

Damn, I want to be naked already. I slip my thumbs beneath the waist of my thong, but Arnold places his hands on mine.

"No," he says. "Let me."

But he doesn't pull my thong off. Not right away. Instead, he lowers his head and takes one if my nipples into his mouth. He grazes it with his teeth, flicks his tongue over one, then the other. The feeling is utterly delicious.

I place my hands onto his shoulders and moan. I explore the hard planes and muscles of his shoulders while he nibbles his way down to my thong underwear. He secures the waistband in his teeth.

"Rip it," I tell him. "Rip it off."

I don't have to tell him twice. Arnold grabs one side of my Victoria's Secret thong and easily snaps the elastic. Then he does the same with the other side. He pulls the fabric away and covers my pussy with his hand.

"When I told you this morning that you had the sweetest pussy I've ever seen, I wasn't lying." He strokes my clit with his thumb. "I love the way your clit peeks out from your luscious lips. It's not shy. It knows what it wants."

A shiver snakes down my spine. I expect Arnold to go down on me, but he doesn't. Instead, he rises and kicks his jeans off, then strips out of his boxers. I allow myself a moment to ogle his beautiful, erect penis before I bend to take off my shoes.

My walk is slow and seductive as I cross the room. I step into the tub and slip down into the hot water and bubbles.

"Get in," I tell Arnold.

He does, easing his body across from mine. I position one of my feet between his legs and brush it across his cock.

"Would you believe it if I said that I was thinking about you all day long, regretting that I hadn't fucked you this morning?"

"Would you believe if I said I turned down going out with some friends tonight—because I was hoping to hear from you?"

"Really?" I ask doubtfully.

"Really. I've been dreaming of your pussy all day." He strokes my leg. "I couldn't bring myself to accept that I wouldn't get to know it a little better."

"By the end of the night, you'll know it a lot better."

"You're not a shy one, are you?"

"I told you—you have no clue what I can handle."

Arnold narrows his eyes as he looks at me, as though he's trying to determine how serious I am.

"One thing." He holds up a finger. "Tell me one thing that no man has ever done to you. One sexual thing that might've gotten you off but you've never asked for it before. I want to do that to you."

I stroke his penis with my foot, then inch it upward along his chest until it appears above the bubbles. I skim my big toe along his bottom lip. "No one has ever done this," I tell him. "Sucked my toes."

He holds my foot in his hand. "No?" he asks, his tone saying he's surprised. "And damn if you don't have the prettiest feet."

Arnold takes my big toe into his mouth and doesn't just suck it—he makes love to it. Gently nibbles on it, suckles it softly. Flicks his tongue over it the way I imagine he would a clitoris.

I close my eyes and savor the pleasure. Never would I have considered my feet an erogenous zone, but damn, this toe-sucking stimulates me. Maybe it's about power—enjoying the feeling of a gorgeous guy literally worshipping your feet.

My body temperature starts to rise, and it's not just because the water in the tub is so hot. Arnold excites me, turns me on in a way I didn't imagine possible for a guy I just met.

The rich girl and the bad boy.

A totally appealing fantasy.

As Arnold works his tongue over my other foot, I play with my nipples. The rush of pleasure is overpowering, and I want more.

Need more.

I slip my hand into the water and run a finger over my sex. My nub is swollen and hard. My pussy is slick with my juices.

Lifting my hand out of the water, I move toward Arnold. I offer him my fingers. "Taste me. Taste how much I want you."

Arnold takes three of my fingers into his mouth and greedily sucks on them. He laps up my essence without reservation. It's so erotic I almost come.

"I want more," he tells me.

I dip my hand into the water, finger myself, and offer him more of me.

"More," Arnold rasps when he's had his fill.

Every time I touch my pussy, I don't want to stop. As Arnold sucks on my fingers once more, I say, "I just thought of something else…something else I haven't done."

"Anything you want, baby. I'm game."

"I…" I can't believe I'm going to say what I'm going to say, but I want raunch. I want naughty, uninhibited sex. "I want to masturbate, and I don't want you to touch me. I just want you to watch."

Standing, I begin stroking my clit.

"Holy fuck, you are beautiful."

I sit on the tub's edge and spread my legs, giving Arnold a complete view of my sex. I rub my fingers over my clitoris before pushing them into my folds. "I want to come like this. With you watching."

Honestly, I can't tell you how exquisitely sexy I feel doing this. It's so friggin' naughty. It's taboo. But exposing myself to a stranger this way is the most incredible thrill I've ever experienced.

Moans escape my lips as I finger myself, massage my nub, and tweak my nipple. Arnold's eyes never leave my pussy.

My breathing starts to quicken. Arnold moves forward in the water.

"No," I tell him. "No touching. Let me come…with only your eyes on me…"

Arnold keeps moving, positioning his face about a foot from my pussy. "Jeez, I don't know if I can do this. Watch you and not touch you. I want you to come with my tongue on your clit."

I moan when Arnold puts his hands on my legs. I want to tell him no, that his eyes are enough, but I'm powerless to say a word. I can only watch as he moves forward and buries his head between my thighs. He presses his hot tongue on my clit, licks it as though it's a lollipop.

My orgasm catches me off guard, takes hold of my body and doesn't let go for several seconds. My legs tremble as I cry out, scream Arnold's name, and all the while he doesn't stop suckling me, making one exquisite orgasm roll into a second one.

Finally my moans subside and are replaced by my heavy breathing. Only then does Arnold's hot tongue relent.

Standing, he grins and reaches for my hand. "You ready to get out of here?"

Still taking in deep breaths, I only nod. I'm too spent from my orgasm to do anything else.

Arnold gets out of the tub and takes a thick towel off the rack. I stand as he approaches me, and he wraps the towel around me. I appreciate the gesture, as I'd started to feel chilly.

My eyes follow Arnold's body as he pads across the marble floor. There's a robe hanging on the back of the bathroom door, and he brings it to me.

"You wear it," I tell him.

He slips it on. "How do I look?"

"Sexy."

He makes a show of modeling the robe, and even checks himself out in the mirror.

At the bathroom counter, he picks up the small bottle of lotion. A moment later, he lifts his jeans and digs a couple condoms out of the pocket. The robe is open as he saunters over to me and his cock is hard. Ready to pleasure me.

He gives me a deep, urgent kiss. I want to drop my towel and let him fuck me right here, but Arnold apparently doesn't want that. Instead he takes my hand and leads me out of the bathroom to the king-size bed.

He sits, and I sit beside him. Once again we start to neck. Kissing like this is normally reserved for intimate couples, but with Arnold, it doesn't feel strained. It feels incredible.

His tongue sweeps over mine, delves deep into my mouth. Arnold's hands slowly move up my arm, to my neck, then to my face. He frames it delicately as he continues to kiss me. Kiss me like we've done this a million times.

A moan sounds deep in Arnold's throat, and he pushes his body forward, forcing me backward on the bed. His lips move from my mouth to my neck, across my jawline to my earlobe.

"You're making me crazy," I tell him. And he is. He knows just how to touch me to make my body sing.

When Arnold eases his body off mine, the cool air hits me. I sigh with disappointment. I want him to stay on me, spread my legs and fuck me. Instead he opens the bottle of lotion.

"We can do that later," I tell him. I'm way past wanting more foreplay, and the massage he gave me earlier already worked wonders for me.

Arnold pulls my towel apart. "You know what I want?"

"You gave me a fantastic massage this morning," I tell him.

"That's not what I want." He lathers lotion between his palms, then runs his hands up one of my legs. He stops when he reaches the top of my thigh and rolls me over onto my stomach. Now he rubs his hands over my butt.

There's a pause before I feel the cold sensation of fresh lotion on my behind. "This is what I want," he says. He skims his fingers over the crack of my ass. "To fuck you like this. Come in your ass."

A delicious jolt hits my body.

"You said you wanted naughty," he says after a moment.

"I do," I tell him. "I just didn't—"

"Didn't what?" I hear the sound of Arnold opening and rolling on the condom. When he finishes, he stretches his body over mine. He fingers my pussy from behind before resting the head of his cock there. "You didn't think I'd fuck you like this?"

As Arnold says the words, the thrusts his cock inside me, and I gasp.

His cock deep inside me, he doesn't move. "You didn't think I'd want this sweet pussy?"

"I...I didn't know..."

His lips brush the back of my neck, and a shiver runs down my spine. Finally Arnold starts to move, pulling back, thrusting deep. Pulling back, thrusting deeper. Going harder, faster.

"How'd you get such a sweet pussy? You feel fucking amazing."

Lying like this, with my legs closed, and his cock burrowed inside me—seriously, nothing has ever felt this good. He pulls out, slips back in, pulls out, enters me again.

"Fuck, Arnold...that's my spot, that's my spot!"

And just like that, my body starts to quiver. I'm back in orgasm heaven.

In a quick motion, Arnold withdraws his cock and pulls me up onto my knees. He licks my pussy from behind while it pulsates with sweet pleasure. I whimper, moan, cry his name.

His tongue travels from my pussy to my ass. Sucks there for a moment and then bites my flesh.

"I want to fuck you this way." He spreads my ass wide. "I *need* to fuck you this way."

"Yes, baby." The words exit my mouth on their own. "Fuck me any way you want."

I hear the sound of Arnold lathering his hands with lotion. Then he's rubbing the scented cream over me. He inserts one finger into my ass, gently stretching me.

"How does that feel?"

"Good…it's good."

More lotion. Arnold inserts another finger. The pleasure intensifies, and I moan.

Even though I've done this before, I'm tense. A little scared that it will hurt like when I did this with Adam. But Arnold takes his time, fingers me, adds more lotion, stretches me gradually.

He puts another finger inside me, the pressure building. Arnold groans shakily. "God, that feels so good? Is it okay for you?"

His words shock me. "You've got it in me?"

"The tip is in. I want to push it all the way."

I can't believe it feels so comfortable. So fucking good.

Arnold reaches for my face and angles it upward. Then he kisses me, all tongue. My breath comes in sharp spurts as Arnold eases his cock farther into my ass, matching what his tongue is doing in my mouth.

"Fuck yeah," he says as he completely enters me. "Claudia, I loved your pussy, but your ass…"

He moves inside me slowly at first, but gradually picks up speed. It's an odd but pleasurable sensation, the way he fills my ass so completely.

The momentum builds, and soon he's fucking my ass as hard as he did my pussy. My moans are louder, more intense, one on top of the other. I drop my head onto the pillow, my butt still high, giving Arnold even more access to my ass.

And, the sensations are far more powerful with me positioned this way. I can feel Arnold's cock hitting my G-spot from the opposite wall. My whole body thrums as though it's one big G-spot.

"Can you come like this?" Arnold asks me.

"Fuck yes!"

Arnold grips my hips and goes at me hard.

"I can't take…much…more." I grip the bed sheet and press my mouth flat against the pillow as sounds of passion erupt from my throat.

And when my body starts to tense, it's like I'm caught in the mouth of a volcano, ready to be thrust forth in a spray of red-hot heat.

"Fuck, baby," Arnold rasps. "I'm gonna blow!"

His words set me free. Then I'm flying, my body molten hot lava vaulting into pure bliss with Arnold.

This is a place where I have no control. My moans are so loud I'm sure someone will hear, but I don't care. I can't care.

I can't stop coming.

When we both stop moaning and groaning, Arnold pulls out and collapses on the bed beside me. I face him, stare into his eyes. I've never shared so much of myself with a stranger before.

Arnold runs a finger along my cheek. Smiles.

Then we kiss, and I know my incredible night with this man is just beginning.

Fourteen

Samera

I'm way past tipsy, but alert enough to know that Rusty is groping my ass on a public elevator and we haven't hit the stop button.

One of his hands slips into my thong, and he wildly massages my clit, moaning like he's about to come in his pants.

A ping sounds, and I whip my head around to see the elevator door opening. It's too late to get out of the compromising position, and when a middle-aged couple sees us, the woman gasps in horror. Rusty doesn't release me, and the couple doesn't step onto the elevator. When the door closes, both Rusty and I burst into laughter.

"You are a naughty boy," I tell him, really enjoying his lust for me. It feels good to forget about my problems, to concentrate on satisfying my body's carnal urges.

"Then you can spank me when we get to the room."

I swat his behind. "Why wait?"

When the elevator stops again, we hurry off. Rusty pulls me to the right. His room is the second door down on the eleventh floor. Before he can open it, I brazenly grope him. I run my fingers down the backs of his thighs and squeeze his firm ass.

Rusty opens the door and we tumble inside. No sooner than I slam the door, Rusty grips my shoulders and jerks me to him. I feel his cock—hard, and what I guess to be about eight inches in length. Just what I need to send me into orgasm heaven.

This guy's hands are superfast. He pulls me down to the floor, and before I hit the ground on top of him, he's got my thong halfway down my thighs. He spins me over onto my back and spreads my legs. And then his hot tongue is all over my clit.

"Holy shit." I grip his hair, hold him in place as he eats my pussy. "Oh, fuck!"

His hungry moans turn me on. Rusty spreads my lips wide, then sucks on me like he's competing in an Olympic sport and determined to win. He's not gentle; in fact, he's a bit rough. But I can handle it. I don't want gentle lovemaking right now.

I want wild fucking.

"Your pussy…God, I love this pussy."

"Stick your fingers inside me!"

Rusty's tongue doesn't let up its delicious pleasure as he inserts one, then two fingers into my sex.

"More!" I cry out. I want it hard, I want it rough….

Rusty slips two more fingers inside me, and I moan long and hard. I lift my head and gaze down at his head between my thighs.

"You taste fucking great." He breathes raggedly. "I want to eat your pussy all night long."

I drop my head backward and arch my hips, gyrating

them against Rusty's mouth. He thrusts his fingers harder and faster, and soon I'm moaning like a veritable porn star.

"You like that?" he asks. I look at him again, and he meets my gaze. He moves four fingers in and out of me with lightening speed.

"Fuck, yeah."

With his other hand, he plays with my anus. "Have you ever had two guys inside you at the same time?" he asks.

"Yes…" I moan.

"Fuck, I think I just creamed my pants. Baby, I am gonna fuck you all night. In your pussy, in your ass."

I moan in agreement.

"But not yet." Rusty drives his fingers inside me as far as they'll go. "Man, I want to put my whole fucking fist in you."

"Do it," I tell him. I want to be so lost in sexual pleasure that I forget the outside world.

In goes his thumb, and I gasp. It hurts, but I don't want him to stop. Slowly Rusty tries to work his whole hand into my pussy. I moan and pant, wanting him to fuck me in a way no one has before.

But the pain is suddenly too much, and I can't take it anymore.

"Stop…"

"I'm almost in," he tells me.

"No—"

"You are so fucking sexy—"

Now I jerk my body backward. "Fuck you, I said to stop!"

Seeing how serious I am, Rusty pulls out his fingers and rests them on my knee.

"Baby—"

"Don't you fucking do that again, you hear me? When I tell you to stop, you fucking stop!"

"Okay, okay."

I stare at him, try to figure out if the guy is a creep or just got carried away.

"I'm sorry," he says, and he sounds earnest.

"I make the rules, got it?"

"You make the rules, baby."

"Kiss me," I tell him.

When he hesitates, I pounce on him, knocking him onto his back. His hands settle on my hips. "From now on, this is my game—all right?" I think about the woman I am onstage, the one in the Dominatrix outfit with the whip. "What I tell you to do, you do. Understand?"

Rusty nods.

"Take your clothes off," I demand. I ease my body off of his. "Now."

A smile spreads on Rusty's sexy face. "I get it. I think I'm going to like this."

"Stop talking and get naked."

Rusty starts to unbutton his shirt. As he does I spread my legs wide and massage my clit.

"You are fucking delicious," Rusty tells me, his eyes on my fingers. "You keep that up, and I'm gonna come in my pants."

My fingers move faster. "Let me see your cock. Let me see how large it is."

"You don't have to worry about that. I'm hung like a horse."

"I'll be the judge of that."

Rusty pushes his pants and boxers down, and juts his penis forward, as if to prove to me he's all I need and more.

"Nice." I lower myself to my knees.

"Nice?"

I take him in my hands. "It's beautiful." I flick my tongue

over the tip of his throbbing shaft. "Fucking gorgeous. I am gonna ride you so hard, baby…"

Rusty rasps loudly, grips my hair. I take his cock deep into my throat, as far as I can, then pull back to run my tongue around the tip of his shaft. I lift my eyes to gaze at him, and his expression says he is in absolute heaven.

Now I move away from him. When his eyes fly open, I say, "The bedroom. Let's get off this floor."

"Don't like it rough?"

"Baby, *I* defined *rough*."

A rush of pleasure flows through me as I see the look in Rusty's eyes. He looks at me like he's never met anyone quite like me before, and that makes me feel powerful.

I own him. He'll do anything I fucking want.

He gathers me in his arms and cements his mouth to mine. I wrap my legs around his waist, and he carries me like that to the bedroom.

When we're there, I tell him, "Lay me on the bed and eat my pussy. Don't stop till you make me come."

"As long as you need, sweetheart. I can stay down there for hours. But first, let me get out of my pants."

"Ask my permission," I tell him bluntly.

"Samera." He draws out my name on a sexy breath. "May I take off the rest of my clothes?"

"Yes. You may." I use the time to slip my dress over my head, exposing my breasts.

"Please—leave the shoes on," Rusty begs me.

"Of course." No doubt about it, guys love these stilettos.

While Rusty gets completely out of his pants and briefs, I lick my fingers and massage my clitoris.

Fully naked, Rusty faces me, and I can't help but be impressed.

"My, my, what a nice cock you have," I chime, in a tone reminiscent of Little Red Riding Hood. Truly, it's awesome. Not only is it a good length, the girth is magnificent. I can't wait to take him inside me.

"Eat me, Rusty. Nice and slow."

Rusty positions himself on the bed between my legs and does exactly what I asked of him. He licks my pussy with gentle flicks of his tongue, then suckles me softly. I arch my back and whimper, because nothing gets me off more than a guy sucking softly on my clit.

Rusty spreads me wide and runs his tongue completely over my opening. Then he dips his tongue inside me, a little at first. He takes his time going further, until his tongue is as far inside me as it can get.

"Oh, fuck. Rusty, you are so fucking hot. So—"

My words end on a cry when Rusty sucks my clit into his mouth again. The delicious pressure inside me builds. Any second, and I'm gonna come.

"Oh baby, just like that. Don't stop…"

A few more seconds is all I can take before my body explodes. It's so intense, my moans turn into a scream.

I'm too weak from my orgasm to be in control, and Rusty knows this. Not giving me a moment to catch my breath, he settles between my thighs, spreads my folds with one hand, then enters me in one hard thrust. It leaves me breathless, all thoughts in my mind one big scramble.

"Fuck, you've got a sweet pussy." Rusty's movements are quick, each one leaving me gasping in ecstasy. "And you've got the most spectacular tits I've ever seen," he goes on. He reaches for one of my nipples and tweaks it.

I can't believe I'm going to come again so quickly, but Rusty's movements make my body start to tense once more. He's fast, he's hard and he hits my G-spot with every stroke.

"Do I own this pussy?" he asks.

"Y-y-yes! Yes, you fucking own this pussy!"

A splash of cold disappointment washes over me when Rusty pulls his cock from my vagina. I whimper in protest—until he covers my pussy with his mouth.

"Come again, baby. Just like this. I want to taste your sweet juices in my mouth."

"No…no, please…" I pant.

"In my mouth, baby. I want you—" He licks me. "Weak and quivering—" He suckles my clit. "And calling my name while I suck on you."

He pushes a finger inside me and sucks me softly at the same time, and holy fuck, I come again. Harder than before.

More explosive.

And, God help me, I'm lost.

Rusty and I take a break to use the bathroom, catch our breath and regain our energy. Rusty uses the toilet first, and when he's finished, I head in.

Like the bathroom in my suite, this one is also large, though it doesn't boast the large Jacuzzi tub. Still, if we decide to take our fucking from the bedroom to the bathroom, the shower stall is certainly big enough.

I've been with a lot of guys, and no doubt about it, Rusty ranks among the top five for skill and stamina. The man knows how to ram a pussy good and hard. I'll bet his six-pack abs are in part a result of his active sex life, which means he and his wife must have been very happy.

I finish using the toilet and head to the sink. For a

moment, I stare at my reflection in the mirror. My face is flushed, and there's a thin sheen of sweat covering my skin.

First I wash my hands, then splash cold water on my face and neck. The cold on my skin invigorates me, so I do it again, this time also splashing water on my arms.

Sufficiently cooled, I reach for one of the plush hand towels near the sink. As I dry myself, I head back to the bedroom. That's when I hear talking, and at first figure Rusty has turned on the television. It takes me another second to realize that it's Rusty talking, and that he must be on the phone.

Rusty sees me as I appear at the doorway to the bedroom, and winks.

"Gotta go," he says somewhat hurriedly into the phone. "Talk to you later."

Hmm. Interesting.

I know I'm not Rusty's girl, and it's not like we've professed our love for each other. But I wonder if he's got a girlfriend back home, one he'd be brazen enough to call while I was in his bathroom.

I'm no longer wearing my heels, since they were getting in the way. But that doesn't stop me from strutting my stuff toward him the way I would on stage. I plop my ass onto his lap and wrap my arms around his neck.

"So." I nibble on his ear. "Who was that?"

"My buddy. The guy you met downstairs."

"Ahhh." Relief washes over me. I didn't want this to be the moment that I find out I'm the other woman.

"Did you think it was a woman?" Rusty asks.

"It wouldn't surprise me," I confess.

"I get the feeling that not much surprises you."

"And you're right." I cover Rusty's mouth with mine, easing him backward on the bed as I do.

"Haven't had enough?" he asks.

"Not nearly," I whisper hotly into his ear. I reach between his legs and feel his hard-as-concrete erection. "And clearly you haven't either."

Rusty kisses me deeply, and my entire body ignites. I'm one of those women who simply love to fuck. I don't do it just to please my man. Hell, many a man hasn't been able to keep up with my sexual needs. To me, there's nothing sweeter than sharing my body with a man in the most intimate way possible.

Rusty breaks the kiss and rasps in my ear, "I want you to sit on my face so I can eat your pussy while you deep-throat my dick."

"My favorite position." I quickly turn my body and straddle my legs over his face. His hot tongue covers my swollen nub instantly, and I savor the blissful sensation for several seconds before easing my body down to take him in my mouth.

"This pussy, this ass…" Rusty's words trail off on a throaty groan. "I swear, you're the hottest woman I've ever fucked."

I take his cock deep in my mouth, hold it there as I flex my throat around him. At the same time, I massage his balls. After a couple of minutes I can feel him tense, and I'm sure he's going to come. But he moans and pushes me forward, away from his erection. A second later his mouth is on my vagina from behind, running along the opening of my lips to my anus. And just like that, I'm writhing and panting, the tension inside me building.

"Oh, fuck. Rusty, I'm gonna come…again…"

My orgasm is a long and rapturous scream of pleasure.

"Fuuuuuuuuuuuck!"

The sound of a door clicking shut has me whipping my

head upward and effectively kills my orgasm. Since Rusty's mouth is on my pussy, who the hell—

A man appears at the doorway to the bedroom. I recognize him instantly as Rusty's friend. And instead of looking shocked, jumping backward and apologizing for intruding on us at this most intimate moment, he stands there with a smug smile on his face that gives me the creeps.

I quickly scramble backward, grab the bed's comforter and cover what I can of my body. Then my eyes dart to Rusty. Why the hell isn't he trying to cover himself? And more important—why he hasn't he kicked his friend out already?

Horror slowly spreads over me. My God, Rusty is *smirking* at his friend. As if his being here is cool.

"You were right, Rusty," the friend says. "She's one hot bitch."

Bitch? Rusty referred to me as a hot *bitch?*

Okay, so maybe Rusty did say that. I know how guys are. They don't necessarily speak in loving terms when they describe their fuck partners. But still. I'm wondering why the fuck Rusty isn't telling his friend to leave the room.

"Rusty?" I practically croak. Do I have to spell it out for him?

"It's okay," he finally says. "You remember my friend, Peter? The guy you've seen me with a couple times. We were kinda thinking that this would be fun—two guys to please you in every way possible."

Peter starts to undo his belt, making it clear that he and Rusty have already made their decision without including me.

"Are you out of your mind?" I ask Rusty.

"Come on," he says, a chortle in his voice. "You don't strike me as a prude."

"And you didn't strike me as an asshole."

Peter now unzips his dress pants. I edge slowly off the bed, my eyes scanning the floor for my dress. Shit, it's across the room. But it's not like I should be concerned about modesty right now. I have to get out of here.

"Trust me, sweetheart," Peter says. "We are going to give you the best damn night of your life." As if to emphasize his point, he flicks his tongue out in a circular motion.

"I don't know what kind of game the two of you want to play, but I'm not interested." I try not to sound scared, but the truth is, I am. Something has seriously changed right now, and I don't like the vibe.

"I think we forgot to mention that we'd pay her," Peter says to Rusty.

"Hell, yeah." Rusty wiggles his eyebrows at me. "We'll pay you, babe."

"Like I'm some kind of whore?" I gape at Rusty. Where is the guy who was giving me one incredible orgasm after another?

"No one has ever paid you for sex?" Peter asks disbelievingly. "Come on. The minute I looked at you, I could tell you were some kind of pro. And what Rusty told me about how you fuck…"

"You do fuck like a pro," Rusty agrees.

"A *pro?* That's what you think of me?" Maybe I'm being stupid, but the way Rusty spoke to me before his friend arrived…the way he touched me… How can he think of me as a pro?

"So which one is it?" Peter goes on. "Stripper, hooker, porn star?"

Maybe this asshole's been drinking, but how dare he talk to me that way?

"You're a fucking creep," I snap. "And so are you, Rusty."

I drop the bedspread and hustle across the room, but before I make it to my dress, Peter grabs hold of my arm.

"Let go of me, you sick pig!" I jerk my arm, but his grip is too strong.

"Name your price." Rusty, naked and hard, starts slowly toward me. "Whatever you want."

"I don't want shit from you."

"Stop playing games. A woman like you always has a price."

I want to belt him, but I'm too shocked. Too hurt. Too frightened.

Peter drops his pants, exposing an unimpressive erection.

Rusty says, "You told me you've experienced double penetration. That's all we want to do."

"And you can start by sucking my dick," Peter tells me.

"Go to hell." I hastily pull my dress over my head. Fuck, where are my shoes?

Peter grabs me again and roughly pushes me down onto my knees. "You do what I tell you, bitch."

"Fuck you!" I ram my hand as hard as I can into his balls. He screams and goes down.

I scramble to my feet, but now Rusty grabs me by the hair. All this time, I've been hoping that Rusty simply didn't have to guts to tell his friend to stop being an asshole. But he's just as rough with me as Peter was.

"What the hell's the matter with you?" Rusty spits out.

I thrust my elbow backward, and it lands in Rusty's solar plexus. He groans, releases me.

And I take off. I pause only to scoop up my purse near the door before charging out of the room.

I stumble down the hallway, pulling up my dress strap as I do. Behind me I hear loud cursing, but I don't turn around. And I'm not stupid enough to head for the elevator. I have to get out of here, escape before Rusty and his fucking freak of a friend come charging through the door.

I break into a panicked run and sprint to the left, where the door to the stairwell is. Moments later I push through the exit door and barrel down the stairs. I make it down three flights, panting and now crying, before I pause and look upward. No one is coming. I pause a moment longer, drag my hand over my face to dry my tears.

"Fuck you, Rusty."

Certain that no one is following me, I head onto the eighth floor, for the elevators. When it opens and I step on, two twentysomething women eye me with scorn, both their gazes landing on my bare feet.

I ignore them and pound on the Lobby button so the door can hurry and close already.

I get to the lobby and burst through the elevator doors like the devil himself is chasing me. Immediately I'm surrounded by the dinging, ringing, and screams of excitement that fill the casino floor.

I spin one way, then another. It's like I'm lost in a maze of neon lights and crazy sounds.

It finally dawns on me that I have no clue what I'm doing. I'm so distraught I'm not even thinking. I should be heading upstairs to my room, not to the friggin' lobby.

Sniffling, I turn around. Forcing myself to be calm, I walk back to the bank of elevators. But as I press the Up button, a hand clamps down on my shoulder.

I scream.

"Fuck, Sammy. What the hell happened to you?"

Oh my God.

Slowly, I turn. And instantly, my heart fills with hope.

Reed.

Like he did in Costa Rica, my ex has completely shocked me with his appearance.

I don't have to ask. I know that Maxine betrayed my whereabouts to Reed.

And for that, I could kiss her.

"Sammy?"

I want to speak, but I can't. Instead, I step toward Reed and bury my face against his chest.

And then I break down. I sob in his arms.

"What happened?" Reed demands. "Who hurt you?"

I don't speak. I can't. I'm still crying.

"Damn it, Sammy. It was some guy, wasn't it? I'm gonna kill him. What'd he do?"

"No!" I grab Reed's arm when he starts for an open elevator. Not that he knows where he's going, but I don't need him getting all steamed and wanting to bash Rusty's face in. "Look, just forget it."

"Someone hurt you," Reed says, anger simmering beneath his words.

"No, that's not true." At least not in the way he thinks. "I…I hurt myself."

"What the fuck does that mean?"

"Please, Reed." I don't ask him why he's here. Right now I don't care. "I just need you to…" I don't finish my statement. Instead, I rest my head against his shoulder, reveling in the comfort that it brings. Reed and I might not have ended things on a decent note, but the familiarity of his touch brings me comfort nonetheless.

"You've got a room upstairs, right?" he asks.

I catch a breath, nod. "Where are you staying?"

"At Bellagio. Jesus Christ, that place is expensive. But I came here for you, Sammy. Looks like I got here just in time."

"Why don't we go there?" I suggest.

"But you're right upstairs."

"And so is my sister. We're sharing a room."

"Ah. Gotcha."

Reed offers me his arm, and I take it, resting my head against his shoulder as I walk with him.

"Miss," someone calls out. I turn to see a man dressed in a hotel uniform walking briskly toward me. "You need to be wearing shoes in the hotel's lobby."

"Bite me," I snap.

The man stops, jerking backward, as if afraid I might break his neck.

Reed scoops me into his arms. "How's this?" he asks the bellman. "Is it legal for a guy to carry a girl across a hotel lobby? Or are you gonna sue me?"

Not surprisingly, the man doesn't answer. I snuggle close to Reed as he carries me out the front door. Even though we're outside now, he doesn't release me, and I have to admit, it feels good to be in his familiar arms.

He doesn't lower me to my feet until a taxi arrives for us. And even then, when we're safely inside, he wraps his arm around me as though he wants to protect me from all the evil in the world.

I settle against his shoulder and close my eyes.

Fifteen

Annelise

Where my sister's concerned, I don't tend to worry. Tough and feisty, she's more than able to take care of herself. But now that a new day has dawned and I haven't seen her since last night, my concern radar has shot right up.

Yeah, she could have spent the night in bed with some hot man. But since we arrived in Vegas, sex has been the farthest thing from her mind. Which is why I can't relax this morning.

I'm really worried that something bad has happened.

As I finish the last of my coffee, paranoia takes total hold of me. I slip on a brown knit shirt and white skirt, then head across the hallway to Lishelle's room. I guess I could just call her, but I need the company.

I ring the doorbell to Lishelle's room. And only as the door swings open do I remember that she might not be alone.

Lishelle, dressed in a robe and her hair pulled back, smiles when she sees me. "Morning, babe."

"Morning," I reply. "Are you alone?"

"Yeah." She stands back and pulls the door wide. "Come in."

I walk into the suite. "So, how was your night?" I ask to be polite, but what I really want to do is ask about my sister.

"Ah, could have been better."

"Oh?"

"Yeah. I was with someone, but things fizzled."

"Nothing you want to talk about?"

"Maybe later. What'd you do?"

"I won twenty-five hundred at the dollar slots."

"Get out."

"Yeah, I did. Total long shot, but I won."

"And you sound absolutely thrilled." Lishelle frowns. "What's up, hon?"

"Speaking of long shots—do you have any idea where Samera could be?"

Lishelle shakes her head. "No. I have no clue."

"Damn."

"What's going on?" Lishelle asks.

I exhale loudly. "She didn't come back to the suite last night."

"Okay… But she's a big girl."

"I know. The thing is, she wasn't interested in getting with anyone. So, what could have happened to her?"

"She changed her mind?" Lishelle suggests. "Found some hottie that made her melt?"

I suddenly remember the guy in the restaurant, the one she said had been flirting with her since our first day here. "There was someone."

"Then they hooked up. And hell, they're probably still fucking."

"I'm sure you're right," I agree. Though there's still part

of me that can't shake the worry. I don't know what's gotten into me.

"You had coffee yet?" Lishelle asks.

"Yeah, but if you're making a pot, I could use another cup."

"How about I order room service so we can get a decent jolt of caffeine. Maybe a couple of cappuccinos. Have you eaten yet?"

"No."

"Eggs, bacon, toast?"

"Sounds good," I say.

I settle on the sofa while Lishelle orders breakfast. Because worry is still nagging at me, I reach for the remote control and turn on the television. I channel surf until I get to CNN.

"What are you doing?" Lishelle asks as she heads into the living room.

"You never know," is my answer.

"You think Samera has made it onto CNN in twelve hours?"

I continue to flip through channels until I reach a local news station. And I swear, I'm as jittery as hell because when I see "Breaking news story" written below the newscaster, I immediately think this has to do with Samera.

"Hey, doesn't that look like our hotel?" Lishelle asks.

"My God, it does." I turn up the volume, expecting to hear the worst regarding my sister.

"…body was just removed. Again, if you're just joining us, I'm standing outside of the Venetian hotel on the Las Vegas strip, where a body was discovered early this morning on the pool deck."

My stomach lurches. "Oh my God."

Lishelle squeezes my hand.

"According to witnesses, there was the sound of a loud crash, then a body was seen falling from a window. Whether the man committed suicide or was a victim of foul play, the police aren't sure, but I can tell you, the scene here is gruesome."

"The man. Did he say *the man?*" I ask Lishelle. I know it's not even right to feel good about someone else's death, but I desperately want to know that my sister wasn't the victim.

"Yeah, it was a guy."

An audible breath oozes out of me. If the victim is male, it can't be my sister.

"I can't believe it," Lishelle goes on. "Right here at this hotel."

I shush her as a picture flashes on the screen. And then my stomach lurches.

"…Rusty Nickell of Chicago."

Now I point frantically at the television screen. "That's him! That's him!"

"Who?"

"The guy! The one who was flirting with Samera!" My mind starts to work overtime. "What if Samera was in his room, what if—" I can't verbalize my fear. It's too horrifying.

Lishelle's hand tightens on mine in a gesture of support. "Did you call her?"

"I did, but I got her voice mail."

"Call again," Lishelle tells me.

"Okay."

"But I can't imagine your sister being in this guy's room given the circumstances," Lishelle says as I hurry to her phone.

"Unless she's in custody! Shit, one minute I'm relieved, the next I'm more worried than ever."

"Try not to panic until you know what's going on."

Easier said than done. As I punch in the digits to my sister's cell phone, my hand is shaking.

"There's no answer," I say when the phone goes to voice mail. "What should I do?"

"Call the police?" Lishelle suggests. She shrugs before continuing. "But what would you say? We have no clue what's happened, and you just might implicate your sister if it turns out this guy didn't commit suicide."

My head is pounding. "I know my sister isn't a murderer. God, I can't believe those words are even coming out of my mouth."

Lishelle approaches me and wraps an arm around my shoulder. "And I know it, too. Let's get real—Samera isn't involved in this. But until we know where she is, I don't think you should call the cops. If she wasn't with Rusty, she was with someone else. And hey, we'll call Claudia. Maybe she's heard from her."

I look at Lishelle doubtfully.

"Okay, maybe not. But, sweetie, don't worry. Your sister will show up. And I bet she'll have some crazy story about where she was." Lishelle wiggles her eyebrows. "Who she spent the night with."

I nod shakily. "Of course. You're right."

But despite my words I can't help feeling spooked. Like something with my sister is very, very wrong.

Part Three

What happens in Vegas…
doesn't always stay in Vegas.

Sixteen

Samera

As my eyes slowly open, I feel an immediate sensation of warmth.

I feel safe.

The same moment I apprehend it's now morning, I also notice that arms are wrapped around me.

And that's all it takes for the memory of last night to come rushing back to me. Drinking with Rusty, then taking our lust for each other upstairs. Peter showing up and creeping me out. The panic of what almost happened. Reed finding me in the lobby and ushering me away to safety.

I place my hand on top of Reed's and sigh.

I know I was over Reed, but everything about this feels so right. The way Reed's hand is gently slung around my belly, not perched on one of my breasts—which was a fairly common thing whenever we fell asleep together during our relationship. And if he's erect right now, I can't tell, since he doesn't have his cock pressed against my ass.

My God, it's odd—me and Reed like this. Odd because in the past whenever we've touched, the passion between us burned out of control and we both knew we'd end up fucking.

Just like in Costa Rica.

I almost didn't think Reed capable of tenderness. But that's definitely the vibe I'm getting from him right now, even in sleep, and I can't help but view him differently.

I shift my body until I'm on my back. Reed's eyes pop open, frightening me for a second.

"You're awake," he says.

"I thought you were sleeping."

"I woke up a few minutes ago. But I didn't want to get up."

I try to sit up—but a killer jolt of pain across my temple stops me cold. The effect of a hangover.

No surprise there.

"What do you need, babe?" Reed asks me.

I place a hand on my forehead. "Some sort of painkiller. And coffee. Preferably Starbucks."

Reed sits up and glances around the room. "I know I don't have any Aspirin. Will you be okay while I go downstairs to get it?"

"Yeah, sure."

Reed squeezes my hand before getting off the bed. He's already dressed in blue jeans and a T-shirt, so he doesn't need to throw anything on but his shoes. Though my brain is fuzzy, I notice that I'm also fully dressed. Which means Reed didn't try to get any action from me last night.

He flashes a little smile before heading out of the room. Glancing at the digital clock, I see that it's nearly eleven in the morning. My God, I was out like a light. But again, no surprise.

I shuffle off the bed and head to the bathroom, and after I'm finished in there, I turn my cell phone on, then lie back on the comfortable pillows and close my eyes.

The sound of the door turning has my eyes flying open, and I realize that I must have drifted off to sleep.

"Sorry I took so long," Reed says. He's carrying a very large paper bag in one hand and a coffee holder with two Starbucks cups in the other.

I get off the bed and walk toward him. "Smells delicious."

"I figured you could use some breakfast. I picked up some grub at the café."

I reach for the coffee. "You're a sweetheart."

"Here, take this." He rotates the coffee holder, and I see that there's a small white bag on it. "I got Advil. I hope that's okay."

"It's perfect."

I take the coffee and bottle of Advil and head back toward the bed. I busy myself opening the bottle and popping out two pills. I wash them down with a swallow of coffee, which is so hot that it scalds my throat.

"Motherfucker!"

"What?" Reed is at my side in a flash.

"Nothing," I say. "The coffee…" And shit, I start crying.

Reed folds me in his arms. It's not the coffee, of course. It's everything. The reality that I don't know what the hell I'm doing most of the time. First, I broke Miguel's heart in Costa Rica. Then I found the worst guy on the planet to use as a palate cleanser. And here I am, back with Reed, a guy who fucked me over royally.

I feel completely lost.

Reed coos softly. "It's okay, Sammy. I'm here now."

"Why?" I ask. "Why are you here?"

"You're kidding me, right?"

I ease backward and stare into his eyes. "No, I'm not kidding. You showed up in Costa Rica, and I thought you'd changed. I believed that you loved me. That you were sorry for cheating on me. But then you acted like a prick, trying to tell me what to do. So why are you here?"

Reed doesn't answer right away. "You have every reason to doubt me. I fucked up when I screwed Lilly. And I fucked up in Costa Rica. I can't defend what I did. I can only tell you that sometimes it takes a while for a guy to get it. I finally get it."

I don't say a word. I simply examine Reed's face, trying to determine if I can trust him.

"Come on, Sammy. You think I'd come all this way— knowing you could tell me to fuck off—if I didn't love you?"

His words give me pause. My brain says I shouldn't believe him, but my heart—God, I've trusted my heart before and been steered on the wrong path. But still, ever since seeing Reed last night, I've been feeling better about him. Like maybe we truly are meant to be together, and that this is our time to do it right.

Maybe my brain is clouded right now because he was there for me after a harrowing ordeal. I'm not sure. All I know is that right now, being with him feels good.

"Why don't we eat?" Reed takes the large paper bag to the table in the room and starts to pull out the contents.

After a moment I join him there. Reed shares a plate of scrambled eggs and sausage with me. I place my hand on the small of his back, and he gives me a quick kiss on my temple.

This is when I really start to believe that Reed has done a one-eighty. Because the Reed I know wouldn't need more than a touch like that to turn to me, sweep me into his arms, and get all hot and heavy. In less than a minute we'd be naked, his tongue on my nipples and his fingers playing with my clit.

Instead, Reed pulls out a chair for me, and I sit.

We eat in silence for several minutes. The toast is like manna from heaven, helping assuage the queasiness in my stomach after all the alcohol I consumed last night.

"Thanks, Reed," I tell him when I finished. "This really hit the spot."

His eyes roam over my face, but never venture lower. He doesn't make the obvious joke about hitting my "other" spot.

"I do love you," he says. "I want you to know that."

"I believe you."

His lips curve in a smile. "You know what I was thinking?"

"What?"

Reed lifts my hand and kisses my palm. "You might think this is crazy, but I was kinda thinking that maybe…maybe we could get hitched."

I sip my coffee, buying time. "Married?" I ask weakly. I might be feeling good about Reed again, but marriage is a huge step.

"Why not? Hey, this is Vegas, and I'm feeling lucky."

When I don't answer, Reed edges his chair closer to mine. "You believe that I love you."

"Yes."

"And I know you have feelings for me."

I don't say yes. But I don't say no, either.

Reed kisses my hand again. "I know I'm not the most traditional guy, nor the most romantic, but you have my heart, Sammy. That's just the way it is. I can't change that. I'm done being scared of what I feel for you. Done thinking that marriage means a ball and chain around your ankle."

Wow—everything Reed is saying sounds absolutely perfect. He's acting sweeter than he ever has.

"What do you say?" he asks me.

At that exact moment, my cell phone rings. *Saved by the bell,* I think.

"Hold that thought," I tell him. I scoot across the room to retrieve my purse. My sister's number is etched on the call display.

I press the button to speak. "Hey, Annelise."

"Sam! Oh my God! *Where are you?*"

I pull the phone away from my ear for a moment. "Annie, what's with all the drama? Did you think I'd been abducted by aliens or something?"

"I have been out of my mind with worry. Are you okay?"

"Yes, I'm okay. A little hung over, but okay."

"Where are you?"

"I'm…I'm with someone."

"You've been with this person all night? Why couldn't you call, leave a note?"

"Actually, I was with someone who turned into a fucking asshole." Reed shoots me a glance, and I turn away. "I'm not there anymore," I add in a quieter tone. "It's a long story."

"So you haven't heard the news?"

"What news?"

"It's about that guy. The one you showed me in the restaurant. Look, it'll be easier if I just talk to you face-to-face. Are you in this hotel?"

"No."

"Can you come back here? There's a lot of shit going down."

"Right now?"

"Yes, right now. I have no clue who you're with, and I don't want him hearing your end of the conversation."

"You're freaking me out a little."

"It's that serious, Samera. How long will it take you to get back here?"

I glance at Reed again. He's got a curious look on his face.

"Ten minutes," I tell my sister.

"See you then."

I end the call and put my cell phone back into my purse.

"Trouble?" Reed asks.

I cross the room to meet him at the table. "Sounds like something serious is going on. My sister wants me back at the hotel to talk to me about it."

"Serious like what?"

"So serious she didn't want to talk about it on the phone." I don't add that it has something to do with Rusty, the guy I'd fucked last night before running into Reed in the lobby.

I wonder if the motherfucker's been arrested for rape.

At that very thought, a chill sweeps over me. I feel the same eerie sensation I did only moments before I made the decision to sleep with Rusty.

At the time, I'd thought the feeling had to do with something else, like someone following me, and I'd figured I would be safe with Rusty. Now I know that I was lucky as hell last night, because he and his friend could have raped me, then strangled me—all for a cheap thrill.

"You've got this weird look on your face."

I jerk my head in Reed's direction.

"Babe?"

"I...I'm just thinking. Wondering what my sister wants to tell me."

Reed rises and slips his arms around my waist. "You want me to go with you?"

"No."

"You gonna come back?"

I nod. "As soon as I'm finished with my sister, I'll come back here."

"I hope so. Because I have a flight out of here this evening."

"You're leaving?"

Reed nods. "Maybe you'll go with me. Just a suggestion. Whatever you want to do is cool."

"We'll see," I tell him. This is all happening *way* too fast.

I expect him to pressure me, to not let up until I agree to leave Vegas with him. But he doesn't. Instead he gives me a soft kiss on the lips.

"See ya, babe."

"Yeah. See ya."

When I get back to my suite at the Venetian, Annelise is sitting on the sofa with her legs folded under her, the remote control in her hand as she watches the television.

Her eyes fill with relief when she sees me. She jumps to her feet and flies toward me, then wraps me in a long, hard hug.

"Oh, Sammy. Thank *God.*"

"Whoa, whoa, whoa," I say. "You're acting like you thought I was dead." As we pull apart, I plant my hands on my hips. "Want to tell me what's going on?"

Annelise sighs. "I'm afraid you're not too far off."

"Huh?" I ask, not getting her meaning.

"When you came in, did you see any reporters or cops downstairs?"

"Both. Why—" My question dies on my lips as I realize what my sister is saying. *I'm afraid you're not too far off.* "Are you telling me that someone—someone actually *died?*"

"Not just someone. I think it was that guy you showed me—the one you said you'd been flirting with."

I gasp. "Rusty?"

"Yes! That's the name they said on the news! I knew it was him when they showed his picture, but I guess I didn't want to believe—"

"Rusty's dead?" I ask anxiously. "Are you sure?"

"Ever since I heard the news, I've been freaking out. And when I didn't see you this morning...I thought for sure you spent the night with him."

I'm too shocked to speak. Slowly I walk to the sofa and plop down onto it. I stare at the television. Some newscaster is reporting on the story of a fire somewhere in the city.

Annelise sits beside me and turns down the volume. "I'm sure the news will feature the story again. It's bad, Sammy. He either jumped or was pushed out of his window."

A mangled cry escapes from my throat. "H-how could this have happened?" I hated Rusty for what he did to me, but the thought of him being dead after being very much alive with me last night... "He was fine last night... He—"

"You were with him last night?" Annelise sounds mortified.

"Part of the night, yeah," I answer somewhat cautiously, my eyes narrowing as I look at her.

"But not the whole night?" she presses.

"I told you on the phone I was with someone who turned into an asshole."

"Why not?"

"I feel like I'm on trial here, Annie."

"You tell me Rusty became an asshole. Now his brains are splattered on the pool deck. And now you're with someone else? You think I don't want to know what happened?"

I hesitate for a moment. "I'd had every intention of spending the night with Rusty, but he became a first-class jerk." Over the next few minutes, I fill Annelise in on all that happened.

She groans. "Oh, sis."

"I'm fine," I tell her. And then an awful thought hits me, hits me so hard I inhale sharply. "Fuck, I wonder if he felt guilty for being with me. The way he talked about his late wife… He'd been so in love with her. And maybe what happened with his friend was a bad idea that simply went too far." I exhale a shaky breath.

"If he jumped… Well, he chose his fate."

"Annelise!"

"It's true."

"I've never known you to be so cold."

"There's a bigger concern here, Sammy. If he didn't jump… Think about it. He and his friend were out of line with you. If he was murdered, don't you see that you'd be a suspect?"

My sister's words settle over me heavily. "I never even considered that."

"Does anyone know you were with him?"

"No. Yes! His friend, Peter. But if Peter was in the room with him, he would know if Rusty jumped."

"Maybe. Maybe not."

"Oh my God. If Peter wasn't in the room… He knows how pissed I was. What if he mentions me to the cops?"

"That's exactly my concern—that you might get implicated in this. And you should know that one of the bartenders told a reporter that he saw Rusty last night with a big-busted blonde. Sure, that could be half the population in Las Vegas…"

I grip my stomach. "I can't be involved in this."

"You're obviously being a bit secretive about this, but since you weren't with Rusty last night, who *were* you with?"

"Reed," I answer.

"*Reed?*" My sister's eyes bulge.

"I know. Total shocker. Maxine must have told him where I was and—"

"And what? I thought you were over him? You said he ruined everything in Costa Rica."

"I know what I said, but maybe…" My words stop. I think about Rusty. How I let my guard down with him and he turned out to be a jerk. "Maybe I was wrong," I finish.

"Never doubt your instincts," Annelise tells me. "And all I've ever heard you say about this Reed character is that you can't trust him."

"My instincts told me Rusty was a nice guy. Someone who'd lost his wife and wanted to reconnect with a woman. And I was wrong."

"That has nothing to do with Reed."

"You know," I begin defensively, "I can see you dismissing his trip to see me in Costa Rica. But he came here, too, Annie. After how ugly things got when I ended our relationship, he didn't have to, but he did. That tells me a lot."

"That tells me he likes a challenge," Annelise mutters.

"Don't." Anger starts to bubble inside me, but I know it's not Annelise I'm really pissed with. I'm pissed with the situation. Still, I press on. "Don't lecture me, okay? I need you to be my sister. I need you to fucking support my decision."

"I don't want to see you get hurt again," she tells me. "And Reed—I'm sorry, but I don't like him."

"Because he runs a strip club instead of pushes papers all day?"

"I didn't say that."

"You didn't have to. I know you never liked me stripping, and I'm not stupid enough to believe you'd accept any of my friends from that world."

"You think that's what this is about?"

"I'm leaving," I tell her, ignoring her question. "I'm packing my stuff now and heading back to Atlanta with Reed."

"You're kidding me."

"No, I'm not. We're heading back to Atlanta tonight."

"Samera, Samera," Annelise says pitifully. "That's exactly what Reed did in Costa Rica. Show up and demand that you leave with him on *his* schedule."

"For God's sake!" I lash out. "Can't you listen to me without making judgments? Reed didn't demand anything. In fact, he doesn't even know I've made the decision to leave with him."

Annelise is quiet for a moment. "And our trip?" she finally asks.

But her question is now the farthest thing from my mind. Because a photo of Rusty has just flashed on the screen.

"Turn the volume up," I say anxiously.

"…thirty-four-year-old Rusty Nickell. We have now learned that he did leave a suicide note, and there are unconfirmed reports that Mr. Nickell lost a very large amount of money while playing poker at the Venetian's casino. No one from the Venetian would comment on the allegation, but according to a friend of the deceased, he was not in debt and would not have killed himself. Las Vegas police say that they're looking into all angles and that the death of Rusty Nickell is still under investigation."

All angles. I snatch the remote control from my sister and turn the television off. I've heard enough. "I need to get the fuck out of here. Before the police find out I was with Rusty and want to question me."

"You think they will? Now that they've found a suicide note, it's pretty clear—"

"What's clear? One minute you were freaking out that I'd

been with Rusty. Telling me how some bartender told the media he'd spotted Rusty with some blonde. You even said that I could be considered a suspect. Now you think everything's fine and dandy?" My harsh words affect Annelise, cut her like a knife, if the expression on her face is any indication. I jump to my feet. "I'm leaving with Reed."

"All right." My sister slowly rises. "You're a big girl. I can't tell you what to do. And maybe it's for the best that you leave. To be on the safe side."

"I'm sorry." My shoulders sag, the fight gone out of me. "I'm not mad at you. I'm just…spooked. Creeped out. A guy I slept with last night is *dead*. And what if the suicide note is fake, and what if the cops detain me for questioning?" The possibility of the nightmare flashes in my mind. "This is all so surreal."

"I know."

No, Annelise doesn't know. She can't know what I'm going through. That I'm scared to death right now.

And not just because of the possibility that I could be a suspect should Rusty's death be deemed a murder.

But scared by the thought that maybe, just maybe, he jumped because of me.

Seventeen

Claudia

When my bedside phone rings, I answer it right away. "Hello?" I say, my voice deliberately deep and sexy. I'm hoping it's Arnold, even though he left here only four hours ago.

"Wait a second," comes the reply. "I'm not sure I have the right number."

"Lishelle?"

"Yeah, that'd be me. One of your two best friends in the world, remember? Or are you distracted by some guy's face between your thighs?"

"Not anymore," I answer, and completely expect the high-pitched squeal that comes next.

"I'm coming over," she says. Then I hear the dial tone.

I hop off the bed and race to the door. I open it before Lishelle has a chance to knock.

"Hey, you." I grin from ear to ear.

Lishelle strolls into my suite. "Finally, girl. You got laid!"

"I did," I reply in a sing-song voice. "In fact, when the phone rang, I thought it was him calling."

"It went that well?" Lishelle sounds pleased.

"Oh, yeah. And Lishelle, it was *exactly* what I needed."

"No guilt?" she asks as she sits on a bar stool.

"None." I shake my head. "It's weird. I know I'll never see him again—not after this trip anyway. And I don't feel dirty. I don't think I'm a slut. I'm a woman who needed to get laid, and I did. End of story."

"There you go."

"And it was really hot. Completely uninhibited sex."

"You go, girl!"

I climb onto a bar stool beside Lishelle. "Arnold was a total stranger, and yet I felt far worse about some of the things I did with Adam. And I loved Adam."

"Because you didn't *want* to go to a swinger's club. Adam did. You went to please *him*. This you did to please yourself."

"Yeah," I agree. "And deep down, I think part of me knew that something was wrong with my relationship with Adam when he suddenly wanted us to get really kinky. But at the time I couldn't face the truth."

Lishelle pats my hand. "I'm happy for you. New cock is exactly what you need to get over the old one."

"And you?" I eye Lishelle suspiciously. "You could be…happier."

She rolls her eyes. "I could be, yeah. But, I fucked up."

"How? When I left you, you and Rugged looked pretty cozy."

"I know. And we went back to his suite. But I guess I didn't trust him. I kept putting my foot in my mouth, and I offended him."

I tsk. "Lishelle."

"Yeah, it was pretty bad. Especially after he told me that he came to Vegas hoping to find me. Your cousin mentioned we'd be here."

"That's right, I mentioned it to him in passing. Wow—Rugged came here just to see you."

"According to him. I kept testing him, I suppose. Saying stupid things. And then he rejected me."

"No!"

"Uh-huh. I even tried to make things right, because by that point, I really wanted to fuck him. But he didn't cave. He told me to leave his suite."

"Oh, Lishelle."

"It wasn't that bad. He was nice about it. And it's okay. Really. We're working with him on the fund-raiser. It would have been weird sleeping with him. And hey—at least I got a bit of a fix yesterday morning with my masseur. Don't be sorry." She waves off my concern. "Look, now that we've caught up on the girl talk, there's something you should know."

"Oh?"

"Have you turned on the TV this morning?"

"Are you kidding? After last night…" My voice trails off on a dreamy sigh as I remember all the ways Arnold pleased me last night—over and over.

"Well, something really weird happened," Lishelle goes on. "Something downright freaky."

"Don't keep me in suspense."

"Someone died," she tells me, her face growing serious. "Right here, at the hotel."

For a moment I'm speechless. Then I say, "You're kidding."

She shakes her head. "And it looks like Samera knew him."

My mouth falls open. "A friend of hers?"

"No, she didn't know him before this trip. She met him the first day we got here...something like that. Annelise came to see me earlier, worried because Samera hadn't shown up at all last night. My thought was that Samera's a grown woman, no big deal. Then when we found out someone died and who it was, Annelise really freaked out. She figured Samera had likely spent the night with this guy." Lishelle shrugs. "It's a convoluted story, but that's the gist of it."

"No one knows where Samera is?"

"Not as far as I know, but—"

"Why didn't you tell me this right away?"

"Because obviously she wasn't with the guy who died. If she was, we would know that already. Or she'd be in police custody, and I'm sure she would have placed a call to her sister."

I think about that for a minute. "I guess you're right. Have you heard from Annelise recently?"

"No. But I did watch the news, and this guy apparently committed suicide. Took a plunge from the eleventh floor."

I shudder. "Brutal."

"I know. A beautiful place like this? People come here to have fun, to experience some excitement. Who would expect it? From the reports, though, it sounds like he might have lost his shirt at poker. I guess that sent him into depression."

"Ugh." I shake my head sadly. "That's awful."

"It probably happens more than we know."

"We should call Annelise," I say. "See if Samera showed up."

I hop off my bar stool and head to the phone in the small kitchen area. As my fingers touch the phone, it rings. I snatch up the receiver.

"Hello?"

"Hey, Claudia."

"Annelise, hi. Lishelle and I were just talking about you."

"Can I head over?"

"Sure."

Less than a minute later, I open the door to let Annelise into the suite. She's got a glum look on her face, which instantly fills me with alarm.

"Annie…?"

"Sam's okay," she begins without preamble. "But she's leaving today."

"What?" Lishelle asks, her tone laced with shock. "She's that upset about the dead guy?"

"No, Reed showed up. She's going home with him."

"Reed?" Lishelle and I ask at the same time.

"Yeah, *that* Reed. Her friggin' ex." Annelise heads into the living room and drops down onto the sofa.

I follow her. "When the hell did he get here?"

"I don't know," Annelise says, "but apparently she was with him last night. And God only knows what she's thinking. He wants another chance with her."

"I thought stuff like that only happened in the movies," I say. "Guys traveling across the country to proclaim their love to you."

Annelise frowns. "If you ask me, that Reed guy is bad news. For one thing, he's entirely too possessive. First he showed up in Costa Rica, then left angry when Samera refused to head home with him. Now he shows up in Vegas and cuts our trip short?"

I shrug. "Maybe he really does love her. And he pulled out all the stops to get her attention."

"I hope so," Annelise says dryly.

"You don't sound happy about that," I say.

"Can you blame her?" Lishelle asks as she sits on the

armchair. "What's with all the grandstanding? Tracking her down in Costa Rica. Now here in Las Vegas. Couldn't he just wait till she got back to Atlanta?"

"Maybe she called him," I suggest, thinking of how I'd called Adam time and time again when we'd first broken up. "How else did he know she was here?"

"Someone she worked with at the club told him," Annelise explains. "Same woman, I think, who told him she was in Costa Rica."

Lishelle scowls. "Maybe I'm a cynic, but he's trying too hard. The way Glenn did with me. And it was same-old, same-old. Some guys just like a challenge."

"That's what I think," Annelise says. "But I guess my sister has to figure that out for herself."

"And what about the guy who died?" Lishelle asks. "Your sister knows what happened?"

"Yeah, she does. And get this—she was with him part of last night, but he turned into a creep. God only knows when she ran into Reed after that."

"The guy sounds like a stalker," Lishelle comments.

"Stop being so negative," I tell her. "It sounds like he really cares about her."

"When does she leave?" Lishelle asks. "Maybe we can all have lunch before she takes off."

"She's already gone," Annelise tells us.

"Without saying goodbye?" I ask.

"She asked me to tell you both that she enjoyed hanging with you, and that we can get together in Atlanta sometime. This thing with Rusty really spooked her. And of course, Reed influenced her decision to leave." Annelise groans.

"Hey," I begin, "Samera's a big girl. She's gonna be all right."

"I don't know why I'm so worried," Annelise says. "But I've got this weird feeling. Like something's very wrong."

"Something like what?" Lishelle asks.

Annelise's eyes narrow as she shakes her head. "That's the thing. I don't know."

I stare at her for a moment, but I don't know what to say to put her at ease. So I change the subject.

"Anyone hungry?" I ask. "Because right about now, I could seriously use some lunch."

"Need to replenish your energy after your marathon night," Lishelle jokes.

"Hey." Annelise's gaze flies to me. "You got some last night?"

"I did." I take her hand and pull her up from the sofa. "And I'll tell you all about it over some mimosas and scrambled eggs. Just give me five minutes to get dressed, then we can head downstairs."

That at least gets a smile out of Annelise. But the smile doesn't quite mask the worry.

Eighteen

Samera

Later that evening, Reed and I walk into the airport. Ever since I got back to his hotel and told him I'd be going back to Atlanta with him, he's been ultraromantic. He holds my hand whenever he can, gives me kisses for no reason.

And even though we could have fucked when we were in his room, Reed didn't make a move.

Oh, we necked. We got hot and heavy. But Reed pulled away, saying he wanted me to know that he was interested in more than getting me naked.

It's comforting, really. And in a strange way, turned me on even more.

As we head to the ticket counter, I hear snippets of other people's conversations.

"What the hell. You win some you lose some. But at least we had fun." And, "Five thousand dollars! I am *so* going to pay off my car when I get home!" And, "Did you hear about that guy who jumped to his death? I could see everything from my window…"

My stomach curdles. I grip Reed's arm tighter.

He kisses my temple. "What is it, babe?"

"Nothing," I lie. "I'm just happy to be here with you."

Reed accepts my answer. The woman at the counter greets us warmly, takes our IDs, and starts typing into her computer.

A couple minutes later she passes us our tickets. "Ms. Peyton, you have been randomly chosen to go through an added security check."

"What?" Reed snaps, outraged. "You're gonna go through our stuff?" I place a hand on Reed's to quiet him, but he jerks it away from mine. "Jesus Christ, you're treating us like a couple of criminals. This is bullshit."

The woman looks offended, but says politely, "Actually, Mr. McLeod, you're all set. It's only Ms. Peyton who will go through added security measures. Please head to the right," she adds with a nervous smile.

I see a large table and a few security personnel. A man is being wanded by a male security guard while a female guard is sifting through his luggage.

"Is this necessary?" Reed asks.

"It's entirely random," the clerk explains. "And yes, it's mandatory."

Reed huffs.

"It's okay," I tell him.

"You'll need to bring your luggage with you," the clerk explains.

I nod, retrieve my luggage from the scale, and head toward the security table.

I know it doesn't make sense, but my heart starts to beat

extremely fast. I'm nervous, I realize. Nervous about getting out of Las Vegas without incident.

My God, I'm actually afraid the cops might show up and detain me for questioning in Rusty's death.

When I get to the security table, I slowly inhale. Are the two security guys eyeing me suspiciously?

"Hi," I say, trying to be polite.

"Boarding pass, please," one guy says, his voice as stern as the expression on his face.

"What's this about?" Reed asks, his loud voice bordering on anger.

"Reed, it's okay."

"We're gonna miss the damn flight."

The security guard standing in front of me sends a glare in Reed's direction. "Sir, you need to step back. You can't enter this area."

I turn to Reed and place a gentle hand on his chest. "Baby, it's okay. It's probably because I changed my return ticket. No big deal."

I hand the guard my boarding pass, and he instructs me to put my suitcase on the table. I do, then he gestures for me to step forward.

I walk about ten feet forward to a partially enclosed area. There, a female security guard moves her wand over my body.

When the woman is finished, I'm instructed to retrieve my luggage and place it on another table, where a man now goes through my carry-on bag piece by piece. My face starts to flame when the man touches the cloth bag that holds my vibrator. Why I brought it, I don't know.

"What's this?" he asks as he feels it, and I know I must turn beet red. I'm sure this guy isn't a moron, and I'm not the only woman in America to own a vibrator.

He stares at me, waiting for an answer. I roll my eyes. "It's private," I tell him.

He narrows his eyes, as though he doesn't understand. Then he begins to open the bag.

"For God's sake, it's a vibrator," I admit. I meet the man's gaze head-on, not allowing him the luxury of knowing he's embarrassed me.

I've taken my clothes off in front of countless strangers. So what if this guy finds a sex toy in my luggage?

The man stops short of taking the vibrator out and waving it around. The way he stares at me makes me feel like I'm some kind of pervert. Or worse, a criminal. Looking over to my left, I can almost see the smoke billowing out of Reed's nose and ears, that's how pissed he looks. I also see people sneaking peeks at me and my face flushes. They stare at me as though they expect security to announce that they've nailed another terrorist.

Terrorist nabbed at Las Vegas airport. Choice of weapon: neon-pink vibrator…

"All right, ma'am. You can go now."

Thank God, this extended security check is complete.

"Thanks," I mutter. But I don't mean it.

Ten minutes later, as Reed and I walk briskly toward our gate, I throw a glance over my shoulder.

Leaving Las Vegas, and not a minute too soon.

Our flight is direct, but because it's a red-eye I'm totally wiped out when we land in Atlanta at 5:20 in the morning. I never sleep well on planes, and this time was no exception. For a good portion of the night I cozied up to Reed, laid my head on his lap, but still my back and neck ache now that the flight is over.

Having to go through baggage claim before six in the morning is brutal. Especially when all I really want to do is collapse on my bed and sleep the entire day.

Our luggage retrieved, Reed and I make our way to his Ford Explorer. Thank God he's able to drive.

When we reach my apartment, I give him a soft kiss on the cheek. "Thanks so much."

He opens his door. "I'll walk you to the door."

"That's not necessary."

"I'll do it anyway."

Reed gets my luggage from the backseat and carries it up the front steps of the town house where I live on the first floor.

I slip the key into the lock and open the door. Reed steps into my apartment. I'm about to protest, but he moves backward once he's set my suitcase on the floor.

Now he faces me and runs his fingers through my hair before planting both hands on my shoulders. "You know I love you, right?"

I answer honestly. "I know you've been saying that for the past twenty-four hours."

"I'm not just saying it. I do. You're the absolute best thing that has ever happened to me. I mean that."

I smile slightly. It's weird hearing Reed say all this mushy stuff, but still nice. Maybe he finally has gotten it, finally understands.

"Thank you." I wrap my arms around his neck and hug him earnestly. "I appreciate you being there for me."

"You don't want company?" he asks as we pull apart. He raises an eyebrow suggestively, leaving no doubt as to what he's talking about.

"Sweetie, I'm tired. It's been a long day, a long flight. All I want to do right now is hit my pillow—"

"Understood." Reed plants a gentle kiss on my forehead, and I can't help thinking that he has truly changed. The Reed I knew before would get pissed at my reluctance, storm off and expect me to call after him.

"I'll call you when I wake up," I tell him.

"I'll probably be at the club, but call me anyway. No rest for the wicked." He grins, the charming grin that originally won me over. "Maybe you can even come see me there."

And maybe even put in a few hours of work...I don't think so.

But I don't say that. Instead I give Reed a soft, lingering kiss on the lips. "I'll call you later."

Reed heads down the steps, and I watch him. Watch as he climbs behind the wheel of the Explorer. He winds down the window and waves at me.

I wave back.

"Go inside," he instructs me. "I want to make sure you're safe."

I smile at that, liking the way he's being so protective of me.

If only he'd showed up before I got together with Rusty...

I give Reed one last wave, then head inside.

Nineteen

Annelise

Late Sunday night, I turn the key as quietly as I can and enter the apartment I share with Dominic. I didn't call him when I got into town. Didn't warn him that I'd be home soon.

I tell myself that it's because I want to surprise him, but my heart knows that's not the entire truth. I trust Dominic, I really do, but I can't help remembering how when I returned home from a girlfriends' trip once before, I found my husband in bed with another woman.

Effectively changing my life forever.

Don't be silly, I tell myself as I slowly close the door behind me. *You don't have to sneak in like this. Dominic's not Charles. You trust Dom. You know you do.*

But despite my little pep talk, I creep across the hardwood floor nonetheless.

The bedroom door is closed. My heart beats rapidly as I approach it. I listen for sound, hear none.

I close my fingers over the doorknob, take a deep breath, then push the bedroom door open.

My eyes instantly land on the bed. It's unmade, but no Dominic.

Disappointed, I step into the room. And when the en suite bathroom door opens, I'm so startled that I gasp and jump backward.

Dominic steps out. His eyes widen in shock. Will shock change to panic, and will someone else casually head out of the bathroom…

A grin explodes onto Dominic's face. "Annie!" he exclaims, sweeping me into his arms. "I didn't even hear you come in."

Relief washes over me, followed immediately by guilt. I smile and step toward my lover.

"I wanted to surprise you," I tell him. I snake my arms around his neck. And the next instant, we're kissing.

After several seconds we pull apart, breathless. Our gazes meet. Hold. We both giggle, knowing exactly what the other is thinking.

I slip my hands under Dominic's T-shirt and press my palms against his warm chest. "Oh, baby. I've missed you."

His hands settle on my butt. "You saying the vibrator didn't do the trick while you were gone?"

I stroke Dominic's penis, which is now erect. "That vibrator's got nothing on you."

We start to kiss again, a smoldering kiss with lots of tongue. I grab at his pyjama bottoms, shoving them down his hips. He pushes my shirt up, then my bra. And a moment later, his mouth closes around one of my nipples.

His tongue is hot. Ravenous. I practically melt in Dominic's arms. "Baby…" I moan.

While Dominic's tongue plays over my nipple, he slips a

hand into the waist of my skirt. His fingers find my pussy, strokes my clit.

Dominic groans. "This sweet, sweet pussy."

It's only been four days, but his touch ignites me as though I haven't had sex in months.

"Fuck me," I beg, spreading my legs.

"Where's your vibrator?"

"Who cares?"

Dominic's lips kiss a path to my ear as he fingers me. His three fingers stretch me, leave me gasping.

"Let's have some fun with it," Dominic whispers.

"You're serious?" I ask.

Dominic pulls his fingers out of my pussy—slowly. He raises his hand to his mouth and laps up my essence. Then he kisses me.

I want to fuck him already. But Dominic says, "Yeah, I'm serious."

"But baby—"

His kiss shuts me up. He tweaks my nipples, making me entirely too weak for him. When I'm like this, I'll do anything he says.

"My suitcase is by the door."

Dominic takes his cock into his palm. "I'll wait."

As I watch him, I exhale shakily. I want to take his cock in my mouth.

"Go on," Dominic urges.

I head out of the bedroom and hurriedly open my suitcase. My vibrator in hand, I whirl around and head back to Dominic.

"There it is," Dominic says. "My competition."

"Never," I tell him.

"Give it to me."

I raise an eyebrow at that.

Dominic holds out his hand. "Trust me?"

"Of course I trust you. But I also want to do you so badly."

Now he steps forward and kisses me again. "Oh, we will fuck." He takes the vibrator from my hand and lowers himself to his knees. "We've got four days to make up for."

Dominic runs the tip of the vibrator over my pussy. Then he flicks his tongue over my clitoris.

I groan and move backward, my body needing the wall for support. Dominic follows me. He strokes me with his fingers, then asks me to spread my legs.

I do, and he runs the vibrator along my opening. I grip his shoulders, knowing what he'll do next.

But knowing doesn't prepare me for the intense pleasure the first thrust of the vibrator will bring.

I cry out, dig my fingers into Dominic's shoulders. He adds his tongue, suckling my clit as he moves the vibrator in and out of me slowly.

"Oh my God." I writhe my hips and volley my head from side to side.

"Oh, baby. Seeing you like this…you're so damn beautiful."

I've never been so exposed.

Or so turned on.

Dominic picks up speed, moving the vibrator faster as well as his tongue. Soon I'm moaning and panting and so damn close to what I'm sure will be the best orgasm experience ever.

Dominic stops thrusting the vibrator, and instead rotates it inside me. This feels so…dirty. So…illicit.

So incredibly fucking exciting.

I glance down at Dominic, find him looking at me. "God, baby. Just looking at you like this…I think I could come."

I keep my eyes on Dominic, watch as he draws my clitoris into his mouth. And that's all it takes, that delicious visual image, for me to start to unravel. My orgasm seizes me, takes hold of every inch of my body and doesn't let go until I am moaning wildly and thrashing my head and banging my fists against the wall.

My moans turn into soft cries. Finally Dominic releases me from the torture of his tongue and slowly withdraws the vibrator. My energy spent, I wrap my arms around his neck and slide down onto the floor.

"Don't tell me you've had enough," he whispers.

He doesn't give me a chance to answer as he lies on his back and pulls me on top of him. Cradling the back of my head in his palm, he draws me close and kisses me with the passion and tenderness of a man who loves his woman.

My strength slowly builds, my breathing steadies. Ready for round two, I spread my legs over Dominic's body. He reaches for his cock and presses the tip against my folds. Then he grips my hips and pulls me down on him.

Hard.

He rams me with amazing speed and agility from his position on the hardwood floor. I close my eyes, arch my back, and ride every glorious inch of him.

Dominic reaches for one of my hands and links our fingers. I love the way he always brings intimacy to our fucking. How he makes our connection so much greater than strictly physical.

Opening my eyes, I offer him a faint smile. But my smile fades as he quickens his rhythm and leaves me fighting to catch my breath. Dominic's grunts intensify, and I gaze down to see his face contorted with pleasure. Any second now, and he'll be coming.

"Yes, sweetheart," I murmur. "Come. Baby, come…"

Dominic grips my hips and drives his cock into me. I almost orgasm, but I hold him back, wanting him to come first. But after several seconds I sense a change. Dominic has lost his momentum.

I step up my game. I gyrate against him wildly and tighten my vaginal walls around him. Then I stretch a hand behind me and stroke his inner thigh.

When I don't hear his breathing accelerate, I stretch my hand farther and massage his balls. Normally Dominic loves this. But today I'm not getting the excited response I typically would.

"Ooh, baby." I slide my pussy up and down his shaft, hoping that my pleasure will turn him on. Dominic tweaks my nipples, but his touch is different. It's not frenzied, it's controlled.

I ease my body onto his, kiss his cheek, his chin, then suckle his bottom lip. And this is when I know that the energy between us has changed and that Dominic isn't about to experience release, because his cock goes limp.

Pressing my face to his, I sigh. "What's the matter?" I ask without preamble.

Dominic groans but doesn't answer. Instead, he guides my body off of his and rises to a sitting position.

"Your back," I say, realizing what must be the problem. "My knees took some serious punishment as well." I chuckle. Stroke his thigh. "Let's finish this on the bed."

I'm on my feet when Dominic says, "No, Annie. It's not my back. It's…it's something else."

His words are like an injection of poison. I remember my initial fear when I entered the apartment, that Dominic could be cheating on me the way Charles did.

Suddenly, the idea doesn't seem so far-fetched.

"Dom?" I croak.

"I've got to tell you something. And maybe you ought to sit down."

A wave of panic washes over me. *OhmyGodohmyGod. I can't believe this is happening. Not again.*

I don't move. I can't. My body is frozen with fear.

Dominic gets to his feet and takes my hand. He leads me to the bed, where he forces me to sit. Sighing, he sits beside me, but he doesn't release my hands.

Clearly he's going to give me bad news. I don't understand why he keeps touching me. If he's going to break my heart, I don't want him to be Mr. Tender and Wonderful. I don't think I can deal with that. I'd rather him be a jerk.

My heart is beating so hard, I fear I'll have external bruising tomorrow, but somehow I find the courage to speak. "Whatever you have to say to me, just say it."

"All right." He sighs softly, and I brace myself. "It's about Charles."

"Charles?" My heart is still pounding, but damn, I'm confused.

Dominic nods. "I should have told you the moment you came through the door. But I knew that once I told you, you wouldn't be in the mood to make love, and I just wanted some time—"

"Tell me what?" I interject. "Did he do something? Has the judge changed his mind about giving me half the proceeds from the house? What?"

Dominic glances away before meeting my gaze head-on. "Annie," he begins slowly. "I hate to have to tell you this, but Charles is dead."

Complete silence fills the room. I don't think I even blink as I stare at Dominic for several seconds.

"Annie—"

"Dead?" I ask. "What do you mean he's dead?"

"It happened late Friday night. Early Saturday, really."

"An accident? What?"

"No." Dominic pauses, then says, "Annie, he shot himself."

Now I gasp.

"I should have called you in Las Vegas, but I didn't have the heart to tell you that way, over the phone while you were on vacation."

Slowly I stand.

"Are you okay?" Dominic asks me.

I don't answer. I'm not sure what I feel, really, other than profound surprise.

Hugging my torso, I head for the window. It's dark outside, but I stare out at the trees nonetheless. Stare and try to make sense of the reality that Charles took the coward's way out.

Dominic's hand clamps down on my shoulder. I don't even jump, that's how numb I suddenly felt.

He turns me to face him. "Annie, are you okay?"

"I'm absolutely fine," I tell him. "Couldn't be better."

He flashes me a look that says he knows I'm lying. "I don't believe that."

"Why wouldn't I be okay? Charles is a loser. If he's taken his own life, well, at least that will spare the city of Atlanta a long and ugly trial."

And words I said only yesterday pop into my mind. Words I said about Rusty.

If he jumped…well, he chose his fate.

My God, I'd been so callous when I'd said those words. So…so lacking any sense of empathy. I'd thought only about my sister, how she'd been hurt, and my relief that she'd been okay.

Then I remember something else. The bad feeling I'd had that entire morning, fearing something was terribly wrong. Even after I'd seen Samera, the sense of foreboding hadn't truly left me.

Suddenly it's like a lightbulb has gone on in my brain. All this time I was sensing something bad about Charles, not Samera.

And what a horrible coincidence that Rusty killed himself the same day that Charles did.

"Annie?"

"What?" I bark.

A wounded expression passes over Dominic's face, but he quickly recovers.

"I'm sorry," I tell him. "I didn't mean to bite your head off."

"I know."

"I'm not mad at you."

"I know."

"On the plus side, you don't have to worry about the trial driving us apart," I say, trying to be funny. Instead my voice cracks.

Dominic wraps his arms around me. "Annie."

"No." I try to resist him pressing my head to his chest. "I am not going to cry. Charles is a piece of shit."

"But you were married to him."

"For too long."

"The point is, you cared about him. It's okay to feel something now that he's gone."

Suddenly, I am crying. "Damn him. Taking the easy way out. I should have known."

"I was hoping the news didn't reach you in Vegas. I wanted you to hear it from me."

Now I slip my arms around him and squeeze.

"Some reporters have already called. I don't think they'll go away until they get to talk to you about this."

"Oh, for crying out loud." I wipe at my tears.

"Hey." Dominic lifts my chin upward, forcing me to look at him.

"What?"

"You are right about one thing. With your husband dead, the case against him is over."

"Please don't refer to him as my husband."

"I'm just saying… Forget it." He wraps his arms around me. "You want to head to bed?"

"To finish what we started?" I joke. Lamely.

"No," Dominic says. "So you can get some sleep. I don't know how you'll feel about this in the morning, but I want you to know that I'll be here for you every step of the way. Whatever you need to do. The funeral—"

"Funeral?" The thought that I'll have to bury my estranged husband is too much to bear. "You don't really think I'll have to bury him?"

"Forget I said that. We'll figure things out in the morning."

"Great. Just great. Charles has found yet another way to screw me."

"He's got no other family?"

"A brother somewhere." My head starts to throb. "No one I cared to talk to. Do you think it's my legal obligation to start making calls?"

Dominic leads me to the bed, where he forces me under the covers and tucks the sheets around me.

"Dom—"

He places a finger on my mouth to quiet me. "I know you have a million questions. A million concerns. But nothing's gonna get solved tonight, all right? You take the time you need to let this sink in, or to cry, or whatever you need to do."

"I need you," I tell him. "Please, lie with me. Hold me."

Dominic slips into the bed beside me and snakes an arm around my waist.

For a long while I don't sleep. But when I do drift off, Dominic's arm is still wrapped around me.

Twenty

Lishelle

When a person returns from a vacation, she expects to be refreshed. She expects to have a smile on her face for at least a couple weeks.

But when Claudia, Annelise and I returned from Las Vegas, life changed immediately for the worse. No longer were we happy women who'd gotten our grooves back. Because suddenly, with the news of Charles's death, we were thrown into tragedy.

As you can imagine, Charles Crawford's suicide was big news. With the city anticipating his trial for embezzling money from the Wishes Come True Foundation, the news hit Atlanta hard. Some felt Charles had received the justice he deserved, while others felt that he'd taken the easy route to escape what was sure to be jail time, and a lot of it.

As far as I'm concerned, what's happened has happened and we all have to deal with it. I only care how this has affected Annelise. Sure, she's put on a brave face, even when she gave me an exclusive interview on the news. But inside, I think she's suffering more than she's letting on.

The funeral was yesterday—a week and a half after our return from Vegas. Annelise helped Charles's brother with the arrangements, and she sat at the front of the church during the service, and was front and center at the graveside. I think her religious and moral convictions kicked in, and she dealt with Charles's passing the way a committed wife would.

While Annelise hasn't admitted it, I'm sure that Charles's death has hit her hard. My hope now is that with the funeral over, the healing will begin.

I'm at work now, and I reach for the phone on my desk. I dial Annelise's number.

The phone rings three times, and I'm about to hang up. But then someone picks up. It takes a couple seconds before I hear, "Hello?"

"Annelise, hi. It's Lishelle."

"Oh, hey." She sounds tired.

"Did I wake you up?"

"No. I was just lying down."

It's four o'clock in the afternoon. I wonder if she's even gotten out of bed today. "How're you feeling?"

"All right. I've got a bit of a headache, that's all."

"I'm worried about you."

"Why?"

"Come on, Annie. You know why. Your husband died, and you haven't talked about how this has made you feel. I don't know if you're sad, happy, angry."

"You sound like Dominic."

"Normally you tell me and Claudia everything. Remember when you found Charles in bed with Marsha, and you thought you were going to have a nervous breakdown? You leaned on us for support, and we helped you get through that."

"I'm not in love with Charles anymore. I'm not going to lose it."

"You just spent the last week and half dealing with funeral arrangements like you were his doting wife."

"He needed to be buried."

"I know that. And I'm not saying you shouldn't have done what you did. What I am saying is that you've kept all your feelings bottled inside. You need to know that it's okay to not be okay. It's okay to call me in the middle of the night in tears. It's okay to feel like you want to dig him up and kill him again. Whatever."

"It's over. I'm moving on."

"And why are you in bed at four o'clock in the afternoon? I really don't like that you're home alone."

"Claudia came over earlier. She brought me lunch."

"Oh, okay. Well that's good."

"I'm not drowning my sorrows. I'm not on the verge of an emotional breakdown."

"I'm only worried because I love you to death," I explain.

"I know."

I glance at my watch and sigh. It's time for me to head over to hair and makeup. "Sweetie, we'll talk later, okay? Maybe I'll visit you tomorrow before work."

"Like I'm a grieving widow." She pauses. "My God, I *am* a widow." Annelise says this as though she has just realized that fact. "The asshole died before we could get divorced."

"Yes, but—"

"You know what really sucks? Now that he's dead, I don't know if I can revert to my maiden name."

That's not what I expected to hear Annelise say. "I'm sure you can," I tell her.

"But what will people think of me? That I'm some callous bitch? My husband's body is rotting in his grave, and I can't let him rest in peace. I've got to hurt him one more way by dropping his name."

"Who cares what people think? And let's face it, Annie. It's not gonna matter to Charles one bit."

Annelise starts to cry. "My God, he's dead. He's *dead,* Lishelle. This past week and a half, it's like I've been starring in some really bad off-Broadway play. Playing this part I never thought I'd have to play, doing things I never imagined doing. And I had to smile and be polite so I didn't offend the audience. But you know what? I'm really angry. Charles took so much from me already. And now he had to go to the grave and rob me of my plan to divorce him while he was alive…"

"Maybe you should call Claudia. Ask her to come over." Or better yet, I could give Claudia a quick call myself.

"Dominic and I haven't made love since he told me the news. It's like he's afraid to touch me. And with all this, 'Your husband' from the funeral directors and media and strangers, I feel like some kind of harlot for living with another man."

"You're not a harlot."

"And where was Marsha Hindenberg in all this? The supposed love of Charles's life? The bitch broke up our marriage, and she didn't even make a fucking appearance at the funeral."

"Isn't she in jail?"

"No, she's out on bail while awaiting trial. It's probably

a good thing she stayed away, because I might have pummeled her."

This is good, Annelise's release of all these emotions. If only the timing for me didn't suck.

There's a knock at my door.

"Annie, sweetheart? I really do have to run. But we'll talk later, okay."

"Thanks for calling. I do feel better."

I end the call and hurry to the door. The first thing I see when I open it is a bouquet of flowers, an explosion of lavender and purple. Then Bernie from the mail room peeks his head out from behind the bouquet.

"Oh my God." I laugh giddily. And the thought that immediately pops into my mind is, *Roger*.

Since I've been home, I've thought of him often, wondered when I would hear from him and if we'd be able to pick things up from where we left off. Which is weird, since I'm not really into him.

Well, not totally.

Now that I've been able to look at the situation with some perspective, I know the guy's not my type. He's good for a one-night stand or a short-term affair. I figure what I truly want is to assuage my bruised ego.

"You have one helluva fan," Bernie tells me as he walks into the room with the arrangement. "Where do you want this?"

"My desk is fine." I scoot ahead of Bernie to clear off a corner of my desk. And the moment Bernie is gone, I rip the card open.

The message on the front of the card makes me laugh out loud:

"What happens in Vegas doesn't always stay in Vegas."

I've got to hand it to Roger. He's got a sense of humor. This is his way of saying that we can take what we started in Vegas and finish it in Atlanta.

I flip the card over.

"Your dirty little secret is about to be exposed."

My eyes narrow. What the hell?

I turn the card over again, and this time when I read the front the words have an entirely different meaning.

There's no name on the card. I search the envelope and also find nothing about a name. Then I dig through the flowers for a sign of another piece of paper.

But I find nothing.

I know I'm supposed to be in makeup, but I get on the phone and call Bernie. There's something I've only just realized, something that has struck me as odd.

"Hey, Bernie. It's Lishelle."

"Hey, babe. What's up?"

"That bouquet you delivered for me. Do you know where it came from?"

"Naw. The card should say."

"It should, but it doesn't."

"Was it unsigned?"

"Yeah."

"Something you're worried about?"

I hesitate. "No," I lie. "Just wondering which of my friends is playing secret admirer." I force a laugh. "Don't worry about it."

"All right. Call me if you need me."

"Will do."

When I hang up with Bernie, I stare at the bouquet of flowers. Filled with lavender roses, chrysanthemums and purple and white carnations, it's the kind of floral arrangement that speaks of romance.

Who would send such a beautiful bouquet with such a sinister message?

Twenty-One

Claudia

If anyone knows that life can change on a dime, I do. That one day you can happily be trotting down one path, only to have a gale-force wind knock you straight onto a path you didn't even know was in the vicinity.

What you don't know at the time is that the new path can be much more scenic, more beautiful, more peaceful. Even if it does have some twists and turns that continue to surprise you.

When Adam Hart, my fiancé of four years, broke up with me, I was catapulted onto a path I didn't expect. That was jarring, but I got up and kept walking.

What happened today, however, has straight-up pulled the paved path out from under me and left me on a bed of sharp rocks.

I'm sitting on my living room sofa, staring at the arrangement of purple flowers that had just arrived and rests on the coffee table. Maybe I should throw the damn thing out. Dump it in the trash where it belongs.

But dumping it in the trash isn't going to change the reality that it brought. It's not going to erase the implied threat.

> "What happens in Vegas doesn't always stay in Vegas. Your dirty little secret is about to be exposed."

Part of me wants to dismiss the crazy note that accompanied the flowers. And I would—if it hadn't arrived at my home.

Maybe Arlene learned I was in Las Vegas and figured I must have had a scandalous affair. After seeing her in the salon before my trip, she's probably been itching to get back at me for standing up to her. She's that kind of bitch.

And I wouldn't put it past her to think I'd start sweating at the prospect of her telling Adam all about my "dirty deeds" in Sin City.

It's plausible, yes, but is it likely? How the heck would Arlene know about my trip? And even if she does know, she'd have to have had someone tailing me to know I fucked a man I barely knew.

No, the more I consider Arlene's possible guilt in this, the less it makes sense.

I call Lishelle's cell phone and leave her a message. Lishelle's good at giving level-headed advice, and if she thinks the bizarre note is someone's idea of a bad joke, then I'll dismiss it.

In the meantime I'm restless, so I decide to call Annelise. I saw her earlier today for lunch, and she appeared in good spirits. But I also suspect that the dam holding her emotions in check might bust at any moment.

Annelise answers on the first ring. "What's up, Claudia?" she says, which tells me she saw the Caller ID before she picked up.

"Nothing much," I answer. "Just checking in with you. Wondering how you're doing."

"Well, I had a good cry."

"Because of—"

"Charles, yeah. I talked to Lishelle about an hour ago, and out of nowhere, I started to feel again. First, it was anger. Anger at Charles for killing himself and leaving me to deal with his mess. Anger at all the bullshit I've had to endure because of him. Anger because he made sure he'd never have to pay for his crimes. But then... Then the sadness came. Claudia, I just cried and cried, and I don't even know why I was crying."

"You've been through hell in the past few months. You're entitled."

"I know. And I feel better now. Especially since I got this gorgeous bouquet of flowers from Dom. He's been so sweet and supportive."

Annelise's words make the hairs on the back of my neck stand on end. "Flowers?" I ask.

"Yeah." I hear a smile in my friend's voice. "They just arrived when you called. It's a beautiful summer arrangement, with lavender roses, carnations—"

My heart starts to pound so loudly, I hear it in my brain. It drowns out the sound of Annelise's voice.

"—trying to find the perfect place to put it," she's saying when I can hear again.

"Did you open the card?" I ask urgently.

"Not yet. Like I said, I got the bouquet, then you called."

"Open the card."

"What?"

"Open the card, Annelise. And it's not because I want to find out how romantic Dominic is."

"You've lost me," she says.

"I just got a bouquet of flowers, too. About half an hour ago. A beautiful, purple floral arrangement."

I hear the sound of an envelope ripping. "This is what mine says. 'What happens in Vegas doesn't always stay in Vegas. Your dirty little secret—'"

"'—is about to be exposed,'" I finish for her. "Damn it. I got the same one."

"Claudia, what does it mean?"

"I have no clue. And there's nothing on the card to indicate where it came from."

"But the nicest guy delivered these to me," Annelise says, as though that means something.

"You saw him?" I ask. And before she can answer, I continue. "Did you see the delivery vehicle, which company it was?"

"He had dark hair. I think. He had sunglasses on. He smiled a lot and seemed friendly."

"And the vehicle?"

"A van, I think. White. Oh, God. I'm not sure."

There's silence for several seconds. "What are you thinking?" Annelise asks me.

"I'm remembering that story here in Atlanta from about ten years ago. The one where a woman opened her door to a flower delivery guy and he shot her. Hired by her husband to kill her."

Annelise gasps. "That's right. You don't think… Charles couldn't have set this up? He didn't even know where I was."

"I'm thinking that we don't open the door to any more flower delivery guys," I say.

"What could this be about? What dirty secret?"

"That's the thing. What *could* it be. So what if we went to Vegas and messed around a bit. Who doesn't in Sin City?"

"You think Lishelle got one?"

"Likely," I answer. "And maybe your sister, too."

"I'll call her and ask, then let you know."

I hang up feeling even more alarmed. My eyes land on the flowers.

"Who the heck is behind this?" I ask aloud.

But of course the flowers can't answer.

Twenty-Two

Samera

The sound of the office door opening has me slamming the college brochure shut.

Reed breezes into the room. "There you are, babe!" he exclaims a little too loudly, and I roll my eyes. Reed has been drinking, something he can't seem to abstain from when he's at the club.

He charges around the desk, spins his chair around so that I'm facing him, and smothers my mouth with his. I taste bourbon, his drink of choice.

"What are you doing in here?" he asks. "Why don't you come onto the club floor?"

"I figured I'd wait for you in here," I tell him.

Reed's eyes narrow as he glances over my shoulder. He lifts the college brochure. "What the hell's this?"

"Nothing."

"Doesn't look like 'nothing.'" Now he scowls at me. "You planning on going to college?"

"I told you that already, remember? When we got back from Vegas? You said you wanted me to come back and work at the club. I told you I wanted to find something different to do with my life."

"And *this* is what you're gonna do? Go to school and do what—become a nurse or something?"

I stand and snatch the brochure from Reed. "I was thinking maybe something artistic. I like dancing, obviously."

Reed laughs, and I swallow a spate of anger.

"Dancing?" he says, and wraps his arms around my waist. "Baby, you wanna dance—why don't you go on stage and do what you do best? We can dress you up in a nurse's outfit if you want. China didn't show, so I could use you."

I groan softly. The time might come when I'll have to do some more stripping, but while I still have some savings, I want to spend my time figuring out a new path for myself.

"Reed, I'm gonna leave."

"No, no, no." He tightens his arms, making my escape impossible. "You think I'm not listening to you, but I am. So this is the real me, the new, sensitive me, who's gonna talk now, okay?"

I don't say anything, just try to keep my mouth turned so I don't have to inhale Reed's foul breath. I've never liked it when he drinks, and this is bringing back bad memories.

"You don't wanna dance, fine. We can run the club together."

"Huh?"

"Me and you. A team."

Running the club with Reed is not exactly my idea of career advancement. But I don't tell him that.

"I'll run the books, hire the girls. And you…you can train

them. Make them into stars." Reed's eyes light up. "Great idea, huh?"

"Yeah, great," I say, but there's not one ounce of enthusiasm in my voice.

"And I was thinking that maybe I could branch off into porn. Make some really hot, all-girl action videos. I could make you into a star, babe. I wouldn't mind you eating all that pussy."

"Okay." I squirm in Reed's arms. "I'm tired. I'm gonna head home."

He pushes his leg between my thighs and urges my legs apart. "Why don't we fuck? I haven't tasted your pussy in two friggin' days. Let's have a quickie before you leave."

Reed's already reaching for the snap on my jeans as he pushes my shirt up and sucks on my nipple. But the knock on the door has him raising his head.

I quickly cover myself and turn around.

Standing at the doorway is Laci, a twenty-two-year-old who's new to the club. She seems startled to see me and Reed together. But then her eyes narrow.

"Reed?" she says, her tone clipped.

"Hold up, Laci. I'll come out in a minute, okay?"

She whirls around and disappears.

I look at Reed, and I guess my question is obvious. "No, I haven't fucked her," he tells me. "Not that she hasn't been asking."

Shaking my head, I twist out of Reed's arms.

He grabs me by the elbow. "Don't get pissed. All I want is your pussy. Remember that."

Each day that passes, I'm wondering more and more why I got back together with Reed. For maybe five days after returning from Vegas, he was the living example of sensitivity, especially after the news of Charles's suicide. Even when we made love, he was a different person. Slower, gentler, telling me he loved me often.

And I was enjoying it, this new Reed. But then a few days ago, he came home from the club drunk and I saw the old Reed again—the one I don't like.

I know that if I'm going to be with him, I have to accept who he is. But that night, when he was drunk on bourbon and fucked me like he was some wild animal, I saw exactly where my life with Reed will lead.

And it's not a place I want to go.

One of these days, I want to have some children, and I don't want to raise them amid the environment of a strip club, or worse, the porn world.

So Reed being who he is—and yeah, I loved him once— I'm slowly realizing that whether or not he ever cheats on me again, we just don't gel.

At least not outside the bedroom.

Despite the warm moisture hanging in the air this night, a chill sweeps over me as I step outside. Maybe it's a bit of melancholy because I'm realizing that Reed and I aren't meant to be, no matter how much we try to force it.

En route to my black BMW, I dig the keys out of my wallet. I press the keyless remote and the lights on my car flash on.

It's not until I'm behind the wheel of my car that I notice there's something on my windshield.

I get out of the car and reach for the piece of paper, assuming it's a flyer. Flyers stuck under wipers are a commonality outside the club.

But as my fingers close around the paper, I realize that it's actually an envelope. The chill I felt earlier creeps over me again when I see that the envelope reads "The Venetian."

Just like the one last week.

Glancing left and right, I try to see if anyone is lurking behind a tree or a bush. I can't tell, but that doesn't mean no one is there.

Hurriedly, I slip into my car and this time lock the door. Then I sit there for a good minute before I get the courage to open the envelope's flap.

The first envelope, one just like this, I found on my doorstep four days after I returned from Las Vegas. But I dismissed it and its seemingly cryptic message:

"What happens in Vegas doesn't always
stay in Vegas. You've been warned."

Now…

I tear into the envelope, figuring that hiding from what it contains isn't going to change a damn thing. There's a note inside, typed like the first one was.

"You made him die, bitch.
Now you're going to pay."

Fear sprouts inside me like a seed growing roots. The roots spread, tangle with my nerve endings, wrap themselves around all my major organs.

Holy shit, I *get* it. What the first letter was about. And this, more sinister, one.

Rusty.

Fuck!

My pulse thunders in my ears. I flip the envelope over, search for some kind of clue I previously missed. A postmark. Anything.

But there's nothing.

"Fuck!" I slam my palm against the steering wheel. Who the hell could have sent me this? And why?

Rusty's friend, Peter? But that son of a bitch knows that Rusty killed himself.

Unless he didn't kill himself…

I admit that I haven't followed up on the story of Rusty's death. I simply came home from Las Vegas and put him and what happened out of my mind.

The sound of brisk knocking on my passenger window scares the shit out of me. I scream bloody murder until I look out the window and see Reed's smiling face.

He asks something, but I can't hear. I roll down my window, my heart thundering in my chest.

"What are you still doing here?" he asks.

"I just, um…had a smoke," I lie.

"Ah."

"Why are you out here?" I ask. "Are you leaving?"

Reed shakes his head. "Just wanted to get out of the club for a minute. I figured I'd come out here and have a smoke."

I nod.

Reed's gaze falls on my hand. "What's that?"

"This?" I quickly crumple the note. "Just a flyer."

Reed nods, but I can't read his expression. I'm not sure if he believes me, or if he knows I'm lying.

"You okay?" he asks. "You look a little spooked."

"A little tired, that's all."

"Is there any reason you have to head home?"

"Other than to sleep?"

"You can sleep at my place."

This is true. And I'm suddenly wary of going home alone. "All right," I tell him. "I'll head to your place, then."

Reed grins like he's won the lottery. "I won't be too long. I'll tell Johnny to close up shop for me so I can get out of here in thirty, maybe forty minutes. Then I'm all yours."

Reed was right. I *am* spooked. So much so that when I reach his town house in midtown, I'm terrified at the thought of getting out of my car and heading to his door. Damn, I wish I'd just waited for him.

Breathing in and out slowly, I try to calm myself.

But it's really hard to be calm when some shithead who wants to hurt you knows where the fuck you live.

How, God only knows. But then, I don't really know much about Peter. He could be some kind of investigator. Or he could have hired someone to track me down.

The only thing I'm certain of is that Peter is behind this. I knew when I met him that he was a total creep, and now I'm convinced of that fact.

I don't think I was followed, but nonetheless, I look all around before even getting out of my car. When my feet hit the ground, I do a serious sprint to Reed's door. Even though I don't see or hear anything suspicious, Reed's key bobs up and down in my trembling hand. I can't slip the damn thing in the lock.

Shit, I have to get myself together. I can't let fear take control of me.

I breathe in, breathe out and calmly insert the key into the lock. It turns, and I open the door to Reed's home.

Once I'm inside, I immediately lock the door.

But I don't feel safe.

I get the distinct impression that someone is calling my name.

My eyes fly open. It takes a moment for them to focus,

and when they do, I see Reed standing over me. My eyes travel from his angry-looking face to his outstretched hand.

Instantly, I shuffle to a sitting position on the bed.

"When were you gonna tell me about this?" Reed demands.

It's too early for my brain to function at full capacity, but that doesn't prevent it from registering the fact that Reed has violated my privacy.

"You went through my purse?" I ask, appalled.

"That's beside the point, Sam." He tosses the note, now uncrumpled, onto the bed beside me. "What the fuck is this about?"

"Nothing."

"Nothing?" His voice raises an octave. "Someone's sent you some kind of threatening note. How does that qualify as nothing?"

"I don't know why someone sent that to me." And that's the truth.

Reed crosses his brawny arms over his chest. "What happened in Las Vegas?"

"Nothing—"

Reed pounces onto the bed, scaring the shit out of me. His arms straddle my body. "Goddamn it, Sam. Don't tell me nothing. If someone's threatening my girl, I need to know about it. How am I gonna protect you if you don't tell me what's going on?"

"If I tell you what happened, do you promise not to get mad?"

Reed clenches his teeth. "Sure."

"No, I'm serious. You have to remember, we were broken up when I went to Vegas, so whatever I tell you, you have to be able to deal with. 'Cuz if you can't, I'll be out that door so fast."

Reed is silent as he ponders my words. "All right. Just tell me."

I draw in a shaky breath. "Remember when you ran into me in the lobby of the Venetian?"

"Yeah. When I touched you, you screamed like you thought I was going to murder you."

I nod. "You asked me who hurt me, and I didn't tell you. Because all I wanted to do right then was forget."

Reed's eyebrows shoot up. "Someone *did* hurt you."

"Not just someone. Remember the news about the guy who killed himself? Well, it was him. Him and a friend."

"What the fuck happened?" Reed asks, his anger barely contained.

So I tell him. And I don't leave out any of the dirty details.

"You should have told me," he says when I'm finished my story.

"Why—so you could bust someone's kneecaps?"

"Yes, damn it."

"Which is exactly what I didn't want you to do." I sigh. "If it makes you feel better, this guy got what he deserved. He *killed* himself."

"And what about his friend? This Peter guy?"

"It's over, Reed. I don't need you trying to be Rambo. I've learned my lesson. Trust me, no one is ever gonna be able to do that to me again."

"That's not what I care about. Don't you think this Peter guy is behind the notes you got?" When I don't answer, Reed continues. "I need to find him. Make sure this guy doesn't even *think* of hurting you."

"I don't know anything about him."

"What about this Rusty guy? You know where he was from,

right? You didn't just drop your pants for him without a little conversation first, did you?"

I glare at Reed. "Don't you dare. You promised you wouldn't get mad. And you have no friggin' right to be mad. So just stop it."

Reed spins around and marches to the window. He stares outside for several seconds. I can hear his angry breathing, even from my spot on the bed.

I get to my feet.

In a flash Reed whirls around and pins me with his eyes. "Where are you going?"

"To take a piss. That okay?"

He doesn't say anything, and I disappear into the bathroom. A couple minutes later, I'm finished my business, and I almost head back into the bedroom. But when I see the phone on the wall, I pause.

For some reason, I haven't been able to find my cell phone, but I can check my messages from a landline. I lift the receiver and punch in my home number. I'm not in the mood to rush back to Reed right now, knowing he's still got to be seething.

I smile when I hear Annelise's voice, but the smile quickly fades when I hear what she has to say.

"Sammy, where are you? I just got something really weird. And Claudia, too. A bouquet of flowers with a note saying that what happens in Vegas doesn't always stay in Vegas, and that my dirty little secret is about to be exposed. Did you get anything like that?"

I quickly hang up, then call my sister. When she answers, I begin without preamble, "You got some weird message about Las Vegas?"

"Yeah. You, too?"

"Uh-huh." My head starts to throb. "Look, maybe we should meet somewhere. Talk in person instead of on the phone."

"I agree. Let me call Lishelle and Claudia, then call you back."

"Wait, why don't I call you back in ten minutes. I'm not at home, and I can't find my cell."

"All right."

I end the call and get into the shower. I quickly wash my body, and when I'm finished, I call Annelise again.

"We're gonna meet at eleven-thirty," she tells me. "A place called Liaisons. You know where that is?"

"Yes. I'll be there."

When I exit the bathroom with a towel wrapped around my body, Reed seems to be in a better mood. His eyes roam over me from head to toe, and then he smiles.

I head to the chair where I placed my clothes last night. Reed slips his arms around me from behind and loosens my towel.

"Reed…"

He pulls the towel from my body. "Let's fuck."

"I can't."

"Why not?" He strokes my nipples while pressing his groin against my ass. He's already hard.

"Because I've got to go. My sister got a note about Las Vegas, and so did her friends. We're going to meet to talk about it."

A full minute passes before Reed speaks again, and in that time I put my clothes on.

"Do me a favor," he finally says.

"All right."

"Don't go back to your place."

"Why not?"

"Because there's some freak out there who wants to hurt you. I think you're better off staying with me."

I can't argue with Reed's logic. "I'm going to need to get some clothes. Other necessities."

"Then I'll go with you. Promise me you won't go back to your apartment alone."

"Okay. I won't."

The corners of Reed's mouth lift in a warm smile. He strokes my face. "I love you, babe."

I give Reed a peck on the lips, hoping that will suffice for my inability to utter those same three words back to him.

Twenty-Three

Annelise

When I approach our table in Liaisons, Lishelle and Claudia are already there. They both look up at me expectantly.

"Where's your sister?" Lishelle asks when I reach the table. Worry is etched on her face.

"On her way," I answer. "She called to say she'd be about ten minutes late."

I slide into the booth, sighing as I do.

Claudia drops an envelope onto the table, one that reads "The Venetian" in the top-left-hand corner. "I got this this morning. It was left outside my door."

I dig a similar envelope out of my purse. "I got one, as well. Mine said, 'Payback's a bitch.' What did yours say?"

"The same thing," Claudia responds.

"Guess mine is waiting for me at the office?" Lishelle comments sourly.

"Payback for what?" Claudia asks, frustration lacing her tone. "I don't get it."

"If this is someone's idea of a joke," Lishelle begins, "this shit ain't funny."

"I'm starting to get scared," Claudia admits. "Yesterday, it was those flowers. This morning, a note on my doorstep. Whoever is behind this is here, in Atlanta." Claudia pounds a finger on the table to emphasize her words.

"I know," I say. "Trust me, I know. Dom found the letter outside his door. He wondered how it got there, without any postage."

"Shit." Lishelle's eyes widen. "Wait, what'd he say about the flowers?"

"He didn't see them," I say. "Once I realized they weren't from him, I tossed them in a bin before he got home." It was a knee-jerk reaction, but I had no clue how I'd explain the flowers to my boyfriend."

"You probably should tell him what's going on," Claudia says.

"Not until *I* know what's going on."

The waitress arrives, and we each order cosmopolitans. Sure, it's the lunch hour, but we need them. We spend the next few minutes sipping on our drinks and not saying much. My friends are worried—I can see it in their eyes. Heck, I'm worried too.

"Thank God," Claudia mutters, and I swivel around in my seat.

Samera, wearing jeans, a supertight white T-shirt, and those clear pumps strippers are so fond of, strolls toward our table. My body shudders with relief. Then I hop out of the booth and give my sister a long, warm hug.

We don't say anything as we settle in the booth, side by

side. Lishelle looks at Samera pointedly and asks, "Do you have any idea what this shit is about?"

Samera gazes at each of us in turn. "I think so, yeah."

"Don't keep us in suspense," Claudia says.

"Something happened when we were in Las Vegas," Samera goes on. "Friday night."

"What?" Lishelle demands.

"Lishelle, give her a second okay?" I say. "If it's what I think it is, then this isn't easy for her."

Lishelle doesn't look pleased while she shrugs, but at least she bites her tongue.

"The night before I left," Samera begins, "I was with a guy in Vegas. I saw him the first day we got there, and kept running into him. Ultimately we got together."

"Wait a minute," Claudia interjects. "Is this the guy who killed himself?"

Samera nods.

"Let her finish the story," Lishelle says. "Because I'd love to know what this has to do with any of us."

I scowl at Lishelle, but she doesn't notice.

"We hit it off," Samera continues. "It's not like I thought we'd end up happily ever after or anything, but he was cool, you know? A guy to spend the night with who'd make me forget all the shit going on in my life. In the beginning he seemed so fun, so decent. We took things upstairs to his room. And in the middle of fucking our brains out—"

Samera stops abruptly, her gaze flying to her left. I glance that way as well, and there's the waitress. She grins sheepishly, then mutters, "I'll give you a few more minutes."

The waitress gone, Samera picks up her story where she left off. "We were in the middle of things. And the next thing

I know, some guy comes in the room. The same guy I'd seen Rusty with a few times. A guy named Peter. His friend."

Samera stops, bristles.

"Don't stop now," Lishelle tells her.

"His friend wanted to join the action. I thought Rusty would be appalled. But he *wanted* him in on the action. I told them to fuck off, but they got nasty, calling me a whore, saying they knew I had a price. After that, Peter got a bit rough with me and so did Rusty. I think those two mother-fuckers wanted to rape me. I fought my way out of there, and they eventually let me go."

"Oh my God," Claudia says.

"And after that," I say, "this Rusty guy plunged out of his hotel window."

"And I think that's what this is all about," Samera says.

"But why?" Lishelle asks. "Rusty killed himself."

"I have to assume Peter's pissed about that," Samera answers. "Pissed enough to send all of us threatening notes."

For a moment none of us says a word. We take in what Samera has told us. Samera glances away, and I get the distinct impression that she's trying to keep herself together. Which is hard for me to see, because I'm used to her being so strong.

I reach for Samera's hand and give it a squeeze. And I can't help it—my eyes mist.

"And you *never* went back to the room?" Lishelle asks. "Not even to tell them off?"

Samera shakes her head. "You think I wanted to see them again? I went downstairs, ran into Reed, and then went to the Bellagio with him."

"Odd," Claudia says. "That he would commit suicide after that. But even more odd is why Peter would blame you for his death?"

"I think," Samera says, then pauses. "I think he must blame me. My feeling is that maybe Rusty felt guilty about what he'd done after I left. Maybe he even thought I'd go to the police. Before we went upstairs, he told me how much he'd been in love with his wife. She died of cancer only six months ago. Maybe everything got to him and he couldn't live with himself." Samera shrugs. "That's my best guess."

"We should go to the police," Claudia says.

"I don't want to do that," Samera admits.

"Why not?" Lishelle asks.

"Because what if they start thinking that Rusty didn't kill himself. Remember, Annie—you told me the cops were looking for the blonde Rusty had been in the bar with. That blonde was *me*. What if they think I had something to do with his death?"

"Why would they think that?" Lishelle asks doubtfully. "You said yourself that you met up with Reed right after that. That you spent the night with him. He's your alibi."

"How convincing of an alibi do you think he'd be?" Samera asks me. "He's in love with me. The cops will know he'd say anything to protect me."

"But you don't need protecting," Claudia points out. "You didn't kill him."

"I know that. But why does his friend think I did? Why's he going to these elaborate lengths to scare the shit out of me? He told the police that he didn't believe Rusty killed himself. And who most likely killed him if he didn't commit suicide? Me." Samera points to herself. "I had reason to want to kill the piece of shit. He crossed the line with me. It won't be too hard for the police to come to the same conclusion and issue a warrant for my arrest."

Now Samera starts to sob, and I stretch my arm across her shoulder. "It's okay."

"How can it be okay? This asshole knows where I live. Maybe he's watching my every move. Following me where I go."

I notice Lishelle's eyes flitting around the restaurant. "We need to go to the cops."

"Did you hear a word I said?" Samera asks her pointedly.

"Yeah, well, you're not the only one in danger here," Lishelle shoots back. "We all got letters."

"Fine. I guess that's fair. I go to jail, but at least everyone will be safe."

"That's an illogical conclusion," Lishelle replies.

"Lishelle," I begin as an idea hits me. "Can't you get someone at the station to investigate this? Hell, you can call the Vegas police yourself, ask if they consider the death a suicide or homicide. Then we can go from there."

"Yes," Claudia agrees. "I'm not saying we shouldn't call the police, but Sam's right to be concerned. If she's identified as the last person to be with Rusty—and one who had a reason to be angry with him—she could be in serious trouble."

"I think that's a stretch," Lishelle says dryly.

"Easy for you to say, since it's not your ass on the line." The words pour out of me, all on their own. I'm doing something I haven't done since childhood—defending my sister.

Lishelle meets my gaze dead-on, and I see a challenge in her eyes. Then she looks away, and I know I've won this battle.

"All right," she says. "I'll get Ruben at the station to look into this. He's the one who tracked Glenn down in Arizona."

"Thank you," Samera says, and a small smile forms on her face.

Lishelle nods. "You're welcome. You'll have to tell me everything you know about Rusty. His full name, where he lives—if you know."

"Rusty Nickell. I saw that on the news. He was from Chicago. All I know is that his friend's name is Peter."

"It's a start," Lishelle says. "First, I'll head to my office and do some preliminary digging myself. Find any news articles relevant to Rusty's death. Then I'll go from there."

"You think that this Ruben guy can find out Peter's last name?" Samera asks. "Maybe from the hotel or the police, and even tell you where he lives?"

"Ahhh." Claudia nods, understanding.

"Great idea." My heart fills with hope. "Because if he can find out who this guy is, where he lives—then we can contact him. Tell him we're gonna go to the cops if he doesn't smarten up."

"Yes," Samera says.

We all look at Lishelle, waiting for her response.

"I'm sure it's completely unethical," she begins slowly, "but it's not like I didn't cross ethical lines when tracking down Glenn. And this situation is a whole lot more serious."

"That's for sure," Claudia says.

"So, yeah," Lishelle continues. "Let's find out who this son of a bitch is and make him sorry for ever messing with us."

An hour later I'm at Kroger's with a cartful of groceries when my cell phone rings. The display reads "Unknown Number," and I assume it must be Lishelle.

I press the talk button. "Hello?"

"Annie, it's Lishelle."

"Did you find something already?" I ask.

"Yeah. And your sister isn't going to like it." Lishelle pauses. "It looks like Rusty didn't kill himself."

I gasp.

"Yeah, I know. The autopsy showed that he died before the fall. His throat had been slit."

"*No!*"

"Yes. And, it gets worse. They found a woman's shoe in the room. A clear, high-heeled shoe."

Lishelle is silent, and her words settle over me. "Oh my God."

"And…the concierge remembers seeing a busty blonde walking through the lobby barefoot. She was rude to him when he told her she needed shoes, which is why he remembers her. The police are apparently looking for anyone who can come forward to supply this woman's identity."

"Shit!"

"Yeah. So now we know why Rusty's friend is hell-bent on getting to Samera. He probably sent you, me and Claudia those notes just to steer Samera off his trail."

"Why doesn't he just go to the police then?" I ask. "If he thinks my sister killed his friend, and he knows where she lives, why doesn't the shithead just go to the police?"

"Because he wants to take matters into his own hands?"

Lishelle's suggestion makes me shiver. "So this is real. Peter is out to hurt my sister. Or worse."

"Seems so. Look, you better call Samera. Tell her not to go to her house under any circumstances. I'll get Ruben to track down this Peter person and find out his full name, and then we can cross-reference that name with hotel reservations in the city. It might take a while, but it can be done."

"Thanks," I say softly, emotion filling my throat.

"Listen, sweetie," Lishelle says. "I wish I could say something to make this all go away."

"But you can't. I know. Just try to find this guy, okay?"

"You bet."

I stuff my phone back into the purse and look around. Could Peter be in this grocery store right now, watching my every move?

I release my grocery cart and hustle toward the store's exit, not about to take any chances.

Twenty-Four

Samera

My heart has been beating at an accelerated speed ever since I left the restaurant. Not knowing where to go, I drove to a strip mall and parked outside a Ross Dress For Less store. That's where I am now, slumped behind the wheel of my BMW. I sit there and try to figure out what I'm going to do.

Five minutes pass, and I have no answers.

Finally deciding that I have to do something, I start the car. The engine purrs and the air-conditioning comes on full-blast. The only thing I'm sure of right now is that I can't go back to my place. At least not by myself.

I remember Reed's anger this morning, his desire to beat Peter's head in. At the time I'd told him to forget the issue, as though I wanted him to take the high road. Now I know the truth is that I need the Reed that can be a hothead, the guy who'll hunt Peter down and make him sorry for messing with me. Because if I'm alone somewhere and Peter confronts me, there's no way I'll be able to handle him by myself.

I start for the parking lot's exit, then think better of it and pull the car to the side. Thankfully, I found my cell phone under the seat in my car, and I use it now to call Reed.

He doesn't pick up his home phone, so I call the cell, which he does answer.

"Sam," he says.

"Hey, Reed."

"How'd your meeting go?"

"Creepy," I admit. "I'll tell you all about it when I see you. Where are you?"

"I went out to get some wine."

"Do you have time to head to my place now? I don't want to go there alone, but I need to pick up some of my things."

"Sure, I've got time. Why don't you meet me back at the house? There's no point in taking two cars."

"Right. Okay, see you soon."

My stomach twists painfully as I drive back to Reed's house. I glance in my rearview mirror often, fearing that someone's following me.

And I see Peter many times. In cars driving beside me, behind me, on the opposite side of the road.

Of course, I don't really see him. My mind is playing tricks on me.

Living in fear…it's no way to live.

Still, when I pull into Reed's driveway and see his Explorer there, I sigh in relief.

I'm opening my car door when Reed appears at his doorway. He grins, waves, then steps outside.

I stay behind the wheel. Moments later Reed approaches the passenger side of my car.

"All right if we take your car?" he asks.

"Sure," I say.

Reed gets in beside me and kisses me on the cheek. And as I stare at him, I feel conflicted. Just last night I hadn't been sure if I wanted to continue my relationship with him. Now I'm thankful that he's here with me.

I start to drive. Reed turns on the car radio and searches until he finds a station he likes, one playing pop-rock. He turns the volume high.

With the music blaring, we don't talk. And that's fine with me. Reed's presence is enough.

Twenty minutes later we're at the town house that houses my apartment. I pull into the driveway and turn off the car's engine. Then I reach for the door's handle, but Reed puts a hand on my arm, stopping me.

I turn my head to look at him. "What?"

"Don't just get out of your car like that. Look around first." He looks left and right, showing me what I ought to do. "If that Peter asshole is hiding somewhere in the bushes, you don't want to be blindsided."

I nod.

"Wait here, okay?" Reed opens his car door and gets out. He does a three-sixty, scanning the area, and then heads over to my door.

He opens it, saying, "It looks like the coast is clear."

I exit the car, and Reed immediately takes my hand. Together we head up the steps to my home, but I'm anxious every step of the way, even with Reed here.

At the front door Reed turns and takes another look around while I insert my key into the lock. But the door pushes open, and I frown.

Without thinking, I step into the foyer. And what I see hits me hard. Before I have a chance to scream, I'm slipping. My stilettos sliding through the sticky, dark red blood covering the floor.

Everything happens in slow motion. I fall backward, my hands flailing, a silent scream bubbling in my throat. I'm unable to fight gravity, and my head pounds on the hardwood floor.

Right beside the severed head.

It is then that my scream becomes audible. I scream uncontrollably, like some psycho killer is standing over me with a knife. My fingers and arms slide through the thick blood and I try desperately to move away from the bloodied head beside me. But I keep slipping and going nowhere.

"Holy fuck!"

Reed charges into the foyer. He drops to his knees, gathers me in his arms, but still I don't stop screaming.

"My God!" Reed runs his fingers over my face and upper body. "Motherfucker!"

Hot tears spill onto my cheeks. "It's a head!" I scream. "It's a fucking head!" I know I sound hysterical, but given the circumstances, I have every right to be.

"Motherfucker," Reed repeats.

Carefully he climbs to his feet and pulls me up with him. I grip him, hold on to him for dear life. I cry until my throat is hoarse.

After a few minutes I chance a look over my shoulder. The head is in bad shape—its skull bashed and brain matter exposed.

"Stay here," Reed instructs me, pushing me toward a corner in the foyer. "I'm gonna check that thing out."

"N-no. Maybe you shouldn't."

"We're covered in blood here. It's not gonna matter."

Glancing at my hands, I feel like Lady Macbeth. There's

blood everywhere. I can't stand to see it anymore, and I close my eyes. I huddle in the corner, shaking and crying.

"I don't think it's real," Reed says after a moment.

I open my eyes and scream when I see him lifting the head.

"It's too light," he explains, bobbing it up and down.

"Reed, don't…don't do that."

"And this blood…" He gestures to the foyer floor. "It smells kinda sweet to me."

Once again I examine my hands. I lift one until it's close enough for me to smell it.

"It does smell sweet," I concur, and my heart finally starts to slow its frantic pace. "Kind of like strawberry."

"Syrup," Reed concludes. And to be sure, he licks the substance off his finger. "Yep."

A long, relieved breath oozes out of me. Then I realize what has happened. "Someone went to serious lengths to scare the shit out of me. And it worked."

Reed drops the head, and even though I know it's fake, I jump as it bounces. "That son of a bitch."

I nod. What else can I do?

"One night in Las Vegas." Reed shakes his head as he stares at me, and I see anger in his eyes. I know at this moment, that anger is for me. "One night of fun, right? I bet that's all you thought it'd be."

I sniffle and move toward my living room. Fuck, my ankle hurts. I'm about to sit on my living room sofa, but I abruptly stop myself. I'm covered in strawberry syrup. I can't very well sit on my furniture like this.

Instead I plop my body onto the floor and take off my heels.

"Do you see how real this shit is?" Reed asks. He sits on the floor beside me, stares at me with a stern look. "Goddamn it, you brought this shit to Atlanta—"

"Fuck you, Reed, I know!" I yell. "I know better than anyone else what the price of that night was. So spare me the lecture!"

Reed breathes heavily as he stares at me, his anger evident. I do the same as I meet his irate look.

"Honestly, Reed, if you can't deal with what I have to say, then you can walk out that door right now."

"I'm scared, okay?" He takes my hand in his. "I love you more than anything, and someone wants you dead. How am I supposed to feel about that?"

"How did he find me?" I ask. "I mean, it's not like Peter knew anything about me. I don't understand."

"People can find all kinds of shit on the Internet, Sam."

"I guess so," I agree, knowing that's the only thing that makes sense. Cold, I run my hands up and down my arms.

Reed rises. "You're definitely never coming back here. Pack your bags and make it fast. You're not staying here another minute. This son of a bitch means business."

"What about the police? I'm not keen on calling them, because God only knows if they'll take me into custody, but maybe they can protect me."

"I'll protect you." Reed extends his hand to me. "Come on."

My heart slams against my rib cage as Reed pulls me to my feet. I glance every which way in my apartment, as though someone might come out of a door or round a corner any second.

"Reed, what if he's still here?"

"I should have brought my gun," Reed utters.

I want to run out of my apartment and never return. But I can't leave like this, wearing clothes covered in fake blood. Even Reed has the strawberry syrup all over his jeans, which will be suspicious as hell should anyone see us leaving my apartment.

"Babe," Reed says, "you stay close to the phone. I'll take a look around."

Reed heads off, and I hold my breath. I don't think I breathe until he returns to me and proclaims that all's clear.

I rip off my shirt before I even get to my bedroom. Then, I shimmy my jeans off my hips. I toss both pieces into the hamper in my room before retrieving my suitcase from the closet. Then I spend a couple minutes going through drawer after drawer, dumping contents from my dresser into the suitcase without even caring what it is.

Five minutes later I'm dressed in a pink sundress. I wanted to shower, but the sooner I get out of my apartment, the better.

Reed offers me his arm. "You ready?"

"Absolutely. Let's get out of here."

Twenty-Five

Lishelle

Two days ago, when I received that bouquet of flowers at the office it was the beginning of a nightmare. So you can imagine that I'm none too pleased to open my office door and see another stunning bouquet. This time it's a gorgeous arrangement of red roses, and for a moment it takes my breath away.

"Not more flowers, Bernie."

Bernie doesn't say a word, just steps into the room. And that's when I see that it *isn't* Bernie holding these flowers. It's Rugged.

"So I have some competition," he says when we make eye contact.

"Rugged?" I ask, as though I can't believe he's really here.

"Roger. Remember, my friends call me Roger."

I glance at my wristwatch. It's not even one in the afternoon—a time of day when I normally wouldn't be here.

"How did you know I'd be here?" I ask him. "I don't usually come in until later." And something niggles at the back of my neck as I ask the question. A hint of suspicion.

"I didn't know," he replies. "I wanted to bring these here to surprise you."

I breathe in and out slowly, eyeing Roger warily. He places the vase of roses onto the desk beside the other bouquet. Yeah, I kept the flowers. I didn't want to rouse curiosity by dumping them.

Roger looks at me and asks, "What?"

"You didn't by chance send me flowers a couple of days ago, did you?"

"If I sent you flowers, you'd know it."

"Hmm." I'm not sure if I should believe him.

He chuckles nervously. "You're not happy to see me?"

"I don't know."

Now he narrows his eyes. "The way we left things in Vegas...I thought you wanted to see me again."

"I'm gonna say something, and I want an honest answer. Did you send me and my friends flowers? Possibly as a bad joke?"

Roger's expression turns serious. "No. What's this about?"

"Just...we got some flowers. The notes were weird. Vague," I add. "And now you show up with roses..."

"I got into town this morning." He reaches into the pocket of his baggy jeans and produces a cell phone. "Call my manager if you want."

My rigid stance softens. "No, that's okay."

"You're not happy to see me?" he asks.

"I didn't say that." And then I smile.

Roger matches my smile and heads toward me. He scoops me into his arms and kisses me deeply.

"Damn," he says when we pull apart. "I've wanted to do that ever since you walked away that night."

"Walked away? You *sent* me away, remember?"

"And I've been suffering ever since."

I'm obviously crazy because I flush at the statement. Since when did I become such a pushover?

Roger nuzzles his nose against my ear. "Did you miss me?" he whispers.

"A little," I admit. But my body screams, *A lot!*

"Damn, you know how to bring a brotha to his knees. Crush his ego."

"Oh, let's not talk about crushed egos! And then you didn't call…"

"I had ta work. Concerts on the West Coast. You know."

"And all those groupies to keep you warm at night." I soften the accusation with a smile, let him know I'm joking.

"You said you got some time, right?"

"A little," I tell him.

He takes my hand. "Then come with me."

"Where?" I ask.

"My place ain't far from here. We can finish what we started in Vegas. And this time, no games."

Talk about direct. "I don't have much time," I tell him. "A little less than three hours." Not nearly as long as I'd like, but certainly long enough to quench my thirst.

"Enough time for an appetizer. Something to whet yo' appetite."

I smile sweetly, my vagina already thrumming. "Let me grab my purse."

Rugged's place is a stately home in Buckhead, complete with magnolia trees and a wrought-iron gate lining the property.

I'm impressed, yes, but I'm more impressed with his huge cock. I've been playing with it ever since we left the news station, and it's stayed hard all that time.

The gate shuts behind Rugged's Navigator once the vehicle is on the property. I unbuckle my seat belt and go for gold. Dropping my head onto his lap, I immediately swirl my tongue over the tip of his penis.

"Damn, woman!" he exclaims, then laughs. "Let me park the car."

I ignore him and continue to flick my tongue over his shaft, pumping it as I do.

The car comes to an abrupt stop, and I expect Roger to recline his seat and enjoy. Instead, he grips me by the shoulders and urges me up.

I flash him a confused look.

"I'm all fo' a quickie in the car," he tells me, "but what I wanna do ta you? Nuh-uh. I need you inside."

I groan slightly in protest, but I'm not really disappointed. I'm excited at the idea of finding out exactly how Roger plans to whet my appetite.

I make my way out of the car, and he meets me at the front of the SUV, where he's struggling to zip up his pants. Then he takes my hand.

"Don't look so disappointed," he tells me. "I promise, you're gonna love this."

My body shudders from the promise, that's how hot and bothered I am.

The walk to the front door seems like an eternity, but really it's less than a minute. Roger opens the door, and we step into the house. He takes my hand again and leads me upstairs.

The blinds are drawn in his massive bedroom, and very little natural light is coming into the room. Enough for me to see his face, and little enough that I don't mind getting completely naked.

Roger gathers me in his arms and kisses me, a startlingly gentle kiss considering I know we both can't wait to get naked. It's a reminder that sex can be tender, intimate, and to my own surprise I appreciate that.

He moves his mouth from my lips to my neck, where he sucks softly on my skin and gently nips it with his teeth.

"I think you're sexy," he whispers. "And I'm mad attracted to you."

"I kind of figured that out," I joke, and offer him more of my neck to tease.

"Even if you are stubborn as hell," he goes on, and we both chuckle at that.

Roger's mouth finds mine again, and we kiss deeply. After a few seconds he abruptly pulls away.

"Wait a second, okay?"

I moan and nod at the same time.

Running my hands over my breasts, I watch as Roger heads to the stereo in his room. He flips through a CD case, finds something he likes, then puts it into the CD player. As he does, I pull my dress over my head.

And I have a twilight moment sensation. Here I am, standing in a rap star's bedroom in only designer shoes and lace panties. Never in my wildest dreams would I have pictured myself in this situation.

Turning, Roger sees me and grins. Soft music fills the airwaves, and I soon recognize the voice as Usher's.

He heads back to me and immediately wraps his arms around me, splays his hands over my back. And then he sways first to the left, then the right. It takes me a moment to realize he wants me to dance with him.

So I do. Together, we move our bodies in sync to the romantic beat. Roger's fingers play over my back. His touch is light—he's only skimming my skin—but it's electric.

We dance for the entire song, until another person's voice fills the airwaves. This time it's a woman. Tamia.

Now I wrap my arms around Roger's neck and hold him close. We don't have all night, but still this feels nice. Nice to enjoy the moment as though we have all the time in the world.

Roger moves his hands lower, to the small of my back.

I'm the first to raise my lips to his. The kiss is slow at first. Soon it turns hot and passionate. His touch is no longer light. His hands roam all over my back, over my ass, kneading my flesh.

I reach for his shirt, tug it out of his jeans. He raises his hands high and I pull the shirt over his head. Then I run my fingers over his chest, playing with the strands of dark curls I find there.

Roger slips his hands between my thighs and covers my pussy through my panties.

I moan. "Oh, that feels good."

"I love everything about you," he tells me. "Your body is perfect."

"You're pretty perfect yourself."

And he is. Forget a six-pack. He's got eight well-defined muscular ripples across his torso. And his arms are strong. The kind I love to have wrapped around my body.

I stroke my fingers over his arms, his abdomen. I move them lower, to the snap on his jeans.

"I'm all yours, baby," he tells me.

I undo his jeans and shimmy them down his hips, enjoying the feel of his long, muscular legs as I do. But it's the shape of his penis, erect beneath white cotton briefs, that has me inhaling sharply.

"Wow."

Only when I hear Roger's chuckle do I realize that I said the word aloud. In the car I couldn't see the entire length and girth. But now…

I glance up at him and grin. "This is…fucking impressive," I tell him bluntly.

I pull down his briefs, hold his cock in my hands. He's got to be a good nine, ten inches. More than enough.

As I stroke him, inhale the scent of him, my pussy gets wet. I lower myself to my knees and take him into my mouth.

Roger starts to groan. Up and down, I move my lips over his shaft. He tangles his fingers in my hair as his groans grow louder. I take him as far into my mouth as I can, to the back of my throat. My fingers travel up his inner thigh, to his testicles. I massage them as I continue to work my mouth over his cock.

"Jeez," he mutters, and then he grips my shoulders and pulls me upward. "I don't want to come yet," he whispers in my ear. He licks my earlobe, then my jawline, and then sucks my bottom lip into his mouth.

A moment later he urges me backward onto the bed. I land on the mattress with a soft thud. I love Roger's smile. It's hot and sweet at the same time.

He spreads my legs, and soon his smile disappears between my thighs.

The first brush of his tongue against my clitoris is pure heaven. His tongue moves slowly at first, back and forth across my clit. Then he picks up speed, lapping at my pussy as though he can't get enough of me.

I moan, arch my back. Roger splays a hand across my

stomach, holding me in place. Then he draws my clitoris completely into his mouth and sucks on me so softly and sweetly the pleasure is torturous.

"Oh my God." I thrash my head around, and my hands. After a moment I settle my hands on my nipples and squeeze.

I cry out when Roger spreads my lips and dips his tongue into my opening. And when he flicks his hot tongue over my nub once again, I start to come.

"Fuck, Roger!" My orgasm moves through me like a giant wave. "Put your cock in me right now. *Please.*"

But he doesn't stop eating my pussy until another orgasm rips through me. The second one leaves me quivering and whimpering. Only then does Roger's tongue relent. My breathing ragged, I lie with my eyes closed. I hear the sound of a condom opening, and seconds later Roger's body covers mine.

He kisses me. Lord, the man knows how to kiss a woman.

With his tongue in my mouth, he guides his cock into my pussy. The first, sweet thrust leaves me breathless.

"Damn, baby." I gasp as his cock fills me. I run my hands over Roger's back, grip his flesh, dig my nails into his skin. "Gawd…"

Roger braces his hands behind my knees and thrusts his cock in and out of me. Pleasure flows like liquid heat through my veins.

"Wrap your arms around my neck," Roger tells me, and I do.

With my arms around his neck, he spins onto his back, taking me with him. His cock reaches deep inside me, and I gasp from the intense pleasure. He lifts his head and takes one of my nipples into his mouth. He sucks on it hard.

"Roger…"

"Damn, baby. Your pussy! *Shit!*"

I move my hips up and down, sliding my vagina up and down his penis. Just when I think I might come again, Roger moves me off his body and onto the bed.

I moan in protest, but he moves behind me and pulls me to my knees. Then I feel his tongue on my pussy again, and I bite down on my bottom lip to quiet my scream of pure bliss.

And when Roger enters me from this position, it's the ultimate ecstasy. He doesn't even have to thrust to intensify my pleasure.

But he does thrust, in and out, in and out, the velocity increasing with each stroke.

He pulls out completely, then enters me fully and asks, "You like that?"

"Yes…"

"Damn, I love the way yo' pussy feels on my dick. Tight and wet." He slips his hands between my legs and massages me. "I wanna fuck this pussy all damn day, and all night…make you come a hundred times…"

Every stroke tickles my G-spot. Any second now and I could come again.

"Harder!" I cry. Roger moves faster, harder. Wrapping an arm around my upper body, he pulls me upward in a swift motion. Both our bodies upright, our rhythm doesn't slow, not even for a second. Roger's hands urgently caress the front of my body, playing with my nipples and my clit while I ride his cock. I throw my head back onto his shoulder and moan like a woman possessed.

I am possessed. By one amazing cock.

Now Roger pushes my body forward. My upper body goes all the way down so that my breasts press against the mattress.

Roger grunts and pushes himself deep inside me, so deep

I shudder. "Pound my pussy!" I yell. And Roger pounds me so hard, the sound of our bodies colliding fills the air like staccato clapping. "Yes, Roger. *Yes*. Harder!" I start to whimper. "Harder, baby. Make me co-o-ome!"

I explode. My orgasm spirals out from my pussy, through my stomach and to my breasts, and down my legs to my toes. I grip the bedspread as my body convulses over and over again.

Roger's groans getting wilder, he squeezes my ass and spreads my cheeks wide. "Fuck, I'm coming!" he exclaims, and pushes his cock deep inside me. He holds it there, his penis jerking as his semen flows.

I fall completely forward onto the bed, and Roger lies next to me. I'm aware once again of the soft music playing. Mariah Carey serenades the two of us as we lie side by side, breathing heavily.

Roger angles his head to look at me and flashes me a soft smile. I return the smile and reach for his hand.

"So," he begins. "How was that for an appetizer?"

"With that kind of appetizer, a girl doesn't need the meal!"

"That mean I ain't gonna see ya tonight?" Before I can answer, Roger plays with my nipple, then takes it into his mouth. He sucks the taut peak until I'm moaning again.

"You know I want to see you, baby," I tell him as he continues to suck my nipple. "The moment I get off work." He runs the pad of his thumb over my clitoris, and I start to writhe. "Please, Roger. No more."

His hand stills. He lifts his head. "Had enough?"

"Trust me, I'd love nothing more than to play hookey and stay here all day. But I have to get to work—"

Roger's abrupt kiss silences me.

I tear my lips away to finish my point. "And if we fuck

any more right now, I don't think I'll be able to walk. Seriously. Roger, you put a hurtin' on my pussy!"

He howls at that.

"All right," he whispers in my ear after a moment. "I can wait till later. 'Cuz I got *all* night. And I hope you do, too."

"Ooh, I love how that sounds."

"And you're gonna love how it feels, too."

Of that I have no doubt.

Twenty-Six

Samera

A tongue is traveling up my thigh. A hot tongue that makes my body tremble.

"Mmm," I moan. "Oooh, baby."

The tongue makes its way to my vagina and swirls around and around my clitoris. I arch my back and moan, deep and throaty.

"I love it when you wake up horny."

The words are like nails on a chalkboard, jarring me from my pleasure. My eyes pop open. And when I see Reed, I'm momentarily confused. Then I realize that I was dreaming.

The man in my dream had dark hair, dark skin and a Spanish accent.

Damn, I was dreaming about Miguel.

My fingers are on my pussy, and Reed's hand is on top of mine.

"Looks like someone was having a very nice dream," he says.

I quickly scoot backward, and move my hand, and thus his, off my body. Then I glance away.

"What's the matter?" Reed asks. "What—you embarrassed because I caught you masturbating?"

"I guess a little." Which is a big, fat lie.

"We've been a lot kinkier than that, babe." Reed strokes my leg, and I don't think. I simply react, moving my leg out of his reach.

Now he raises an eyebrow. "Something bothering you, babe?" But he asks the question in a suspicious way, not a sincerely concerned way.

"My head." Another lie. "I just felt this splitting pain." I massage my temple to prove my point. "I really have to stop drinking tequila."

Reed looks at me doubtfully. "You were just fingering your pussy. It didn't look like you were in any pain."

"In my dream, no. Too bad I woke up," I joke.

"Hmm."

Reed stares at me to the point where I'm uncomfortable. "What?" I ask.

"I don't know." His gaze is pointed, unwavering. "Every time I touch you lately, I'm sensing some resistance."

I shrug. "There's a lot going on right now, Reed. Can you blame me for not being in the mood for sex? Someone broke into my apartment. *My apartment.* I'm in hiding, for God's sake. My whole life is one big mess right now."

"And me? I'm part of that mess? That's what you think?"

"Why are you saying that? Why are you starting a fight with me?"

"Oh, I don't know. Maybe because you sound really friggin' ungrateful. You're the one who fucked that guy in Vegas. You've brought some psycho maniac into your life and *my* life. I'm trying to keep your ass safe, and all you do is sit around and bitch and complain."

"Reed—"

"Don't worry. I'll shut the fuck up." He leaps off the bed, cursing under his breath.

I sit, stupefied, wondering what the hell his problem is. And more so, wondering why I'm here.

Reed slips his boxers on, then cutoff jeans and a muscle T-shirt. I know he's waiting for me to tell him that I *do* appreciate what he's doing for me. But for the life of me, I can't bring myself to.

The thought going through my brain is that I'm in the middle of a mess I don't want to be in. I have no clue what I'm going to do with the rest of my life. I'm hiding from some freak who wants to hurt me. And I'm living with a guy I don't love anymore because I'm hoping he'll protect me, when what I really need to do is figure out a way to protect myself.

Reed storms out of the room.

"I don't love you anymore, Reed," I whisper. And then the reality of my words comes crashing down on my shoulders. I really don't love him anymore. And they're not words spoken in anger. It's simply a truth I've finally come to accept.

There's no changing my mind tomorrow. There's no changing my mind when he starts acting sweet again. I'm over him.

Completely.

The truth is, I have been for a while now. The man in my heart is the man I haven't been able to forget, even after returning to America.

Miguel.

Nearly two months have passed since I left him in Costa Rica, and I still think of him, still dream of him, still wonder how he is. Wonder if he's found some other woman to love. And if he has, if that woman's pretty and nice and worthy of him.

And if they click sexually the way he and I did.

The bedroom door flies open, and I reel backward on the bed. Reed steps into the room and tosses the cordless phone onto the mattress beside me.

"The phone's for you," he tells me.

I swallow. Take a deep breath. "Who is it?"

"Your sister."

"You heading out?" I ask.

"Do you care?"

I don't bother to answer, because I'm not interested in round two with Reed. Instead I lift the phone and place it at my ear.

"Annie," I say tentatively.

"Is everything all right over there?"

"Sure, why?"

"Reed sounded *very* pissed. Are you two arguing?"

"I don't feel like talking about Reed."

"Okay," Annelise says. "Then I'll tell you what Lishelle found out."

Hope swells inside me. "She found Peter?"

"Yes. And no."

I frown. "Meaning?"

"Meaning that yes, she tracked him down. His name is Peter Bartlett, thirty-five years old. Works as a high school phys-ed teacher."

"A *teacher?*" I couldn't be more shocked. I don't expect someone entrusted to guide and protect young people to be such a perverted snake.

"Yeah. And he's nowhere near Atlanta. In fact, he's not even in the state of Georgia."

"I don't understand."

"Personally, I still believe he's the one behind the threats. The investigator was able to find out that he's had quite the interesting past—including assaulting some guy in a bar."

"And he's a *teacher?*"

"I don't know why the board would keep him on, but they did."

"Good grief."

"Yeah, tell me about it. The only thing is, he hasn't been in Atlanta since he left Las Vegas. He's been in Chicago. Actually, in Evanston, a Chicago suburb."

"But if he hasn't been here—"

"Then he hired someone to harass us. At least that's what I think, and Lishelle agrees."

"Harass, right." I snort. Last night, after I had officially temporarily moved into Reed's place, I called my sister to tell her about the fake head in my apartment, and how I might have nightmares about it for weeks. "Terrify is more like it."

"Since he hasn't physically been here, we can't prove anything. But like I said, I'm sure he hired some thug to do his dirty work."

"Great. So we're still not safe. Or me—if I'm the one he's really after."

"For what it's worth, Lishelle called him. And she tore into him something good. Told him to stay the hell away from us, and that if he harassed us again, he'd be up on charges."

"And what did he say?" I ask anxiously.

"That he had no clue what she was talking about. But what else is he gonna say? 'Oh, okay. I'll stop making your life hell. Sorry.' I don't think so."

I drag a hand over my face. "This whole thing is wearing me out, Annie. I feel so damn trapped. I've had to move in with Reed, and now I'm starting to question that decision." I sigh. "Do you think Dominic would let me stay with you guys? Just for a little while? Until I find my own place? I'd ask Maxine, but she lives with her loser boyfriend—"

"You don't have to give me a hard sell. Of course you can stay here if you need to. There's not a lot of space, but I don't think Dominic would mind."

"Just in case," I tell her. "Who knows...maybe things will still work out for Reed and me."

There's a moment of quiet. Then Annelise says, "I could say 'but,' because I sense a 'but,' but I won't."

I sigh, then blurt out, "But I'm in love with Miguel."

"*What?*"

"Clearly, nothing I do in my life can be easy. I have to choose the hardest path, every single—"

"You're in love with Miguel?" Gone is Annelise's shock, replaced by a wistful tone.

"I know. Talk about complicated. Miguel was supposed to be a fling. But just this morning I finally realized that he's much more than that."

"Sammy..."

"And I've totally fucked my life up. I never should have left him in Costa Rica. He was the one guy in my life who was really decent to me, treated me with respect, believed in me. And I left him. You don't leave a guy like that. What is wrong with me?"

"Sweetie, there's nothing wrong with you. It's not a crime to be confused."

"You say that because you're my sister."

"I say it because it's true. Look at how long I stayed with Charles? Basically, I had to be hit over the head with a hammer for me to see the light."

"Maybe it's in the Peyton genes." I sigh. "Oh, Annie. What do I do?"

"First and foremost, if you don't want to stay with Reed anymore, leave."

"But he's been so good to me."

"And for that, you buy him a nice shirt at Macy's. You don't fuck him."

I close my eyes and nod. "Maybe you're right."

"I am right."

"And you've never liked Reed."

"I can't deny that, no. But listen, I need to talk to you about something else."

"What?"

"Now hear me out completely." There's a brief pause, then my sister says, "I think you should go to the police."

"No way. Are you kidding me? How can I go to the police?"

"I know you're afraid, but here's the thing. You're *innocent*. Right now, it looks like you're running. And you have no reason to run, no reason to hide. If you go to them, tell them what you know, it'll be over and done with."

"Unless they want to charge me for murder."

"I don't think it'll be long before the police call me, anyway. The hotel has probably given them guest records."

"That still won't tie me to Rusty. How many people visit Vegas every day? Anyone could have killed him."

"I agree. But while Peter might have some sick revenge plan up his sleeve, I think it's wise to go to the police, tell them you'd been with Rusty before his murder, and what happened with him and Peter. That way they can open a file for this harassment. Lishelle's scared Peter off for now, but what if he shows up in six months?"

"That's why I'm gonna move."

"And you'll always be running."

"I'm not running. I didn't do anything."

"All right." Annelise sighs, the fight going out of her. "That's my suggestion, and do with it what you will."

"Yeah."

"And if you want to come over to talk—"

"Whatever."

"You're angry."

"No, I'm stressed as hell. Look, I'll talk to you later, okay?"

I hear Annelise sigh again. "Okay."

I click the cordless phone off. If only I could click my problems away as easily.

Twenty-Seven

Claudia

"So," I begin, "do you think that's the end of it?" I ask Lishelle. "You think you put the fear of God in this guy and he's going to leave us alone?"

"I did my best," she responds. "I can't imagine him even trying to mess with us from this point onward. Let's face it. Guys like that—they're bullies. They prey on you if they think you're weak. My phone call to that shithead told him we're anything but weak."

I mull that over as I reach for my mimosa. It's Saturday morning, and Annelise, Lishelle and I are in Liaisons for brunch. We normally do it Sunday, but with all the crap that's gone down this week, we wanted to get together earlier.

"You know what's insanely weird?" Annelise asks. "One minute we were in Vegas having a great time. The next, we were back home and I found out that Charles had killed himself. Then some creep started stalking us. My house sold and I get a nice, fat check on Monday. So much has happened in the span of a couple weeks that it feels like so much more time has passed."

"I know what you mean," I agree. "Seems like we went to Las Vegas months ago."

Lishelle's lips curl. "Are you saying you're already ready for another vacation?"

Annelise's eyes brighten. "Not a bad idea. Maybe we can all head to Costa Rica, and take Samera."

"Costa Rica?" Lishelle asks. "Not that I object to the idea of gorgeous, Spanish-speaking men—but why there? I wouldn't think you'd want to go back there after the whole ordeal with Charles."

"Personally, I'm happy to go to Hawaii or some other exotic place. But my sister…well, it seems she left the love of her life in Costa Rica."

Lishelle swallows her mouthful of eggs, then says, "You're joking."

"No. I'm not."

"What about Reed?" I ask.

"Reed was convenient," Annelise replies. "He's not the man of her dreams."

I smile, my hopeless romantic feelings coming to life. "So your sister's in love. Sweet."

"With a guy who's not an asshole. Do you see why I'm anxious to get her back together with him?"

"No offence," Lishelle begins, "but your sister knows how to find trouble. I don't know that I want to go anywhere with her again."

I wash my Belgian waffle down with a swig of coffee. "At least life is never boring around her."

Annelise chuckles. "You've got that right."

"And to make things even more interesting," I go on, "I can call my fabulous masseur from Vegas and ask if he wants to come along. And you can bring Dominic," I say to Annelise.

"Of course," she agrees.

My gaze lands on Lishelle. "And you can bring Rugged."

Lishelle rolls her eyes. "Talk about stalkers. He has called me at least ten times since we got together on Thursday— and it's only Saturday!"

"He likes you," I chime.

"Maybe I shouldn't have fucked him. But my God, did he ever give it to me good."

"So bring him to Costa Rica and you're guaranteed a great time," Annelise says.

"I could barely walk on Friday," Lishelle continues, her eyes widening as she looks at me and Annelise in turn. "And I'm not kidding. I had to pretend that I twisted my ankle."

I crack up, and Annelise does, too. I laugh so hard I start to make these wild snorting sounds.

"Go ahead, laugh," Lishelle says. But she herself is smiling.

"The guy's got a big dick and you're complaining?" I ask. "That's not the Lishelle I know."

"Hey, I love his dick," Lishelle says frankly. "The thing is, I'm starting to feel like he's in love with me."

"Already?" Annelise asks.

"You didn't see the absolutely ridiculous bouquet of roses he sent to the station for me—on Friday morning, after we'd had that incredible night together. It was so huge, it took two guys to carry it into my office. It's becoming like a funeral home in there."

"Aww, that's sweet," I say.

"Sweet?" Lishelle balks. "He sent me roses on Thursday, then again on Friday. What next—a diamond ring on Monday?"

"He sounds really romantic," Annelise says.

"He's twenty-four," Lishelle reminds her. "Practically a baby."

"I bet you didn't think he was a baby when you were calling out his name." I smile sweetly.

"I'm not gonna lie. The guy is great in bed. No, beyond great. And the stamina. Holy shit, I think he could have fucked me for two days straight, if I didn't have anything else to do."

"See?" I say.

"No, you're the one who's not seeing the big picture. If it were just sex, that'd be one thing. He could come to town, and we could go at it like rabbits. But I think Roger has fallen in love with me. And love…that's what I can't deal with."

"I know Glenn burned you—" I begin.

"This isn't about Glenn," Lishelle interjects. "It's about me not wanting a relationship right now. Finally I figured out how to fuck like a man—to enjoy the act but leave the emotions aside. And this would have to be the time that the guy decides to get all emotional."

"It's not hard to see why," Annelise says. "You're gorgeous, talented."

Lishelle smiles at her. "Thanks. But I think I need to cool things with him for now. Maybe I can tell him that until we've planned the fund-raiser, we should abstain from sex."

"Or maybe you should continue screwing him until we've finished the fund-raiser," I suggest. "It'd be a fun couple months, in any case."

"I'll figure out what to do after tonight," Lishelle says.

"Why after tonight?" Annelise asks. Then, "Ahh, you're seeing him again!"

Lishelle only grins.

"You little whore," I say, and laugh. "Then what was with all the drama?"

"Hey, do you expect a hot-blooded woman to say no to amazing sex?" Lishelle asks. "I just don't want to hurt him."

"She had me going there for a minute," I say to Annelise. "What about you?"

Annelise nods. "I believed it."

"Shut up, you two!" Lishelle gives us a look, then downs the last of her mimosa. Annelise and I share a heart-felt laugh.

"Tell us we're wrong," I dare her.

"Okay," Lishelle goes on. "I'll admit that I sound like a hypocrite. I'm not quite ready to be done with him. He's fun. Fucking him is fun. I guess I'm just saying that I'm not ready for a long-term commitment."

"Has he asked you for one?" Annelise asks.

"No," Lishelle answers.

"Then don't stress yourself out. Have fun. Lots of it. If he does give you a ring or something crazy, then you break it off. But with the way the guy travels out of town most of the time, it's not like you'll have to see him every day."

"Sounds like the perfect booy call arrangement," I point out.

Lishelle nods slowly. "You're absolutely right. Maybe I'm just afraid of the idea of another relationship."

"But this isn't a relationship," I tell her. "You said so yourself."

"All right," Lishelle says. "I'll deal with this fling with Roger one day at a time."

"You mean one orgasm at a time!" Annelise corrects her.

Annelise and I share a heartfelt laugh, and even Lishelle can't help joining in.

I quickly flag the waitress down and order a second round of drinks.

"God, it feels good to be laughing," Annelise says.

"Does it ever," I agree. "And you know what—I think we're going to be laughing for a long time. I talked to my cousin and there are *ten* rap artists signed on to participate in our fund-raiser. That'll be *ten* concerts around the country. We are going to raise a huge amount of money for the Wishes Come True Foundation!"

Annelise squeals.

"I'm so excited," Lishelle says.

"I was talking about the charity," I say, trying to keep a straight face. "Not your scheduled romp for tonight."

Now Lishelle whacks my arm. *"Shut up!"*

But she laughs. And so do I.

And I can't help thinking that Annelise is right. That it feels so good to be laughing again.

Twenty-Eight

Samera

A week after my sister told me I could move in with her and Dominic, I've finally made the decision to leave Reed's house.

I've stayed out of a sense of obligation, but we're fighting a lot, and the sex is impassionate, and I just don't know why I'm here anymore.

I could simply tell Reed that I'm moving out, but I doubt there'll be anything simple about it. His temper scares me sometimes, and I want right now to make a clean break.

That's why I've waited until Friday night to make my move, one of Reed's busiest nights at the club. While he's there, I take the time to pack my stuff. The clothes I originally brought from my apartment, as well as all the new stuff I purchased.

Yesterday it hit me. Hit me hard. That I can't stay with Reed, play house with him and lead him on when I don't really want a future with him. He saw an application I had filled out for a restaurant job, and he hit the roof.

"You don't appreciate me...what about my suggestion that we work together..." I listened to his tirade, and it went in one ear and out the other.

I was weak, running to him after getting the letters, but I can stay with my sister or even get a new apartment. That's the one great thing about my job as a stripper that I'll never regret. I made tons of cash and was smart enough to save most of it.

And this is perhaps a bit of a chicken-shit way to do this—sneaking out of Reed's house while he's at work—but I don't want to face him. I know he's not going to let me go without a fight, and I don't need that.

What I need is a clean escape. To have him come home and find me gone and just know that it's over forever.

No more playing games.

I take my time writing Reed a note, considering every word carefully. I don't want to hurt him, because as much as I know we're not right for each other, I really do appreciate all he's done for me. When he gets over feeling hurt, I hope that we can be friends.

The note finished, I place it in an envelope with his name scrawled on it, then leave the envelope on his kitchen table.

Then I head to the closet to pack my stuff.

I go through the closet in the spare bedroom, and when I'm through gathering all my clothes, I notice that some outfits are missing. Like the new dress I splurged on at Fendi, and a couple pairs of jeans.

Odd. Because I know I haven't worn them yet.

I head to Reed's bedroom and open his closet. I don't find the outfits there, either.

Maybe I *did* wear them, and Reed sent them out to be dry-cleaned. It's been a stressful few weeks, and much of the time my brain has been in a fog.

My eyes land on the bag at the far end of the slender closet. It's a burlap sack, one I've seen tightly tied since I moved in here. It suddenly occurs to me that it could be a laundry bag, and I wonder if he's put any of my clothes in there.

I sit on my butt and pull the bag onto my lap. I work the tie, which is almost impossible to open. But after a few minutes, I pull it loose. I open the bag and start to sift through it, emptying various clothes items onto the floor one by one.

My hand closes over a shoe. A stiletto heel. Frowning, I pull it from the bag. And immediately recognize it as part of a pair I wore in Vegas.

The ones I wore the night I had my date with Rusty.

The ones I left in his room.

Only now, the shoe has spots of blood caked on the front of it.

Is it mine? I stare at the shoe, study it to be sure. It's size eight, my size. I flip it over, and now I feel a chill. The initials SP are on the bottom of the shoe, written in black marker. When I worked at the club, because other girls would often borrow or steal another dancer's shoes, I took to marking my initials on mine.

The chill slithers down my spine as I hold the shoe. My mind scrambles to make sense of how it could be in Reed's room.

And then the truth hits me like a ton of bricks.

If Reed has *this* shoe—

"Samera."

I scream at the sound of my name. Then I whirl around, my heart beating so fast I'm sure my chest will be bruised.

Reed is standing at the doorway to the walk-in closet, staring at me.

"Jesus, Reed." I breathe out heavily. "You scared the shit out of me."

He doesn't say anything. His eyes volley from my face to the bag.

Shit. I'm on the floor, the contents of the bag beside me, my lost shoe in my hands. I can't explain away this situation.

But more important, neither can Reed.

"Samera, Samera, Samera." Reed puts one foot in front of the other, slowly but surely, until he reaches me. For the life of me, I can't move. I just sit on the floor stupidly.

"You—" I swallow. My throat is suddenly dry. "You found...my shoe..."

Reed lowers himself onto his haunches in front of me. Stares at me. His hard, cold eyes freak me out. "Well, this is an interesting situation, isn't it?"

"Um..." What do I say, what do I say?

"You know why I did it, don't you?"

My stomach lurches.

"Don't you?" Reed prompts.

"I—What do you mean?" Lame!

Reed smiles, but there's no warmth in it. "I know you're not stupid. You know where I found that shoe."

"I, um, I..." Damn it, I can't form a coherent sentence.

But, God help me, my brain is working, and it starts to connect the dots. The notes. The *head* in my apartment. All that fake blood...

Reed freaking out at the airport, worried that they were going to go through *his* luggage...

"It's not just the shoe, is it?" I finally ask. "The notes. The one on my car, the one in my mailbox. And my God, Reed, that elaborate scene with the severed head in my apartment."

I get nothing from Reed—except that cold smile.

"Say something. Tell me I'm wrong, you fucking son of a bitch!" The realization of his deception changes something within me. I no longer feel like I've been caught snooping. Anger rises in me.

"I would have thrown the shoe out, but it was security."

"Against what?"

"Against you leaving!"

I stare at Reed in disbelief. "That's what this is about? You didn't want me to leave you?"

"I wanted to punish you!" Reed yells. "Show you what happens when you decide to act like a friggin' whore!"

"Whore? You run a strip club, sleep with half the dancers, and you tell *me* I'm acting like a whore?"

Reed grips me by my shoulders, his fingers pressing into my skin. "You could have gotten killed. Or have you forgotten already? For God's sake, I found you disoriented in the lobby of the fucking Venetian. You didn't know if you were coming or going. And why?" He squeezes my cheeks like an adult scolding a child. "Because you were in some stranger's room, sucking his cock, instead of here with me, the guy who loves you."

I jerk my face away from his fingers and position myself on my knees. "Love? This isn't love. Trying to scare the shit out of me? That's deranged."

I just say the words, don't think about them, and the moment I do I see I've made a mistake. In Reed's eyes I see his wrath before his hand slaps me across the face.

"No one loves you like I do. *No one.*"

Though the slap hurt like hell, I will not let it show. I will not give Reed the benefit of seeing me cry.

"You're an asshole," I spit out as I get to my feet. "You don't know what love is."

The moment I'm standing, Reed slams my body against the closet wall. I cry out in pain.

"You think you're going to dump me?" Reed asks. "After everything I've done for you?"

I swallow. I'm not sure what to say, but I decide to go for honesty. "Reed, if you loved me so much, you never would have fucked someone else."

"Really?"

"Really."

"And my going to Costa Rica? Didn't that prove that I love you?"

"That was because you couldn't have me," I tell him, and not until then do I realize that all along, this is what I've believed. That it was his ego that had him getting on a plane, not his heartfelt realization that he had screwed up the best thing to ever happen to him.

"Fuck, Samera. I've never known you to be so…so goddamn emotional. I messed up. It happens. It was just pussy. Not about love or caring. What do I have to do to get you to see that you're the one who means everything to me?"

Reed's anger seems to have ebbed away. I'm not frightened of his wrath anymore. "Reed," I say, then sigh. "Look, we had something good for a while. But it's over. It just is."

Reed releases me and heads out of the closet. After a moment, I follow him.

Thank God, it seems like the fight is over. It finally seems to have clicked in Reed's brain that our relationship has run its course.

I open my mouth to tell him that I hope we can be friends, but the stark realization of what Reed has done hits me as if for the first time.

Rusty. *Murdered.*

But how did Reed get into Rusty's room, unless he'd been

spying on us that night. Suddenly I remember feeling as though someone *was* watching me.

And if he killed Rusty, what will he do to me?

It's as though Reed has read my thoughts, because with his back to me he says quietly, "You know why I did it, why I killed him?"

A tear makes its way down my cheek. Hearing Reed admit what he's done—it's overwhelming.

"But I don't understand. You were with me that night. How?"

Reed turns and faces me. "You'd had so much to drink, by the time I brought you back to my hotel room, you passed out."

I don't doubt it. But I still don't understand how Reed knew where to go, how to find Rusty.

"I still don't get it. How on earth would you have found Rusty?"

"That was a bit of luck, I guess," Reed says. "I was in the club at Bellagio the night you came in with him. I saw you right away, and I could tell you were already drunk. You didn't see me. You were so…wrapped up in that guy. But when he went to the bar to get some glasses, I followed him. Chatted to him for a bit. Found out all I needed to know right there."

Oh, God. Reed had been there. Watching me that whole time.

"He told me he was in the restaurant business," Reed continues. "So, I just had to tell him that I own a winery and would love to talk to him about business. He was excited about the idea—but not that night, since he was out with this really hot babe. I told him I could call him the next day and the dumb ass gave me his room number." Reed laughs. "As simple as taking candy from a baby."

I swallow. Hard.

"After that," Reed goes on, "once I found you in the lobby

and put you to bed, I knew I could go back to pay Rusty a visit and you'd never be the wiser."

I close my eyes and breathe in deeply.

"I did it for you," Reed says. "If you were gonna fuck that guy, I could deal with it. But when I saw you in the lobby, all scared and out of your mind…I never would have hurt him if not for that. I did it for you, babe."

"Please, don't say that."

He marches toward me, anger flaring in his eyes. He grabs my arms, squeezes hard. "You don't think I love you, but I killed that fucking pig for you. If I didn't love you… Wait a minute. Are you crying over that piece of shit?"

I sob softly. I can't stop.

"Don't you dare. Don't you dare look at me like that after what I did for you. He and his friend wanted to gang rape you!" Spittle flies from Reed's mouth as he yells. "I should have killed both of them!"

"How can you say that? You, you slit a man's throat! And why—because I fucked him. Because I was stupid. And then you—you sent those letters, not just to me, but my sister, her friends." Every breath is a struggle now. I'm wheezing as I speak. "And the head—"

Reed clamps his hand over my mouth. "Stop that, Sam. Stop fucking freaking out."

Until you're trapped in a room with a madman you know is going to kill you, you don't know what it's like to feel stark terror swallow you whole. Because despite Reed's anger and jealousy, never before today would I have thought him dangerous enough to slit a man's throat and push him out of a hotel window.

For me.

My God. Reed is going to kill me.

I try to force the tears to stop, but I can't. I can't do anything but cry and gasp at the sickness I feel inside me.

"Stop fucking crying!" Reed heaves me forward and throws me to the ground. "You better stop crying, or I'm gonna think you're *real* ungrateful."

I snivel. Wipe my tears. "Reed, you *murdered* him."

"I know what the fuck I did and I know why."

"You left my shoe there. With my initial on the bottom. You want me to go to jail? Is that it?"

"I already told you that shoe was for insurance!" Reed shouts. "You should be thanking me for what I did."

I wipe at my tears and try to catch my breath.

"You had better tell me you fucking appreciate it or I am going to be really friggin' unhappy."

I have to do this. I have to lie. "I…I…appreciate…"

"Fuck that. You're gonna prove it to me."

Reed grabs me by the hair and pulls me to my knees. "Reed, stop!"

He releases me and unbuckles his jeans, then whips out his cock. It's already hard. "Suck it."

I tremble as I look up at him in utter disbelief.

"What the fuck are you waiting for?" he demands. "Show your goddamn appreciation for how I took care of that guy. Suck my dick."

I draw in a deep breath, let it out real slow. "No."

"*What?*"

I get to my feet, anger taking the place of my shock. "Fuck you."

Reed punches me in the face, flat-out coldcocks me. I fly backward. Blood oozes from my nose.

He grabs me by the hair. "You are going to suck my dick right now—"

"Okay," I tell him. Blood drips into my mouth. "Okay. I will."

I ease myself onto my knees, fighting the tears inside me. It's time to go into survival mode and do what it takes to get out of here alive.

I take his cock in my mouth, and Reed groans in delight. "That's right, babe. Deep-throat my cock the way you know I like it."

"Like this?" I kiss the tip of his penis, then run my tongue over it before taking it deep in my mouth, into the deepest part of my throat that I can.

"God, yeah. Babe, don't get mad. But this is kind of hot. Watching you do this with the blood…"

You're a sick son of a bitch, I think. But I moan and continue to give him one amazing blow job, pretending I'm loving every moment of it.

And Reed, the fucking moron, gets lost in the moment. He runs his hands through my hair, groaning softly, like he's not forcing me to do this. I let him enjoy my mouth and tongue for a good couple minutes. I massage his balls, let him completely lose himself in his sick pleasure.

And then I squeeze his balls like I'm crushing a ripe Georgia peach in my hands.

Reed's immediate reaction is shock—then he falters backward and wails in pain. I don't waste a second. I scramble to my feet and start to run.

Behind me Reed cusses a blue streak. I should head straight to the front door, but I make a quick detour to the kitchen to grab a knife. If Reed catches up to me, I'll need to protect myself.

I run out the front door, stumble down the steps. I hear Reed behind me, but I don't turn. And yet I don't know where to go. I don't have my purse, my car keys, my money…not even my cell phone.

I'm running as fast as I can, but the gravel driveway digs into my feet. Despite my fear, my momentum slows. Like an animal predator, it sounds as though Reed is picking up speed at sign of my weakness.

And then I'm jerked down violently. My hands fly out to break my fall, but still my face hits the gravel path. The rocks tear into my skin.

The knife goes flying.

I could give up right now. Accept my fate and let Reed kill me. But damn it, Reed has already taken too much from me.

I won't let him take my life.

Reed grabs me by my collar and spins me onto my back. I throw punches and kick like a woman deranged. But nothing I do stops Reed, who puts his hands around my neck and squeezes.

And then I'm gasping, choking. Grabbing at Reed's hands but failing to loosen their grip.

"You think you're gonna screw me over?" he asks. He loosens his hold on my throat, and I desperately gulp in air.

He drags me back into the house and throws me onto the floor. Now that we're inside, there's no doubt he's going to kill me.

Reed slams the door shut and locks it. Hopelessness grips me. He's tall and built like a Mac truck. Without a weapon, how the hell can I fight him?

As he advances, his eyes wild like a demon's, I push backward on my ass in a futile attempt to escape him.

"Please, Reed." It's all I can do. Beg and hope he'll calm down.

"You're a bitch and a whore and you were never good enough for me."

I keep moving. My hands hit the cool kitchen tile.

"So let me leave," I tell him. "If I'm not good enough for you, just let me walk out the door and you'll never see me again."

Reed chuckles, but there's no mirth in his voice. "Sorry, babe. But you're gonna die."

I'm at a kitchen cupboard now, and Reed is closing in on me. My mind scrambles for a plan, one that will save my life. "No, Reed," I say. "You're the one that's gonna die."

He glances at me oddly, a little stunned. Like he thinks that maybe I've got a gun on me and I'm about to pull it on him.

In his moment of hesitation, I move. I'm on my feet in a flash, my hands reaching for the top of the kitchen counter and the knife rack.

"Fucking whore!" Reed shouts and pounces on me.

Reed yanks on my hair, but not before I'm able to close my fingers around a knife. I whirl around and strike, jab the knife into his flesh over and over again.

"Bitch!"

Reed doesn't let me go, but I feel his fingers loosen slightly. Then he steps backward, an odd expression on his face, but he doesn't fall.

This is it. All I've got. If the knife didn't inflict any damage, then I'm doomed.

Suddenly the expression on his face changes. He becomes ashen as his knees falter. He stumbles backward, and only then do I look down at his torso and see the stain of blood on his shirt.

It's oozing out of him.

"What did you…" His voice fades as he falls in a heap on the floor.

It takes me a moment to realize he's not dead, but he's making this strange wheezing sound. Emotion hits me like a ton of bricks at what I've done.

What I had to do.

Sobbing, I drop the knife.

"Help…help…" Reed stretches his hand toward me, his eyes imploring me to help him.

I stand there and watch him, though part of me wants to drop to my knees and apply pressure to the wound.

But I can't.

"P-please…"

Reed's hand drops. His eyes flutter shut.

I break down and bawl like a baby.

Hours after I've given my statement to police, I'm with my sister in the hospital waiting room.

"I'd walk away and never look back," Annelise tells me.

"I know," I say softly. "And I should. But I just want to know…know that he's going to be okay."

"I don't understand you."

"I don't want him dead, Annie, even if he deserves it. For what he did to me—to Rusty—I want him to spend the rest of his life behind bars."

Annelise grips my hand and squeezes it, saying she understands.

We sit silently for a while. I'm filled with such an overwhelming feeling of comfort having my sister by my side. I don't think I can ever express to her how much this means to me.

"Isn't this strange?" Annelise says after a while. "The two of us almost in the exact same boat. Charles died, now Reed might. Two men in our lives who were so bad for us."

"It is freaky."

"When do you want to get your stuff?" my sister asks me.

"I don't really care about my stuff."

"You say that now—"

"Honestly, I don't care. I don't ever want to go back to Reed's house." I close my eyes and shudder.

Annelise puts her arm around me and pulls me close, and I rest my head on her shoulder. There's something warm about her touch, something comforting the way I'd always hoped for from my mother. So I sit there like that with her, getting strength from her love for me.

"You know what I wish?" I say after a while.

"Tell me."

"I wish I'd stayed in Costa Rica. With Miguel. How could I have been so stupid? He was the perfect guy for me. The perfect guy, period. Then I let Reed ruin things. And I wasn't happy after that. I ran from my feelings for Miguel in Vegas, thought sleeping with Rusty would make me forget him. But now all I can think of is how much I fucked up. Again."

"Maybe you should call him."

"No." I shake my head vehemently. "Look at me. I'm an emotional basket case. Not to mention my face looks like I should be starring in some horror flick. Miguel deserves better than me."

"From everything you told me, the man loves you."

"It's over. I'm sure he's moved on. It's just one of those situations I'll always regret."

"There'll be someone else," Annelise assures me, and she kisses the top of my head. "Someone who treats you with respect, loves you with dignity."

"That'd be nice."

"Have some faith," she tells me.

I wish I could. I wish I could allow myself to believe that a decent guy is lurking around the corner. But I'm not that foolish. The good guys aren't a dime a dozen.

I had one. And I let him go.

Twenty-Nine

Annelise

Reed died.

The very same night that Samera and I were in the hospital, waiting to hear word of his condition after surgery, he slipped away.

And for the past two weeks my sister's been in a slump. Yes, she was fully within her rights to defend herself from Reed's attack. But still, she killed a man. That's been extremely hard for her to deal with.

She's stayed with me and Dominic, and I've tried to help keep her spirits up. Nothing's really helping, but I suppose it's only a matter of time.

We're out for dinner right now at one of Atlanta's upscale eateries, the Capital Grille. We're decked out in elegant dresses, and men all around the room have been checking us out.

But my sister barely smiles. And she only picks at her food, a delectable-smelling dry-aged steak.

"So," I say, "have you figured out which courses you want to take this fall?"

"Not really. I'm not sure I'm ready."

"What can I do to help you feel better?"

"I'm getting there, I guess. It's just hard." Samera sighs.

For the hundredth time, I glance toward the restaurant's entrance. And finally I see my surprise. A grin explodes on my face, one that must be as big as the state of Georgia.

I push my chair back abruptly and stand. "Um, excuse me."

"What? Where are you going?"

"Don't look so panic-stricken," I tell Samera. "I'm just heading to the ladies' room."

"Then what was with that big smile—did Dominic just come in here or something?"

"Or something."

The hostess starts off with Miguel toward our table, and he grins when he sees me.

I sit back down.

"I thought you had to go to the bathroom," Samera says.

"I did, but." I shrug.

"You are acting mighty suspicious. And why do you keep grinning like—"

Samera abruptly stops speaking when Miguel arrives at our table. She doesn't notice who it is right away, considering the bouquet of roses he's carrying is blocking his face. But then he lowers the bouquet and *bam!* Samera's eyes widen as if she's got a piece of beef lodged in her throat.

Her eyes fly from Miguel's face to mine. "Surprise," I say.

Samera stares at Miguel again, her expression saying she can't believe he's here. Heck, she can't even speak.

Miguel is the first to talk. "Samera, *mi bella.*"

"Mi—" Samera croaks. "Miguel?"

He chuckles softly, his dark eyes sparkling. "Yes, it is really me."

"But I don't understand." Samera looks to me again.

"It wasn't hard to find him," I explain. "We knew where he worked."

"And you brought him here?" Her eyes mist with tears.

"Your sister," Miguel says softly. "She said you needed me."

"And you just got on a plane and came to the States?" Samera asks him.

"Yes."

Such a simple answer, but it says so much. It says he still loves her.

My eyes start to water.

Miguel extends the flowers to Samera. "Beautiful flowers for a very beautiful lady."

"Oh, Miguel." Samera takes the roses but doesn't give them a second glance. She drops them onto the table and leaps to her feet, flinging her arms around him.

And she kisses him. A deep, passionate, shameless kiss.

I glance away and dab at my eyes.

And then a funny thing happens. People start to applaud. Maybe they think Miguel and Samera have just gotten engaged. Or maybe they know they're two lovers reuniting. All I know is that as I look at my sister and Miguel, their love is palpable.

I get to my feet and wrap my arms around both Miguel and Samera. Then I say, "Miguel, it's great to see you again. But I'm gonna leave you and my sister now."

"But we haven't finished eating," Samera says.

"I'll pick up a burger somewhere," I tell her.

"But—"

I put my mouth close to her ear and whisper, "Samera, I

know how it was when I got together with Dominic. The last thing I was concerned with was food. I can't imagine you're hungry for anything you can order at this place. You be with Miguel. I already booked a room for you at the Ritz down the street."

Tears fill my sister's eyes. "You did?"

"I love you," I tell her. "In case there was ever any doubt."

She gives me a solo hug, squeezes me hard. Then I hug Miguel, as well. "Take care of my sister."

"I will," he says.

"I'll settle the bill," I tell them.

I leave the two of them standing beside the table, their arms wrapped around each other. When I get to the hostess stand, I explain to the lady there that I'd like to settle the bill for our table.

I glance at Miguel and Samera. They're still holding each other, their faces close as they chat.

I pay the bill with cash, then head toward the elevator that will take me downstairs. I hit the button, then turn for one last look at my sister and her lover.

Samera catches my gaze. She mouths the words, "Thank you."

The elevator door opens, and I give her a wave.

And then I see something I haven't seen in two months. Samera's radiant smile. It fills the entire room with light.

At last my sister is smiling again.

That thought warms me as I descend to the first floor.

Kayla Perrin

Author Kayla Perrin has been writing since the age of thirteen when she submitted her first story to Scholastic Books. Since then she has become the *USA TODAY* bestselling author of several mainstream and romance novels with St. Martin's Press, BET Books and HarperCollins, and has been nominated for many industry awards. Kayla lives with her daughter in Ontario, Canada.

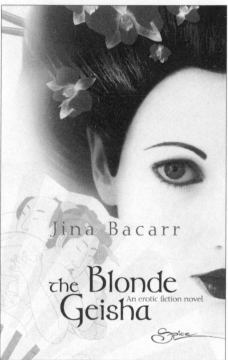